THE DEVIL'S MASK

THE DEVIL'S MASK

CHRISTOPHER WAKLING

ISIS
LARGE PRINT
Oxford

First published in Great Britain 2011
by
Faber and Faber Ltd.

Published in Large Print 2012 by ISIS Publishing Ltd.,
7 Centremead, Osney Mead, Oxford OX2 0ES
by arrangement with
Faber and Faber Ltd.

LP

The moral right of the author has been asserted

British Library Cataloguing in Publication Data
Wakling, Christopher, 1970–
    The devil's mask.
    1. Merchants - - England - - Bristol - - History - -
    19th century - - Fiction.
    2. Bristol (England) - - History - - 19th century - -
    Fiction.
    3. Docks - - England - - Bristol - - History - - 19th
    century - - Fiction.
    4. Slave trade - - England - - Bristol - - Fiction.
    5. Suspense fiction.
    6. Large type books.
    I. Title
    823.9'2–dc23

ISBN 978–0–7531–8932–0 (hb)
ISBN 978–0–7531–8933–7 (pb)

Printed and bound in Great Britain by
T. J. International Ltd., Padstow, Cornwall

For Carole and Balazs

Prologue

The seagull sidestepped along the rail. Against the dull water its back, neck and head were a phosphorescent white.

Too bright for Captain Addison, whose own head throbbed at the sight. Landfall, home, finally, after a year, seven months and nine days at sea, added up to pressure rather than release. Squinting, Addison stamped on the oak deck. The bird screamed once in reply. It was huge — Bristol bred the biggest, meanest gulls in the world, no doubt about it — and it regarded the Captain malevolently. Addison walked towards it muttering, "Get away, get off my ship," and was almost upon the bird before it offered him the insolent semaphore of its wings.

Addison watched the gull flap away, framing his brow with a tanned hand, working his temples with forefinger and thumb.

Homecoming, an end to the voyage, brought with it uncertainty.

At sea a captain knew where he stood. But, looking to the distant village of Pill, home to the Bristol pilots, the tow-boat men whose job it was to intercept incoming ships and haul them from the river's mouth to port, Addison felt weakened; once the *Belsize* had limped those last miles to the quayside

— nine of the most dangerous in the entire round trip — he would step from the ship leached of authority, and each additional step he took on land would threaten to undermine him further still. On deck he walked with a purpose that he never managed ashore.

Which might have explained why the Captain had been in no hurry to take the pilot's lead and proceed to port. For three days he'd stood the *Belsize* at King Road in the Mouth of the Avon, while rushing tides raised and lowered her above the safely distant silt. Three days in which the crew, as desperate to expend themselves ashore as Addison was fearful of finding himself so spent, warmed and boiled and finally raged against one another. Hendryx had knocked the boy Adams senseless over a game of cards, even as Morris buried the blade of his pocket-knife deep in the youngster's thigh. "There'll be nobody left to sail the thing upriver if we don't make a move soon," muttered Waring, the ship's surgeon, as he tended the boy-sailor's leg, only adding "Captain," when he realised Addison had moved within earshot.

"That's a good job you've done there," Addison said, nodding at the stitches. "Now, let me do mine."

Defending his authority, extending his hold on the men by postponing their release, both these things helped explain the Captain's decision to put off his ship's progress to port, but neither was the real reason for the delay. Nor was Addison's reputation for caution, though spilling the *Belsize*'s precious cargo of unrefined sugar, tobacco bales and rum into the swirling mud of the Avon presented a real risk, which would be lessened by waiting to proceed upriver with favourable conditions. An inexperienced captain, mindful of Bristol's notoriety as a port — up a savagely tidal estuary, through a

2

towering, rock-strewn gorge — might well have paused to take stock before deferring to the tow-boat guide, a stranger, in all likelihood. But the weather had been fair all week, and Jacob Swain, the pilot who had beaten off the competition to meet the *Belsize*, intercepting her some seventy miles down the coast, had known Addison for seventeen years, guiding him to and from port on many occasions, even acting as midwife to this voyage, some nineteen months ago.

Still, it wasn't until the ship's fourth morning in the Mouth that the Captain gathered his crew on the foredeck. The rigging buzzed with breeze, timbers creaked, swell slapped at the hull. He drew the sailors close before he spoke, leaving Swain, who was struggling to light his pipe at the ship's stern, firmly out of the circle, and what he said, though muted by the wind, registered in each man's face.

On the rising tide then, the *Belsize* inched towards port. The haze began to lift. The tow-rope, taut between Swain's yawl and the ship, dripped diamonds. Addison stood squinting on deck, the sinews in his legs stiffening as the walls of rock began to rise. In the low morning sun the gorge's scarred sides glowed the pink of a deck running with blood. The Captain shuddered. Either side of his mouth, a dagger of silver in his short black beard emphasised the set of his jaw. His pulse was heavy and dull in his ears, the circuitry of his veins overwrought.

Waring's voice cut through the pounding. "It's a peculiar feeling, coming home. So much to relay, never mind get on with. It's hard to know where to begin!" The surgeon rubbed his hands together in gleeful anticipation.

Addison nodded, grimacing.

Reading the Captain's mood, Waring fingered his ginger whiskers and changed tack. "No, it doesn't matter whether you're a clerk coming back from the counting house at the end of the day, or a soldier returning from war, nothing much ever alters at home. It casts a sort of . . . doubt, don't you think? On the nature of mutability. Yes, in my experience the fact that nothing has changed can make a man question whether he's been away at all."

"Everything changes," Addison stated. "Jessop's diverted the river and completed his ingenious dock, for one."

"Yes, but —"

"Which makes it all the more important for me to concentrate on reaching port safely, much as I'd like to spend the morning philosophising with you."

The surgeon's fingers were plump as sausages, and though they'd switched to wringing one another now in concern, something about his hands still bore the smug look of a farmer whose cow had produced twin calves. Which made sense; although they hadn't spoken of it directly for over a year, the Captain knew the extent to which Waring had put his personal savings behind this voyage. The surgeon stood to see his investment well advanced by the *Belsize*'s safe return.

Addison drove his point home. "You'd not thank me if, for example, distracted by your theories of mutability, I were to split the ship open on St Vincent's Rocks."

"No. Quite right," said the surgeon, backing away from the rail.

In truth the Captain wasn't worried about docking safely. The breeze had dropped in the gorge, the tide bore the *Belsize* forward gently, and Swain was more than competent to pilot the ship into the arms of the new lock. Approaching Hotwells,

4

the plashing of oars ahead and the ringing of birdsong from the wooded cliffs were the only sounds to disturb the still morning air. Yet Addison felt no sense of peace. He took in Dundry church, a notch on the distant blue hills, shut one eye, and thought of a gun-sight. Barbarity, the Captain knew, thrives whatever the colour of the sky.

Jessop's fancy lock, now that he'd completed it, was disappointingly small. Behind it lay a wet dock of some eighty acres, but the *Belsize* barely made it through the lock gates. Tomorrow's ships certainly wouldn't. Galvanising the Merchant Venturers to make this investment had taken the best part of forty years, and what they'd come up with was too little, too late. They'd sooner spend their money on building castles in Clifton than sink it back into the port that made them rich in the first place. Quick cash, made through toil — and the Devil's own risks — undertaken by the likes of Addison, that was their game. The Captain spat and stumped back up to the quarterdeck. What he stood to make from this voyage would barely float him out of the reach of bankruptcy. No, he hadn't even Waring's measure of money; the stuff was like water, forever running through his hands.

"Christ, you'd think banishing the tide would serve to improve the smell," Addison growled. "If anything the place reeks worse than it did before."

"Less of a flow to flush out the harbour now, Captain," a voice said in response. It belonged to Blue, the Negro sailor, who was on his knees, running a hemp rope around itself in mesmerising figures of eight. Aldridge, with whom he was at work squaring away the tackle, underlined his agreement with an oath.

5

In fact the smell, though brackish, did not approach the potentially bad stench of a ship's hold, and both men knew it, and their dutiful charade pleased the Captain, lifting his spirits as the *Belsize*, trailing weed and clouds of sediment, bumped its way through the lock.

For a moment the completed floating harbour, as compared with the old river port he'd sailed from all those months ago, impressed Addison as a miracle. The tow-boat's oars ahead dropped pearls into a lake of liquid silver, and the ship's timbers beneath the Captain's feet, innocent and steadfast throughout the voyage, came alive to him again.

He felt, in the slowing of his heart, the *Belsize*'s shameless relief at returning home safely.

Sheets above him slackened. Lines unfurled ashore.

Church bells vied with those of the cathedral, blurring the hour.

The tension drained from Addison's face. He dropped his head and rolled his shoulders: never mind his own financial ineptitude — the consignment would see him right in the short term anyhow — he had done what was asked of him, and of that he could be proud.

At that moment, high above the docks on Clifton Hill, Ivan Brook was searching for his spade.

To the uninitiated, one spade may look very like another, but no two are the same. Never mind the thickness, smoothness and weight of the wooden shaft, or the balance of the tool in your hands, the real difference lies in the blade. One blade is as distinct from another's, to those who use them daily, as quills are to scribes. A really good one, like the one Ivan Brook had been using the day before, is worn and

6

thin; not so old as to be snag-toothed, but light, sharp at the tip, and — in the right hands — precise.

Ivan should have taken his spade back down the hill with him when they finished up last night. But yesterday had been pay-day, and a spade is no use to a man in the pub. So he'd stood it at the back of the works' shed, apart from the others, before dropping down to the Mandrake first, then the Old King and on to the Admiral's Purse. Where he'd ended up after that, God alone could remember. Still, Ivan Brook understood himself well enough to know the urge to retrieve his spade would help him out of bed in the morning, and drive him back up Granby Hill to work.

Which it had. But although he was first on site his spade wasn't where he'd left it. This annoyed him. It meant that somebody had stayed behind, or returned, to hide the thing, either in earnest, so that they might use it instead of him, or — he had to admit this was much more likely — as a wind-up, a surprise.

Ivan Brook did not like surprises.

And from bitter experience he knew his workmates knew this. So he sorted through the remaining spades, inspecting each one until he found a halfway decent replacement, determined to ignore his loss and deny satisfaction to whoever had duped him. He would keep a step ahead of them this time.

He'd be cutting foundations today. More holes. Lately that was just about all they had him doing, digging the footings for great houses up in Clifton, high above the city and docks. Why anybody would want to live so far from the heart of things baffled Ivan Brook, but then the sort of people he was digging holes for were a mystery to him, too. From up here the big merchants didn't have to tilt their heads so far back to look down their noses at the rest of town, he supposed. Each of these houses had to be bigger than the last, and each footing had to be dug correspondingly deeper, so that Ivan thought, as he trod the planks spanning the trenches and dropped down to where the earth, turned yesterday, was still a dark, reddish brown, there'd soon be more hole in Clifton than hill.

He looked about the trench. Then he looked at the earth flung down the slope. He ground his teeth. A good labourer takes as much care with where he throws the spoils as he does over the shape of the hole he's digging. Somebody had destroyed Ivan's neat mound. The same joker as had hidden his spade, no doubt. He skirted the ragged pile of earth to where butterflies wove amongst the newly flattened buddleia stems. The slope fell away steeply here, so that the dock and sheep-spattered hills of Somerset were visible through the treetops. He put his hands on his hips, felt the breeze on his face, took a deep breath — smelling wet-earth and crushed greenery — and let his gaze fall through the view.

And then he saw it.

His spade!

Flung handle-first into the undergrowth, so that the blade appeared to be raised in salute.

He picked his way quickly downhill, through broken plants and another drift of dirt, which should have given like snow when he trod on it but didn't, because it covered something hard which rolled like a log beneath Ivan's foot, pitching him on to his hands and knees in the nettles instead.

"For God's sake!"

He brushed himself down, took up the spade, then turned and prodded at the offending ground with it, and uncovered a blackened human head.

His breath, hooking on disbelief, hung in his chest.

Ivan bent to look more closely.

One eye gone completely. Lips peeled back. Gums studded with brown teeth. Burnt parchment skin, almost . . . counterfeit. But no, no, no, unmistakably, a real human head. It was attached to a woman's body, complete with arms and legs, all of which Ivan scraped clean of earth with gentle expertise. Adders churned in the workman's stomach: a charred smell filled his nostrils. This body was not long burned, meaning — he guessed — the woman was not long dead. His spade caught on something metal between her legs. Manacles: she had been chained ankle to ankle. And there was something not right about her middle as well, something was missing from it. The snakes rose up Ivan's throat. There was a hole where the woman's belly should have been: she'd been disembowelled.

Ivan threw up. Beer scum. Salty tears.

Voices filtered through the foliage, planks bouncing beneath hobnail boots, shapes moving on the scaffold above. John Booth, it sounded like, and the foreman, Fraser Tremlock, ordering him to make a start. Not a sympathetic man, but Lord, he would know what to do about this, wouldn't he?

And then, all of a sudden it occurred to Ivan Brook that whoever had done this terrible thing — chained a woman so she could not run away, ripped her open, killed her, burnt her, and half-buried her body on a building site — had done so using his spade. Feeling a new sob rising in his chest, he turned it into a call for help, which subsided to a muttering plea as, stamping on the shoulder of his spade, he drove it deep into the unbroken ground, again and again and again.

"Jabbering insanely and digging like a dervish," is how the foreman later described Ivan in his statement. "And covered in goose-grass, and stinking of drink, and generally looking like he'd spent the night in a ditch."

But even as he and John Booth wrested the spade from the labourer, Tremlock earning himself a broken nose in the process, both men heard Ivan holler that he was simply trying to clean the blade.

CHAPTER
ONE

Church bells dissolved in the hubbub as I entered the Thunderbolt Street Coffee Shop. It stood full, but I was unconcerned. Mary always serves us regulars first. Tips, *to insure prompt service*, might help a newcomer up the ladder for his next visit, but I can see the shop's front door from my bedroom window, and have been a patron for six years!

That morning — on which I first heard mention of the *Belsize* — began like any other. I spied the only free seat in Thunderbolts, sidestepped through the crowd and claimed it. Bleary-eyed, I looked down. My flies were undone. Should I risk drawing attention to the oversight by doing the buttons up, or reach for a news-sheet to spread across my thighs? Mary was at my side before I'd done either, bearing my regular order on a raised tray. Mercifully, her attention seemed to be fixed on the back of my head.

"Bad dream? Or have they laid a hedge down the middle of the street?"

I smoothed my wretched curls with one hand, leaving the other in my lap.

"You'd do better flattening that with an iron," said Mary, winking. "I'll lend you mine, if you're good."

For a horrible moment I did not know what she was referring to. My lap-hand leapt up to reveal my innocence, but the waitress was already turning away. Bugger bed-hair! It was Lilly's fault, for encouraging me to grow it long. I resolved to visit the barber's at lunchtime.

"Thank you, Mary," I said to the waitress's retreating back.

Mornings present a circular problem. Until I've had a cup of coffee, I can only ever manage this confused, half-awake state. At its worst, the torpor glues my head to the pillow. But to get that first cup I have to prise myself from bed. Which means that although my desk in Adam Carthy's office is in the same building as my own bedroom (lodgings were part of the deal as an articled clerk: I've not found the time or inclination to move out since qualifying) I invariably manage to arrive at work late.

My pocket watch suggested I was already late that morning.

But I've been a bona fide attorney for six months now. Though my work — and wages — still come through Carthy, it is surely up to me to decide exactly when I do it? As ever, the coffee — venomous, scalding — worked its wonders on my powers of reason, or at least my instinct for self-justification.

I sipped at my cup, considering the travails waiting for me back across the street.

As the week before, and the week after next, I would be spending much of my day sifting through dock records. Reconciliation. Carthy won the Dock Company as a client recently, and consequently the job of cross-checking port records for the past umpteen years, in the hope of rooting out and chasing down ships and traders who hadn't paid their dues. This has necessitated a thorough examination of the documented history of port fees paid and import duties levied and bills-of-lading disclosed and wharfage accounts and . . . I found myself yawning and reaching for my cup again, not halfway through the list. A forced march, infantry work, which Carthy, the cavalry, passed straight on to me, eyes blazing beneath bristling brows (they own his face, Carthy's magnificent eyebrows) when he described the importance of the job. Try as I might, I couldn't quite muster my master's reformist zeal. Where Carthy saw an opportunity to help the Dock Company bring the port into the new century, I could not help thinking that the recently formed authority was made up of the very people responsible for bogging the city down in the corruption of the century just gone. The Society of Merchant Venturers, who also make up most of the City Council, as it happens: the same folk who set the port duties so prohibitively high (double London, three times Liverpool), exacerbating the problem of fee-avoidance in the first place.

Any consternation I might have shared with Carthy in the face of such entrenched crookedness was dampened by the fact that I, and not he, was the man facing months amongst the document crates.

CHAPTER
TWO

Better equipped for that morning, at least, I drained my cup, buttoned my fly (the coffee had galvanised me: I did not care who noticed), and headed across the street to my office, where I discovered that a four-year-old girl had chosen to pitch her tablecloth tent beneath my desk. Anne Carthy has pigeon toes and a marked squint, but she was born laughing and is the only person alive her father considers more important than his work.

"Apologies for the intrusion," said Carthy, appearing in the doorway. He looked from my desk to the mantelpiece clock. "I thought somebody might as well make use of the facilities, until you need them, that is."

I squatted behind my chair, peeled back the tent-flap and asked, "Can I have a pound of eels' eyes and some minced dog?"

Anne squealed and wriggled out from the far side of the desk, then busied herself seriously, reefing in the tablecloth.

I took in the terrain of my desktop. Unread files lay to one side, and the papers I had already examined stood in their neat heap to the other. Between them were the documents I'd been working on last night, corners squared, next to my ledger, inkpot and quill pen. All as it should be. Yet the carefully imposed order was upset by an extra sheaf of papers, bursting from their blue ribbon, plonked at an angle on top of my blotter.

I reached quickly to remove the offending bundle, prompting Carthy to laugh behind me. His office is always a bugger's muddle.

"Keep your hair on!" My resolution to visit the barber hardened despite his jovial tone. "I took the liberty of prioritising that folder for today. Assuming, of course, that it's no trouble for you to do some work. I thought you could perhaps even make a start before lunch."

"I'll consider it. No, really, I will. What's inside?"

"The *Belsize* made port today. She's owned by the Western Trading Company. I thought I might add a bit of urgency to your quest by suggesting you examine their records today. That is the most recent instalment."

"*Ship arrives in port*. Stop the press. Why the sudden rush to welcome the *Belsize*?"

Carthy's lips folded into his beard and his porcupine eyebrows dipped. But he seemed to think better of what he was about to tell me. "Check the file. See if it turns up anything," he said.

He stood aside to steer his daughter, now a ghoul beneath the tablecloth, from the room, following her before I could add another question. This has long been his method as a teacher, to set me off on a journey with the barest clues as to the destination, and let me feel my way there for myself. I hung my jacket on the back of my chair. The strip of wallpaper to the right of the window casement lolled at me, an indolent tongue. It hadn't unpeeled further since yesterday, and the stain behind it had not spread, which suggested that the previous evening had not been Anne's bath night.

I prised up the sash. Fresh air could only help me in my battle to stay awake.

Which I managed, despite the stultifying muddle of paperwork that sprang from the blue ribbon once I'd undone it. Why couldn't shipping clerks sequence forms chronologically? And, given that they could not, why hadn't somebody at the Dock Company imposed order upon the chaos before passing the bundle on? The knowledge that this was what they were paying me to do didn't help. Boredom gnawed at my resolve. Once upon a time, lawyering promised liberty from Father and the family business, but no such freedom has materialised; I am still in debt for the payment he made to Carthy to secure my articled clerkship. What's more, the old man accepted my decision not to join the family firm with an equanimity bordering on relief. He even assured me that my share of the business would be well looked after by Sebastian and John, until such time as it became my inheritance, effectively placing me in the thrall of my younger brothers.

I chose lawyering because it's more sensible than art, but in truth that's where my heart lies. Unfortunately, heart and talent do not always coincide. I have a limited aptitude for pictures: though I can form a drawing well enough, I am completely bamboozled by paint. I've tried watercolours, egg tempura and oils, all with the same, muddy results. So my artistic endeavours are limited to the making of sketches in ink ... and in private. Who would want to hang a scratchy impression of a spade, rain-cloud, or side of beef on their wall, anyway? Nobody. Since those are the sorts of things I find myself compelled to produce, I prefer to keep the results between shut covers. The only time I've made an exception to this rule still makes me wince: in a fit of openness — or to impress her, if I'm honest — I showed a series of unconvincingly optimistic drawings (a robin's nest, daffodil bulbs, a rowing boat) to Lilly not long after we first met. She declared herself "charmed" by them. Ever since then I've kept my sketchbooks in a strongbox with a good lock. The law is at least a realistic means of making my own way in the world.

I ground on through the remains of that morning — more out of loyalty to Carthy than anything else — only pausing once, towards lunchtime, when I came across a document which, when I'd read it, propelled me from my desk to stand before the window again, eyes lifted to the sky. I thought for a moment, chewing on my lower lip. Seagulls knifed this way and that above the rooftops.

"You may as well call on her for lunch if the alternative is such productive mooning."

Carthy had appeared in the doorway again. I would have liked to tell him that I had not paused to think of Lilly all morning, but in trying to persuade him of that, I sensed I would achieve the opposite, and besides, I felt a stab of something approaching shame at admitting the omission to myself.

"Perhaps I will," I said.

"Don't look so happy about it! This phase will soon pass. I remember it well. No sooner have you popped the question than the napkin-and-bunting conundrums begin."

Carthy was avoiding addressing the contents of the folder with this prattle. For now I did so, too.

"After submitting to the colour swatches for half an hour, I'll be sure to return to work refreshed."

"All excitements are relative, it's true," said Carthy, brows creased in mock-concern. "Well, I'll leave you to it. Pass on my condolences to the bride." Continuing in his attempt to lighten my mood, he pushed off the doorjamb as if underwater and lurched down the hall affecting the walk he'd developed for his Caliban in the Law Society's last *Tempest*.

CHAPTER
THREE

I went out. I set off across Queen Square in the direction of the Alexanders' great house, but found myself dawdling, and ultimately doglegged right towards the docks. I would be seeing Lilly soon enough. Now wasn't the moment to go visiting. Instead I allowed the thought of the down on the back of her neck, visible in strong sunlight when she wears her hair piled on top of her head, to buoy me on to the waterfront, where the sun was indeed out, and swarming in the harbour with a violence that made molten gold of the water's surface.

Before my eyes had adjusted to the brightness a cart was upon me — my fault, I had walked into its path — and the horse drawing it, unable to sidestep or stop, had shouldered me into a stall selling fruit, vegetables, and trinkets made from animal parts. This produce was now rolling with me on the filthy cobbles.

"Out of the fucking way!" called the driver, after the event.

I could not recall the last time I'd had the breath knocked from my lungs, but the feeling (and taste, of gunpowder and rust) was instantly familiar, and sickening. I gathered myself on to all fours. The stallholder, a woman with sideburns and a dusting of grey moustache, was also bent double, yammering in my face. One or two of her colleagues from the neighbouring stalls were apparently under the impression that I had launched myself at the woman's mean trestle of goods on purpose. They surrounded me now in a show of solidarity. Try as I might, I could not speak. Shaking my head from side to side in an attempt to clear it only made matters worse. The throng seemed to think I was denying something. Wrapped around one of my hands was a string of severed rabbits' feet. In reaching for my wallet, I must have looked like I was trying to pocket the charm, a manoeuvre the crowd did not appreciate. Having drawn back, one of the circle now saw fit to produce a blade. It winked cheerfully in the brightness. On such a day — how could this be happening? But it was. In the absence of me explaining myself or attempting flight, the stallholders were closing in again. Absurd! I'd have to hold them off until I could find the wind to speak. But when my first breaths came, they exploded from me in threatening gasps. Never mind summon the composure to fight, I hadn't even managed to let go of the wretched rabbits' feet. The circle tightened further.

From nowhere, a presence arrived at my side.

A black man, in baggy cotton trousers and a sleeveless shirt: bull-shoulders and muscle-cabled arms. He nodded at me and took hold of my hand, from the fingers of which he unwound the good luck charm. This he presented to the stallholder. Then he began to pick up the spilled fruit.

20

The man's calm was so deep it felt threatening.

My breathing sawed slower in my chest.

I wanted to apologise, but I found myself taking the sailor's lead instead, picking apples and blackberries from the dirt. When I looked up the circle of assailants had dilated, leaving onlookers, who in turn drifted away. In silence I fished some coins from my pocket and offered them to the stallholder, who wasted no time vanishing them beneath her skirts. When I turned around the Negro was already walking away.

I caught him up, offering thanks.

"You had bad luck." He nodded back down the dock. "I saw the whole thing."

"For a moment there . . ." I trailed off. In the presence of the sailor, the spat seemed inconsequential.

"It was no trouble. Think nothing of it."

I extended a hand. The black sailor shook it, then turned and walked straight up a ship's gangplank. From the look of her, the ship had only just arrived; her sails were still partly unfurled and the stevedores were just beginning to bring her cargo above deck. As often happened in the immediate aftermath of a shot of fear — or strong coffee — I experienced a moment of prescience: I knew before I had advanced to the ship's prow, where her name was painted red in deep carved letters, that I was standing alongside the Western Trading Company's three-masted frigate, the *Belsize*.

I am no sailor. Nevertheless, as I stood on the quayside, looking up at the swaying masts, I felt my heartbeat slow.

The *Belsize* struck me as a tidy ship.

And my ribs ached. I knew they would be sore in bed that night. Yet I had to admit that the confrontation had been more viscerally involving than the morning's work; it had pitched me to a precipice from which I could better contemplate the possible import of the ship.

The document to prompt my early lunch break had detailed investors in the Western Trading Company, among whose number stood my father, Michael Bright. Carthy knew as well as I did that my father's firm had interests in ships which journeyed to the West Indies, but the bulk of the family business lies in refining the trade's fruits, which suggested that my master must be expecting me to turn up something else in the file as well. What, exactly? A sense of disquiet swept over me, subtle as a breeze serrating still water. My eye ran the length of the *Belsize*. She was big, over a hundred feet from bow to stern. There were few sailors visible on board, save an officer, with two grey lines in his beard, standing on the quarterdeck. One hand worked his brow, the other dived inside his coat and pulled out a silver pocket watch. The man checked it perfunctorily, then looked over the rail. When the sweep of his gaze reached me it continued past without snagging, taking in the quay with a look of distrust.

My legs had grown heavy. It would be the shock passing. To counter the leadenness, I returned to Thunderbolts for lunch and to take stock. Though I'd have preferred peace and quiet, the place was abuzz, and Alan Faulks saw fit to include me in the morning's gossip. Something about a drunken labourer in Clifton roasting women over hot coals. The news is always broadcast here first, but it is usually wise to wait until *Felix Farley's Bristol Journal* has sieved it of the worst embellishments. Though Faulks talks with a fat-tongued lisp, the impediment hasn't curtailed his enthusiasm for speech. I found myself explaining that I had to get back to work, then discovered — with some surprise — that I did in fact feel a sense of urgency about returning to my desk. I would have drained my cup in one swig if I'd been a man of fashion: these days it is becoming popular to pollute coffee with cream or milk, which cools it, and so speeds up an establishment's custom.

But I prefer my coffee black.

So I let the man's prattle wash over me, and finished my drink slowly, apprehension shivering beneath my skin.

CHAPTER
FOUR

Though Oni rubs her sides, crouching over the fire of her panic, there is no warmth to be had in the cellar. She shivers in the dark. The crack of light above the door has long since disappeared, leaving cave blackness, a blinding nothingness.

She listens for the other girls. Both are sleeping. Abeni draws deep, regular breaths, waves on a distant shore. Idowu fights a more ragged battle with the damp, underground air. From time to time one of them moves on the straw. The outside noise, which filtered into the hole during the day, is gone now, apart, that is, from the distant song of the bird. It starts, and stops. A bird singing at night is wrong. Oni shivers again, draws her knees to her chest and stands up slowly. She puts her arms out in front of her and, shuffling with the chain, sleepwalks the few paces to the opposite wall.

Her fingers find a hardness, rough as bark, running with cold sap. Wet bricks. The sap tastes of iron when she licks it. Everything about the hole is damp. It has a wet-fur smell, unpleasant, but nothing like the putrid stench of the ship.

Why build a wall underground?

Oni digs her fingernails into her thigh as a punishment because that is a question and she must not ask questions. If you make the mistake of looking for answers, you go mad. She saw that happen so often below deck it became boring.

Didn't they realise? Questions are as pointless as days, hours and minutes. Better to navigate heartbeat by heartbeat, blink by blink, breath by breath.

There is a cough, followed by a shuffling sound as Idowu shifts in her sleep. She will die soon. They all will, but Idowu will be first, because of the wet air. Her lungs can't cope with it; she is coughing up bits of them in protest. No, Idowu's only hope is in following Ayo soon. Again Oni digs her fingers into her thighs.

Breathe in, breathe out. At least that is possible. During the first crossing the air in the hold was so thick that at times she thought she was suffocating. She feared she would choke to death as others around her did. A gap of just three hand-spans separated the boards they lay upon from those above their heads. Here she can stand up, walk these few paces even, right to the end of the chain. Oni bends to adjust its grip on her ankle, then picks up the first links and follows them to their fixing on the wall. The hoop of metal through which the chain passes is as thick as her wrist, the bolt attaching it to the wall is as big as her closed fist. Where do they think she will run? Oni feels her thigh burn and then glow dully with the punishment of another pinch, but it is no use, the next thoughts tumble through her head regardless. So strong a chain cannot be explained by her worth to these devil people; it is instead a warning of how hard they know she might fight to get away if she understood the worse terror that lies ahead.

CHAPTER
FIVE

The paper trail confirmed my suspicions: the Western Trading Company had underpaid import duties and shirked its share of the port fees. Having re-sequenced the file chronologically, I worked my way forwards from the first recorded voyages in which the Company had invested, through to the ships they owned outright, all the while setting declared cargo against duties and fees. The columns did not tally. Since the majority of the Company's shareholders were also members of the Merchant Venturers, who owned the docks and levied the fees, the merchants had in effect been cheating themselves, which . . . I flicked through more receipts, stifling a yawn . . . more or less amounted to cheating nobody at all.

Voices filtered into my office from the landing. Carthy and his daughter Anne, reciting the alphabet together, a prelude to her reading lesson. Though she is laughably young — and a girl — Carthy is fanatical about this daily ritual. He likes to joke that my scepticism is understandable; one day Anne will inherit the practice, making her my employer. With his customary contrariness, Carthy led by mis-example.

"P.I.G. spells HORSE!"

"No, no, no!"

I stiffened in my seat, a new document before me.

"What then? DRAGON? HALIBUT? I can't make it out."

"Pig!" Anne shrieked.

I spread the paper flat upon my blotter. The name upon it did not change. Nor did the figures. Michael Bright, my father, a Western Trading Company member these last two years had, ten months ago, made a payment of two hundred and twelve pounds, nine shillings and four pence, to settle the Company's unpaid balance of dock fees and import duties.

"M.O.O.N."

"That's not a word."

"Yes it is, Daddy!"

"No it's not. It's the sound a cow makes."

I totted up the figures. The remittance, dated 13 December 1808, cleared the substantial deficit owed by the Company at that time. Which ... was a relief, wasn't it? A number of Western Trading Company ships had docked since then, including the *Spirit,* the *Good Hand,* and the *Ranger* this summer, and there were still sums outstanding in relation to them, but the Company would no doubt clear those further debts too, when approached. The receipt detailing the payment made by my father suggested as much, didn't it? I was cross-checking the figures when Carthy, lesson complete, appeared in my doorway.

"Early start. But it'll take more than such grandstanding diligence to pull the wool over my eyes."

I reported my findings.

"Right. So they still owe money."

"Yes, but it looks like they'll pay, as I say —"

"And I look like I might increase your wages one day, but I wouldn't count on it."

"That said —"

Carthy's brows dipped, cutting me off. "I doubt the Dock Company consider it good enough for merchants to remunerate them as and when they feel like it."

Carthy was right, of course, but his objection still rankled. This aspect of the law, the pernickety bit, in seeming so wilfully to ignore the bigger picture, lowers my spirits. Time and again I've heard Carthy's mantra: "detail is the Devil's mask". I know he's right. On a good day I feel equipped to penetrate the veil. On a bad day it blinds me. My shoulders slumped.

"Come now," Carthy's tone softened. "You've done what was asked of us. If these are your findings, so be it. We'll report them to Mr Orton and he can decide what to do. Who knows, he may even be of your persuasion."

Carthy had advanced to the window and was feigning interest in the limited view it gave of the street. The pretence, coupled with his "so be it", further unsettled me. I ran my finger around the inside of my collar. I had not mentioned my father by name to Carthy. Why? Because his involvement was not strictly relevant. If anything, since my father had last cleared the Company's debts, he appeared in the best light. Did he not? Regardless, it was one thing to have chosen not to work for the family business, quite another to strew obstacles in its path. I would hold fire until I'd spoken with Father himself about the matter.

Anne wandered into the office now, a tube of rolled paper pressed to her eye. Carthy's brows immediately unfolded at the sight of her.

"What's that you've got?"

"A telescope."

"Do you mean to inspect Inigo with it?" the lawyer asked, gathering his daughter up. "Or were you going to lend it to him, the more closely to examine his case with?"

Again I stiffened in my chair.

"Neither. It's for you. To look at the moon with," Anne said.

Carthy picked up his daughter under one arm and squeezed her like a set of bagpipes. She duly squealed. He said, "We need to go and practise your piano playing," to her. And to me: "It would be useful if your final reckoning of the sum outstanding could incorporate whatever the Company owes in respect of the last ship, the *Belsize*. Attend to that."

I nodded.

"Then begin again with the rest of the dock records. The crate will no doubt furnish further . . . anomalies." He squeezed a further chirrup from Anne and turned away, muttering, "Hours of fun."

CHAPTER
SIX

That evening I went home. I did not take Carthy's rickety coach, preferring to walk despite the bank of grey cloud which had overrun the clear sky at lunchtime and now pulsed with fine drizzle. A veil of droplets too small to see swept across my face and clung to the wool of my greatcoat and beaded in my hair. I put my head down up the steep hill of Park Street, towards the great house in which I grew up, the home my father commissioned beside Brandon Hill on his return from the West Indies some twenty-one years ago.

Nothing much about the house, inside or out, has altered in at least fourteen years, not since my stepmother, Clarissa, died. Shucking off my coat, I took stock. The worn tiles of the hall floor hadn't moved. Nor had the mahogany chest which squatted upon them, or the silver candlesticks which stood sentry on its dull lid. The portrait of my grandfather astride his black horse still hung on the landing wall. I ran my hands through the damp tangle of my hair, thinking: the house is too big, that's the problem. Carthy's place in town may be taller, but Bright House is wider, squarer, deeper, never mind the stables and grounds.

It's too spread out. That's why Carthy's place feels full but home has always felt empty, even before Clarissa died.

More sameness washed over me: the familiar sound of Sebastian playing the piano upstairs. As a child, my youngest brother played piano to soothe a nervous disposition. Father even credited the instrument with having cured his stutter. I wiped my feet on the faded hall rug and made my way up to the music room. The door stood ajar. I glimpsed the paleness of Sebastian's neck, his fair head bent over the keys.

"Where is everyone?" I asked.

He looked up, shrugged and said, "You're staying for dinner though? They'll no doubt be here then."

"Father keeping you busy?"

"The work does that by itself. It's not called business for nothing."

"What's he got you doing?"

"This and that," Sebastian sighed, then picked out a flurry of notes.

I traced a line in the dust on top of the piano. Did Sebastian think I would not be interested in the detail? The line became a snake. There could be no deeper reason, could there?

"When is Father going to employ a proper cleaner?" I asked. "Either Mrs Watson's eyes are failing or she's working on the basis that you three are blind to her efforts."

"She's loyal, and a bit of dust never hurt anyone." Sebastian played a loud chord. "Since when did you grow so fussy?"

A dog barked downstairs. Hearing my father clunk down his stick and mutter the dog into silence, I felt a sudden surge of tenderness towards Sebastian, and ridiculous for questioning his reticence to discuss business. He simply doesn't care much for work. Like me, he'd no doubt prefer to spend his time doing something else. Composing songs, perhaps. He, however, has never been granted the option to go his own way. Nobody stood between *me* and the door.

Claws clicked and faded, moving from the rug and down the flagstone hall. Dog and master were on their way to the study. I left Sebastian and went downstairs. My father seldom uses the house's formal reception rooms; when not in Bright & Co.'s counting house he is most often to be found here, cocooned in memorabilia. Framed contracts, deeds and bills, and a pair of etchings showing planters in Barbados adorn one wood-panelled wall. Opposite there's a fox-head hung with its milky eye to the window. I stood in the doorway and watched as Father drew a pipe from his jacket pocket, thumbed it full of tobacco and struck a match. The flame painted his square, balding brow, the implacable nose, the boxer's chin. I took a step into the room and, as the flame died, made out the broken capillaries which reddened his weather-worn cheeks. The wall-eyed fox-head had belonged to the quarry of his first hunt, killed some thirty-five years ago. He still shoots throughout the season and rides out with the Aust foxhounds most weeks.

Seeing me now, Father sucked hard on his pipe, advanced, clapped me on both shoulders, turned in a circle, then threw himself into his favoured armchair. He settled himself. Only then did the smoke explode from his nostrils.

"You need a haircut," he said.

I resisted the temptation to flatten my curls. It is unnerving, this ability of his to home in on a person's sensitivities, no matter how trifling, and jab at them with a pin.

"They have good barbershops in town. So something else must have driven you up the hill. The wine. For the wedding. I've already said it'll be my pleasure to furnish it."

Upstairs, Sebastian's piano recital faltered, stopped, then took off again.

"No reason or excuse. I just thought I'd call in."

Father raised his eyes to the yellow plaster ceiling above us and smiled. "Well, it can't have been on account of the entertainment."

"How's business?"

The smile stayed in place — perhaps registering the out-of-character nature of the question — until he saw fit to draw deeply on his pipe again. Smoke rolled from his mouth. Finally he said, "Passable, since you ask. Profitable, even. The same can't be said for Cartwright, Dudley and those other poor fools who stuck at the African trade to the bitter end. But for the more progressive traders, such as us, dealing in humdrum commodities, sugar, tea," he waggled his pipe, "and good old tobacco, all's well. It's a miracle, really. The predicted apocalypse for all merchants just hasn't happened. So yes, we're rubbing along. There's certainly enough fat on the hog's back to contribute to the grand celebration; if the Alexanders will allow our help, that is."

"They're appreciative of the gesture, as I've said."

"I'll wager they are!"

"And your hip?"

Reminded of the injury, Father's eyes darkened. He rose from his seat and stumped to the worktable on which lay the disassembled components of his twelve-gauge pheasant gun. He lifted the barrel to the light and winked down it. He is a young forty-eight, vigorous still, and proud of his prowess both as a shot and in the saddle. Yet he fell from his horse late last winter, injured his leg, and to his dismay hadn't been able to shake off the hurt. The sound of his stick on the hall floor had told me that the hip still hadn't mended, and despite knowing how he would hate to be reminded of the injury, it seemed I had done exactly that. He replaced the barrel carefully amidst the felt cleaning rags, and slapped his hip with a feigned lack of concern.

"Damnable. It'll mend. But the going's slow. That said —"

"I wonder whether the riding is helping?"

"The riding has nothing to do with it."

"Really?"

"Yes. Lounging around never cured anything," he replied. "Now, the sun's past the yardarm. What can I get you to drink?"

One of Bright House's cellar-rooms is stocked with a good range of wine, bought on the advice of Father's old friend, George Heard. Father himself appreciates the value of the collection more than the subtleties of its taste, but is generous with it nevertheless. The offer signalling a truce, I sat back in one of the leather armchairs before the fire while he went to retrieve a bottle. Perhaps Sebastian guessed at the development; he stopped playing upstairs; silence flooded the study. Then the quieter noises — the lapping of flames, Father's uneven footsteps on the wooden floor, the wind through treetops in the garden — or was it distant caterwauling — asserted themselves. The lurcher, curled asleep before the fire, stiffened as the cat-noise broke in upon its dream. Its forelegs twitched and its lip curled to reveal yellow incisors. Did it imagine itself sinking them into the cat, silencing it, as the screech faded?

CHAPTER
SEVEN

Father's mood lifted as the evening progressed. I hoped this had to do with the wine, and not the arrival of Sebastian and John, yet undoubtedly he relaxed in their presence. John, in particular, has a knack of putting him at ease. He has always had a slow-moving complicity around Father that both I and Sebastian lack; it hangs in the heavier set of his bones and fuller figure; you can hear it in the near-ponderous manner of his speech. Wherever a conversation begins with John, it always seems to move towards a joke, with him the willing butt.

"The bear was on a long chain," he was saying now. "We stopped to watch it down by St Nicholas Market. Every time its owner jerked its collar the thing would stand up on its hind legs and clap. Two jerks and it would attempt to keep upright on just the one leg. Hilarious. The man had a tin whistle the bear would dance to. The funniest apparition you ever saw, the great thing lumbering in time to the music on the cobbles! I had to join in, of course, just for a turn, but I got a bit carried away."

"I'll wager," nodded Father. "Two left feet."

"Not at all. Inigo himself must admit I'm the better dancer. It was just the damned chain."

"What happened?" I asked.

"I became entangled. Briefly. Just long enough to lose my footing. In short, I fell headlong into the bear. We ended up in the street."

"Fool!" Father laughed silently.

"Marvellously strong smell on the thing," John said slowly. "And long teeth. Not to worry, though. The owner pulled it back promptly, well out of reach."

"And you informed Jonas Adams of our proposal," said Father. "After this . . . interlude?"

"Of course." John leaned back in his chair and crossed his fleshy calves. "He'll accept."

Both Sebastian and Father nodded sagely at this. I had no idea what they were talking about. As if to underline the point, Father now asked whether I'd had as entertaining a morning as John. Had it involved dancing with a bear?

"I'm afraid not," I admitted. Then I said, "No, my day was altogether more boring. Port fees and import duties. I'm working on a job for the Dock Company. It's a clerk's work, really. Mundane stuff."

John uncrossed his legs. Speaking yet more deliberately than normal, and looking to my father rather than me, he said, "Come, now. No need to play down your more *intellectualised* existence."

A smile passed between my father and brother and the familiar, competitive heat spread across my chest. John's supremacy in the battle for Father's affections has always maddened me, deep down.

Sebastian rose and poured himself a refill from the decanter on the mantelpiece, then bent to stab at the fire with a poker. He abhors confrontation. I quelled my annoyance and stared at my glass. Blood-red wine swam briefly with flame. John repressed a fake yawn. Father twisted his signet ring round his little finger, then muttered, "Wasps' nest, that Dock Company. Be careful not to prod it unduly hard."

Still irked, I replied evenly, "Oh, it's all routine clerking, as I say. Dotting "i"s and crossing "t"s. That's why Mr Carthy has delegated the legwork to me. He has only expressed an interest in the records of one particular ship himself." I looked at Father, found he was still scrutinising his signet ring, and went on slowly. "A ship that docked just yesterday. The *Belstaff* I think she's called. No. The *Belsize*."

Father nodded absently. At length he said, "Did you fear the bear would bite you, John? Was there any intent in its eye when it bared its teeth?"

"Not really," said John. "I think it was more scared of me than I was of it."

I opened my mouth to repeat the word *Belsize*, but refrained. Bright & Co. has investments in concerns beyond the Western Trading Company, which itself takes stakes in many ventures, ships included. Perhaps Father really hadn't heard of the *Belsize*. And even if he had, I knew nothing more of the ship than that its recent arrival in port had raised Carthy's eyebrows. Lord knew it wasn't alone in managing that.

We crossed the hall to the dining room for a dinner of pork chops, cabbage, potatoes and gravy. All of it was overcooked, even the gravy, which swam with caramelised onions. Father, Sebastian and John have always shared a dislike of rare meat. In the Carthy household food has more flavour and meals take time; Mr Carthy himself regards eating as an excuse for conversation about subjects unrelated to work, and his wife's ample figure is testament her commitment to the household's meals. Here we four men sat squarely opposite one another across a table unadorned with cloth or silverware and wolfed our meal in silence. Fuel, untempered by a female touch. Still, there was nothing dishonest about the meal. I took a second helping of potatoes and asked Sebastian to pass the salt.

CHAPTER
EIGHT

Two days later my understanding of the Western Trading Company's records had deepened to a point which required me to talk to Carthy again. Yet he spent his morning taking a witness statement on behalf of a client, and the entire afternoon making an application in court. From there he headed directly to a dinner at the Hot Well. The delay worked upon me with the persistence of rust, blurring my conviction, dulling its edge. Father would be sure to find out I was at the root of the Western Trading Company's misfortune sooner or later, and I knew that "misfortune" really meant "fine". The records showed irregularities above and beyond the sum that Bright & Co. had paid in respect of the Company's debts; put bluntly, the books were impossible to reconcile. In particular, there was insufficient detail about the numbers of slaves the Company had bought and sold before the trade was declared illegal. The Company must have shipped more from the Guinea coast to the Indies than it had declared, or it must have lost fewer in transit, to account for the sums invested in goods subsequently shipped to Bristol. There was outstanding duty on swathes of those goods, too. My father's payment was a sop at best; at worst, it now looked like an attempt to cover up some deeper problem.

The mess could only harm the Western Trading Company as and when it came to light.

If the Company suffered, Father would suffer too.

He'd not keep that suffering to himself. Upon discovering I had been instrumental in bringing it about, he'd be liberal in sharing the harm.

So I waited up to tell Carthy what I'd found, fearful that a night spent sleeping on the matter might fatally weaken my resolve. I spent the time making a sketch. Or at least endeavouring to make one. As so often happened, the blank page had about it something of the quality of a reversed magnet. My attention simply skated away from it. Perhaps I was more preoccupied than I'd realised. That's the trouble with doing the right thing. A man can talk himself out of it so easily. What was the right thing to do about Lilly, for example? I pushed my sketchbook away, dragged my chair over to the window casement and stood upon it to inspect the flap of wallpaper which, Anne no doubt having suffered another bath night, had unpeeled further, a longitudinal slit, revealing a slice of naked plaster wall. Perhaps I could stick it back together with some sealing wax. I rummaged in my desk drawer for a block of the stuff and, candle in hand, was back up on my chair, flame and wax held aloft, dripping red drops down behind the slack wall covering, when Carthy appeared in my doorway.

"You can walk away from the job at any time, Inigo. No need to burn the place down."

"I was just —" I began.

"— but if you're intent on making a statement, there has to be something easier to set fire to than that." Carthy swept his hand in the general direction of my desk. "That lot. I'd set fire to a box of it and throw it into the coal hole. Puff! All our troubles would be over!"

I had climbed down from my chair. I set it before Carthy now, and steered him to sit down. His movements were drink-blunted; he slumped heavily on to the seat and threw an arm over its back. I had seen him the worse for wear before now — often enough through eyes dimmed by the contents of the same bottle — but the warm abandonment Carthy usually exhibited seemed tinged with something more reckless that evening. "You're right, though," he was saying now. "The furnishings aren't up to scratch." He dug at the threadbare rug with the toe of his shoe. "I'll have the matter attended to. Appearances count, after all."

At that moment there was a shout in the street outside. Carthy flinched even before the riposte came, a drunken oath followed by laughter, common enough at such an hour in town. Wondering at his jumpiness, I poured my master a glass of water from the jug on my desk. Then I told him my further misgivings about the accounts.

He appeared to listen. He nodded and sipped and stared at the cloudy water in his glass. Then his toe started tracing the pattern on the rug again. By the time I finished speaking, it was all but tapping.

"Hmm. Yes. Interesting," Carthy said absently.

"I thought so at least."

"And you've been through all their import accounts — anchovies to yams and back again — to spot where duties have and haven't been paid?"

"I have," I smiled. "Anchovies to yams."

"Well, I suppose we must pass all this on to Orton at the Dock Company."

At this I repressed an urge to state my family's interest in the case.

"But it's all a bit . . ." Carthy tossed back the last of his water and upended the empty glass. ". . . a bit dry, don't you think?"

"Dry?"

He kneaded his temples, then rubbed his palm across his furrowed eyebrows, making them bristle all the more. He yawned. I felt impatience prickle across my scalp. I hadn't waited up half the night, struggling with my conscience, to have my findings brushed aside like this. "Perhaps we should continue the conversation in the morning," I said.

Carthy rubbed his eyes and muttered, "No need." Then he yawned again. Something wasn't right with the gesture. Yawns satisfy; this one was perfunctory, over too quickly. It was fake. The drink-blur seemed to have faded fast, too.

"No need?" I repeated.

"I think we need to look somewhere a bit wetter. Juicier detail, that's what we need."

"Wetter?"

"The docks. That ship, the *Belsize*. Have you been on board her yet? Kicked the timbers, sniffed about in the hold?"

"No, I —"

"Well, that's the thing." Another mock-yawn. "The thing to do next. I'll set up a paperwork meeting with Orton for later in the week. In the meantime . . ." Carthy climbed heavily from the chair, stretched out his back, rubbed his forehead again, and waved expansively from the desk to the window. "In the meantime you see if you can't come up with something . . . I don't know . . . something to set fire to the show."

CHAPTER
NINE

As a boy I had a recurring daydream in which every physical thing before me appeared as a prop I'd seen used in a previous scene; likewise, everybody around me was an actor I'd watched before playing a different part. How could they think I would not notice that the man selling mussels on the quay was in fact my Latin master in a poor disguise? Even my own brothers cropped up as market-place extras, my father as the visiting preacher glimpsed from the back of the cathedral. The daydream created the illusion that I was at the centre of things, influencing the deployment of these actors and props, that some inner process of my mind was in fact shaping events, so that the word marigold, say, overheard on my way to the cobbler's, would turn up just minutes later as Mary's gold, a fortune inherited by the cobbler's cousin upon the death of her aged father. Who but me were these echoes orchestrated for, who else could wring meaning from the connections?

Too much coffee. I ordered a refill all the same. Up early, I'd been Thunderbolts' first customer, which in itself had heightened my sense that the story in Felix Farley's newspaper had been written with me in mind.

Now the place was filling up, diminishing my significance, and underlining the foolishness of my delusion. It was a coincidence, nothing more. Nevertheless, I opened the newspaper and read the story again. Until a few days ago I'd never heard of the Western Trading Company. Now it turned out that the Clifton Killer had been discovered attempting to bury his victim's body in the footings of a mansion to be built on the Company's land.

So what?

It was hardly the most interesting detail in the report, most of which seemed to me to undermine its own assertion, in support of Justice of the Peace Jim Wheeler, that the culprit was safely in hand.

The suspect had been named as one Ivan Brook, a local man born and bred. The allegation against this fine Bristolian was that having received his week's wages he'd begun drinking at six in the evening and continued into the small hours, moving from pub to pub and shedding his workmates as he went. The last reliable sighting of the man was at gone midnight, when an aggrieved barmaid he'd just given up pestering had seen him stumbling about outside the Old King. He'd made it across the Welsh Back, from which vantage point he'd relieved himself into the floating dock. Thereupon it was said that he'd staggered off in the direction of Redcliffe, the inference being that he was headed for the alleys beyond that salubrious neighbourhood, in search of a member of the small population of the city's workforce which sees fit to labour at such an hour. His victim, the coroner had reported, was a young woman of no more than eighteen. Nobody had reported such a person as missing, which pointed firmly towards her not having been a Clifton lady, as some were whispering, but instead an unfortunate who dwelt beyond the law. The report ascribed Mr Brook with no motive. It seemed content to surmise that inebriation of the kind he'd already demonstrated that evening was evidence enough of bad character. Perhaps he'd killed out of frustration, too drunk to perform. Or maybe, if he could be given the benefit of the doubt — for it had to be admitted that Mr Brook was of previously sound character — he'd committed his crime out of guilt brought on by a post-coital flash of sobriety. Either way, he'd done his drunken best to vanish the evidence. First, he'd burned the body beyond recognition. The report dwelt upon the detail, telling how the corpse was so badly charred that, never mind its melted face, the coroner had not even been able to deduce the colour of the woman's hair. Conjecture had it that the man might have made use of the brazier at his worksite to carry out the burning. His workmates were evidently now unprepared to light the thing again, preferring to take their break around the flame of rumours instead. Upon extracting the burnt remains, Ivan Brook was said to have made a half-hearted attempt to bury the body in the very trench he'd been cutting before embarking upon his night of evil abandonment. He'd been discovered, still drunk, halfway through the task.

The story did not add up. I took a mouthful of coffee and let it roll burningly across my tongue. For a start, unless they were suggesting the involvement of a horse, it was nonsensical to think that a man, even a labouring man as strong as Ivan Brook, would transport a corpse from beyond the centre of town right up Clifton Hill, simply for the pleasure of burning and burying it on familiar turf. The place was an active building site. Why not just slide the body into the river? It would likely have been discovered sooner or later, bobbing about in the floating harbour, or given up at low tide, but not before the rats, gulls and turbid water had disfigured it, and who was to point then to Mr Brook's involvement in any case? Brook was apparently maintaining that he'd been disturbed in the act of uncovering the body, not burying it. That seemed plausible; all inferences to the contrary appeared to hang on his having been drunk. The man wasn't popular with his workmates, it was alleged. He kept himself to himself. The absurdity of it! A leap of logic that would condemn a man for murder because he'd been observed pissing into the harbour at midnight. By that reckoning half the men in Bristol stood eligible for transportation.

Innocent or guilty, the best Ivan Brook could hope for now would be the remainder of a life lived under a boiling sun, machete in one hand, razor stalks of sugar grass shredding the other, his broad shoulders withering beneath the weight of the work, and the heat, and the disease. Since the abolition of the trade, plantation owners are more desperate than ever for indentured labourers with which to replace those slaves who break daily in the cane fields. Any able body will do. It didn't matter that Ivan Brook's landlady had come forward to state that at an hour she could not be sure of she believed she'd heard her lodger bang his way up the wooden stairs and thump into bed. No, because even if Justice Wheeler failed to cook up sufficient evidence with which to ensure that Ivan Brook swung at home for the crime, he'd nevertheless force a settlement upon the man condemning him to die more slowly on a distant shore.

I pushed the paper away in disgust. Mary, the morning shift waitress, was sidestepping between the nearby tables, tray held high. As she squeezed between two seatbacks her skirts were compressed so that for an instant I saw the real silhouette of her arse, rounded and full. The sleeve of her blouse, rolled above the elbow, revealed a strong smooth forearm, tense with the weight of the tray. Her chest strained against the cotton apron as she set the order down, and a fierce lust overran me, as complete and obliterating a sensation as that of climbing into a warm tub. A long brown indecent stain ran down one side of the girl's apron across her hip and into the material of her skirt. It drifted closer to me.

"Are you all done?"

"Pardon?" I shifted in my seat as the girl stretched across me to take my empty cup.

"Because if there's anything else . . ."

"No, that's fine."

She put the cup on the tray and changed her grip on it, holding the tray flat across her forearm, elbow pressed into the crook of her outthrust hip. I looked up at her face. A tangle of thick brown hair had escaped from the side of her bonnet. She pushed it back with her free hand, exposing the padded pinkness of her cheek, her jaw, throat.

"You'd be sure to ask, if there was, I'm sure," she said, and turned, stepping past me with her backside inches from my face.

More unsettling world, connecting up. Had I noticed Mary before? Not in that way, not that I could remember, though she'd served me on and off for two years. Yet as soon as I'd seen her in that light, or transformed her with my mind's eye, she'd apparently noticed. I turned back to the window. The view through the nearest panes, not three feet away, was of a black frock coat, whose wearer was pulling a chain from its breast pocket, a silver chain attached to a watch. The terseness of the gesture was immediately evocative. I was up and out of my seat before I'd even checked the man's face, but I saw it and was proven right outside. Two shards of grey either side of a dark beard. The officer from the *Belsize*, who turned to walk away, stomping across the flagstones as though he distrusted the very ground he trod upon.

CHAPTER
TEN

I followed the officer down to the dock and along the quayside. He walked more slowly once he was within sight of the water, and before he reached the *Belsize* he paused to fill and tamp and light a pipe. I would have approached the man then, but found myself holding off. I stood at a distance, watching the officer observe the preparations for another voyage with a stillness that presented itself to me as longing. The ship leaving port was called the *Sally-Ann*. Stevedores were loading her up. There on the quay stood the usual barrels of brandy and beer and bolts of carefully wrapped cloth. Beside them were muskets in crates marked Belstan's of Birmingham, and more crates no doubt filled with new kettles and pots and silverware, and there . . . of all things — stood a shrouded grandfather clock whose chimes sounded in protest when two of the dockhands picked it up.

The noise nudged the officer on towards his own ship. It had been moved along the quay and now lay berthed beneath the new Merchant Venturers' crane, the shadow of whose arm juddered across as I watched the man march authoritatively aboard. He was the Captain, presumably: I saw a seaman leap from the rail at his approach; even the gulls flapped from the deck at the pistol-shot succession of his hobnail boots up the gangplank. The crane-arm passed overhead again and I looked up at it, took in the ponderous sweep of the boom as it bisected the flat unfathomable web of lines that comprised the rigging. The sky above was thronged with towering grey clouds. They seemed to be rushing to keep the ship's masts in place. As I watched, the sun edged a valley of cloud with silver, then broke through blue sky and warmed my face. The rigging acquired an extra dimension, turned from cross-hatched lines to a Chinaman's puzzle hanging in space. I imagined myself a gull twisting in flight to skewer the lattice of ropes from bow to stern and was suffused with a sense of the possible; then another cloud overran the sun and the ropes tightened to a flat mesh and the crane-arm swung the dead weight of a pallet strapped full of casks back over my head again.

The gangplank was warped and rutted. I advanced up it and fingered the rope handrail and stared down at the wedge of black water between the ship's side and the dock. It smelt of brackish sweat and rot. Something welled up in my breast, an uncertainty gripping me from within. I was reminded of something I'd known once but lost. I blinked and saw for an instant two parallel scars high on a soft, dark cheek. Then I was staring at the ship's side, which suddenly seemed colossal up close, pulsing with ingenuity and purpose and labour: so much work. Trees planted and grown and felled and hewn into boards cut to size and shaped and steamed and bent and fixed in place and caulked.

52

Bristol, with its tidal port, had a tradition of building ships hardy enough to withstand a dumping, twice daily, fully loaded, on to the mud of the river bed: *shipshape and Bristol fashion*. From this hard start they set off for the furthest reaches. The tension in their sprung sides, the intricacy of their design, now appeared to me as raw capability and vision. I've always known I was delivered to these shores in the cradle of a ship like the one I stood before then, but the knowledge was so familiar that I rarely felt it to be true. Wavering before the *Belsize* I experienced the thing again as a debt I had no means of repaying. I felt belittled.

What exactly did Carthy expect me to look for on board anyway? I didn't know. Yet his blind leads are nothing new. Instead of hailing one of the crew and asking for permission to come on board, I bounced heavy-footed up the gangplank, aping the Captain's assuredness; just as entitlement is evident in a man's bearing, so an assured bearing creates the appearance of entitlement.

I paused on the main deck. Towards the stern it was piled high with more casks on pallets, and crates and barrels filled, presumably, with tobacco and sugar and rum. Two men crabbed sideways round an open hatch, a chest slung between them, and set it with others on a pallet to await the returning crane. The larger of the two figures disappeared immediately behind a mound of webbing up towards the foredeck, but his mate, whose shirt was stuck to his back with sweat, turned to me.

"Yes?" the man asked, wiping his face.

I nodded good morning and pulled a notebook from the pocket of my coat. The book, a present from Lilly, was bound in leather. I flicked through its blank pages, but my tactic — of not appearing hurried — backfired.

"You here in search of your tongue, lad? Or can I help?"

I shifted my weight to my front foot and drew myself to my full height. "How was the voyage?"

The man scratched at the hair bristling from his open collar, which ran uninterrupted into a mess of beard at his throat. "What's your purpose in asking?" he said.

"My purpose? That's my master's business, owed to the Dock Company. But I'm also curious for my own part as to whether or not your voyage was a successful one. Perhaps you can begin by answering that?"

"No, I can't."

I took a step forward and the man held up a hand.

"Which isn't to say that I wouldn't if I could. But I didn't sail with the ship, Sir, so I'd be taking a liberty in guessing how those that did found the voyage."

The man explained this as if to a half-wit, but at least he'd dropped the "lad" in addressing me as "Sir".

"No, all that sailed with her has vanished ashore. Bar the stragglers. If you're quick you may still find one or two sloping around."

"I see."

"Which is understandable, considering. No matter how much they enjoyed the scenery afloat, there's things they'll have missed." The man scratched at his throat again, becoming expansive. "But if you and the

Dock Company are really asking whether she turned a profitable trip, I'm looking around me here and I'm thinking she might have done. They stuffed her full. I know that in every bone." The man's hand moved from his throat to the back of his neck. He glanced up. "Still, it's a marvellous help, the loading gear. That should make sure we get the job done on time."

I looked up too as the crane, trailing its chain and an empty hook, swung back across the deck. Somebody barked an order and the man flinched, then continued more gruffly, "Provided nobody gets in our way, that is."

CHAPTER
ELEVEN

Although the hook passed well above my head, I took a couple of steps backwards and followed its progress with my eye. The Captain was standing at the rail of the upper deck. He appeared to waver there, silhouetted against the rushing sky. It seemed he'd been watching the conversation, for he now forced out a smile — the silver shards in his beard twitched — and called down, "Good morning to you. Maybe I can help."

I shaded my eyes and nodded and skirted a deflated mountain of tarpaulin to make my way up to him, pocketing my notebook again in order to hold on as I climbed the steps. The Captain met me at the top with his hand extended. As I shook it, the sun broke through again and the two of us were enmeshed in a net of shadow cast by the empty rigging and masts.

"I'm here on behalf of the Dock Company," I explained. "My client wants particulars of your latest voyage."

"Captain Charles Addison," he said smilingly. "A pleasure to meet you . . ."

"Inigo Bright, of Carthy and Co."

"And I'd be pleased to furnish you with whatever 'particulars' I can," the Captain went on. "What are you after? Details of the goods we've traded are all set out in the ship's ledgers. As is an account of the delay we suffered. The storm damage. It's all in the log. Our limp back to Speightstown. That's Barbados. The refit costs."

The Captain still hadn't let go of my hand. He pumped it one last time and the white daggers either side of his mouth twitched upwards again. There was something odd about Addison's eyes. They were red-rimmed, sunken deep beneath his weathered brow. He held my gaze and I blinked. The pupils, that was it. Given the brightness, they were too black, too large, too round.

"The log you say. And ledgers. Well, I'm sure my client will want to inspect both."

"You're welcome to them. All of it." Addison waved at the mass of goods stacked on the deck and, smiling at the joke, said, "Everything's . . . quite literally . . . above board."

The Captain's garrulousness did not suit him. It was as unnatural as the light now flashing in his eyes, which appeared less reflected than released, as though it were burning from within. I let him go on.

"Yes, we were away longer than expected, or longer than the owners would have liked, because in a sense they should expect it, don't you see? The Windward Isles. Wind! Christ, did it blow. In all my years. See the mizzenmast, this one here?" Addison advanced across the deck and kicked the foot of the mast in question. "Sheared straight off, below deck! What with that and the damage to the forecastle. But what did us was the rudder. It sprang clean apart. That mast killed a man coming down. Took his legs off and punched a hole in the foredeck for good measure. Waring couldn't save him. We couldn't go on. It was God's will that I got us back round the north of the island and into port."

It seemed Addison wanted me to doubt what he was saying, or at least to question it so that he could restate its truth. He scratched the palm of one square hand with the fingers of the other now, itching to go on.

"Killed a man," I prompted. "By breaking his legs."

"Yes! Not just broke, though. It took them clean off. Look, come below. I'll show you the new joinery, whole sections, green timbers, the repairs amidships."

I let myself be led forward at the Captain's insistence. Had Carthy spoken with him already, prepared the way for a visit? I could think of no other likely reason as to why Addison had required no persuading, no warrant, or other evidence of authority, no proof even of who I was.

I followed the Captain down the steps and across the weathered timbers of the main deck. His rolling gait first appeared to me as right for one accustomed to life on board a ship, but then he stumbled against a low spar and missed the rail he clutched for and ended up down on one knee, his hat awry. He pulled it off and slapped it against his stocky thigh and shouted "Gulls' Eyes!" as he stood and punched the hat roughly and set it back in its rightful place, and I suddenly suspected that the man must have been drinking; at the very least, frayed nerves had put him in this discomfited state.

"No harm done I hope," I said quietly as I waited for him to go forward again towards the hatch.

We made our way below. I had not set foot on a ship such as this since my passage to England as a small child but immediately, before my eyes had a chance to grow accustomed to the dark, the smell of the thing gripped me as something primal and familiar and horrific. There had been a strong, purifying breeze on deck, but even with the hatches open and the hold all but emptied, the dark interior of the ship filled me with claustrophobic dread. It smelt of rotten meat, gaseousness, death. I stifled an urge to retch. One hand was still wrapped tight around a ladder rung: it was all I could do not to bolt straight back up it towards the light. As well as the horrible gloom and smell, the awareness that I was not on land but afloat intensified in me: I felt it as a ghastly weakening in my legs. The ship, tethered tight, was barely moving, but its gentle nuzzling at the dock, the imperceptible bumping and chafing of wood against stone, was magnified in the confinement of the hold, so that to me it seemed the ship was menacingly unstable. I locked my knees, fearful I might otherwise sink to the floor.

"Come along. Mind your head. Wood against timber, timber on wood. That's it, Mr Bright, through here. The mast sheared straight through the bulwark, took a wall of shiplap with it. Infernally heavy. And these timbers here, and those ones, they were splintered by the blow. Something the matter?"

Having staggered after the Captain through a series of low doors with raised sills, past cramped storerooms disgorged of their contents, I now drew up short on entering the wider space between decks. It being impossible not to, I pressed my palm to my mouth and nose. The smell here was . . . raw. The air that bore it had a thick, unholy quality, cloying as earth dug from a grave. A wad of revulsion rolled through me, from my stomach to my chest to my throat, and this time it broke over the back of my tongue, flooding my mouth with sick. I fought to swallow it back down and contain the next wave: the sensation was so overpowering, the effort of resisting it so obliterating, that for long moments I had no idea what the Captain was saying, much less why I had followed the man down here, what I was looking for. My very awareness of where I was faltered; every sense, every shred of reason, all of it dimmed.

". . . and Waring. That's the surgeon as was. Well he . . . impossible to staunch. No point wasting . . . he said, if I hadn't . . . we lashed the man down, against himself you understand, but there was no need . . . my God . . . quickly faded. It was an almighty squall, you see . . . a proper blow."

I took in the new joinery the Captain appeared so keen to highlight, blond wood whose rough-cut grain was still beaded with sap in places. Against it the old timbers looked like something burned and buried and dug up. But they had held firm. Addison stroked a length of black plank and explained how nearly the ship had come to wrenching entirely apart. Perhaps the memory of this recent scare was to blame for having unhinged the Captain? I tried not to breathe in through my nose and nodded with him.

"But she's a marvellous tough tug. The squall would have stowed many a newer vessel in the locker, I'm sure of that."

My legs still swaying beneath me, I steadied myself with a hand on one of the ship's ancient spars. Instantly I recoiled: the woodwork had the greasy feel of cold meat.

Addison stumped off further into the hold, pointing this way and that at the refitted interior as if by doing so he could conjure the nightmare the ship had endured. There was something frightening in his enthusiasm. It was manic, sharp-edged. I could think of no reason to hang back, however, and followed the Captain deeper into the hold's recesses.

"We were broadsided by the swell! The sea shipped itself through that hole, dropping us three feet nearer the waterline. I tell you, by the time we made port, the waves were lapping at the waist!"

Pawing at my coat-tail to rid my hand of the ship's clammy touch, I managed a further sympathetic nod. I did not feel I was beneath the waterline so much as interred; the planks of the ship's hull and deck seemed the walls and lid of a buried coffin. My breathing was shallow, confined to sips of the rotten air. How on earth did sailors manage to survive the long months of a transatlantic voyage? The tour of the empty hold continued aft, past a storeroom strewn with filthy straw. Perhaps disturbed by the sound of our approach, a rat sped out of the open door, around the Captain, and straight over the toe of my right boot. I kicked out instinctively, but missed; the rat fled.

"You have to be quicker than that to catch them," Addison grunted. "The log's still in my cabin. As are the ledgers." He pointed past the stairs to the upper deck and continued, "Back this way."

I faltered. The light pouring through the hatch into the ship intensified at that moment, the sun having emerged from behind clouds above no doubt, so that the block of brightness in the hold appeared suddenly celestial. I walked towards it. "No need," I said. "No need."

"Why ever not? The delay is all accounted for, written down in black and white. You'll need to see it, won't you? Ink! It runs in lawyers' veins, does it not?"

"It does," I muttered, my foot upon the first step.

"Well the log's taut rigged, Sir."

I climbed towards the light. "I'm sure it is. You've no objection to my taking it back to the office, have you? My master will want to review it . . ."

"As you wish," Addison muttered, disappointed. "As you wish."

CHAPTER
TWELVE

Regaining the deck, I found myself blinking and sucking down deep draughts of air. The stink of the port had never tasted so good. I lifted my face to the sun and felt the weight of another shadow pass across it: the crane boom swung from ship to shore where the crate it carried was swiftly unhooked.

"They're making short work of it," Addison said with satisfaction. "Mind you, they need to. The Venturers took five years to erect proper lifting gear when it was needed two decades ago. As with the lock, too little, too late. Still, they're not entirely stupid. With just the one crane they can command an exorbitant price for its use."

"I'm sure."

The Captain's face seemed too mobile again in the bright sunshine. "Yes, well," he said. "If you'll wait here I'll fetch the necessary." He turned on his heel and made for his cabin.

The chain drifted back high above the deck trailing its empty hook. That Addison had volunteered to give me a guided tour of his ship was clearly an aberration; his hot-footed errand to retrieve the ship's log seemed so out of character as to be faintly absurd. Now that I was on deck again and feeling better, I suspected I'd made a mistake in not accepting the invitation to enter the Captain's cabin; I might have spotted something in it, something useful. I watched a stevedore catch the hook as it swung to the deck and stab it nonchalantly into the tangle of ropes above a pallet stacked with casks. Still, if there had been anything untoward in his cabin, Addison would hardly have offered to take me there. The chain rattled itself straight and took the strain and jerked the casks up off the deck to swing immediately sideways in an arc that again cut the air above my head. I stepped back instinctively, before the hook tore through the webbing and one half of the pallet dropped and the casks slid sideways and fell the thirty feet to the deck. One of the barrels smashed a section of the ship's rail; another — filled with rum — exploded as it punched a dent in the ship's deck. And a third cask hit the man who had attached the hook in the first place. He was bent double over a block and tackle when the barrel struck him. In snapping the man's back as it fell, the cask's route to the deck was softened: it did not break open but rolled away lazily across the planks, and as the sound of its rolling died, I realised that the deck-hand had been whistling before he was struck.

One minute a tune, the next nothing.

Instantly, the hot smell of rum swam up from the deck.

I ran forward to the man's side. I had never seen a dead body before, much less a man killed, but I had seen both now, I knew that for sure. There was no blood, and the colour beneath the man's skin had not faded, but the ugly awkwardness of the accident was reflected in the utter stillness of his face. It hadn't even had time to register surprise, much less pain. The blow had been fatal: there was nothing anyone could do. Why then was I working with another of the deck hands to straighten the corpse into a more natural position? Who was I trying to comfort?

Addison was swiftly back up on deck. He broke in upon the circle and his barked questions sounded like accusations. He swore at the stevedores and summoned the crane driver and cursed the ship's surgeon, Waring, for not being there, though the Captain, too, appeared to understand at once that the man was beyond medical help. I retreated a few paces. The crisis, either in itself or because it had eclipsed me, seemed to have given Addison back some of his authority. Within minutes the body had been removed from the deck and the work of unloading the ship began again. A boy — of no more than twelve — set to work clearing the broken casks away.

When Addison turned to me again, his voice was gruffer than it had been before.

"It's all in here," he said, thrusting a leather satchel into my chest.

I took the bag.

"The log, the ship's documentation. Etcetera."

"It was the man's own haste that did it," I said.

"Hmm?"

"The accident. The hurt man (somehow "dead" would not come out of my mouth) hitched the load to the crane. Hastily. In case you were wondering if anyone else was to blame. Not the crane driver, or another hand, just the man himself. Though perhaps if he'd been allowed to work at a more measured pace . . ."

Addison regarded me a while, a yellow incisor working to still his lower lip. "Perhaps," he said eventually, but could not stop himself from going on. "Perhaps pondering, ruminating and whatnot are of use in lawyering. But I can't see that dallying would have helped here. No, Sir. On board a ship, *sloth* does everything but sharpen a man's instincts."

CHAPTER
THIRTEEN

Amidst the rush of the quay, I sat on a bollard to eat a minced beef pasty I had bought from Cousins, the baker. Today more than usual, the warm and wholesome smell of the place, in contrasting so vividly with the docks, had been irresistible. I flicked my foot at a gull. It cocked its head and swaggered just out of reach.

It wasn't the Captain's apparent callousness in the aftermath of the accident which troubled me, but the truth in what Addison had said. Sloth, or drudgery, or thoroughness — call it what you will — did indeed blunt a man's instincts. Poring over documents in search of accounting discrepancies had dulled my own eye. If the Captain had not pricked me with his jibe about lawyering, I might not have noticed. But now, on the quay, I could see every detail, the boy's bare feet, the depression in the deck (like the flattened skin of a bruised apple) where the barrel had hit it, the shard of wood the boy was about to sweep up, branded with a letter: W. And there, beyond the broom, the rest of the barrel's lid, with the remainder of the stamp. I took a bite of pasty and blinked back the initials: TC.

There was nothing untoward about the *Belsize*, owned by the Western Trading Company, unloading a cargo of barrels stamped with the Company's logo. Nothing untoward at all, not when considered rationally. But to have seen a man killed by such a barrel cut through rational thought. It was an omen. My instinct told me that although the documents in the satchel across my knees were no doubt all present and correct, Captain Addison was covering something up.

The seagull had tacked up to within kicking distance again. You've got to admire these birds: nothing short of a blow will warn them off. I stood up and tore the remains of my pasty in two — I was less hungry than I had thought, anyway — and tossed it at the gull's webbed feet.

CHAPTER
FOURTEEN

Kitty didn't want to go in the first place but her brother Edmund said it would be worth their while if she did. He needed somebody to help carry the buckets. Full, they'd be heavy. The track from Leigh Woods to the river's edge was steep. Going down wasn't a problem; you could hop, skip and slide down empty-handed, but the gorge was a trial coming back up, never mind lugging a load.

Edmund was convinced they could make some money out of worms. He always said "We" when he wanted her help. Kitty didn't care about money anyway; she was more interested in colours. It was autumn so the woods were full of golden trees, but she still preferred the yellow a buttercup made if you held it against your forearm. Edmund said he liked gold, too, so long as it was real. He didn't have any of his own yet, but he would, because he was a businessman. Their father laughed when he called himself that. "You mean busybody," he said.

Anyway, Edmund knew you could pull worms out of the mudflats when the river was low. They could sell them to fishermen. It wasn't the money Kitty was interested in, but the walk through the woods at sunset. That was when low tide was today, so that was when they went, and the yellow leaves and red rocks she'd seen on the way down the side of the gorge had been like looking through your fingers at a fire.

Which didn't make up for the fact that she was knee deep in grey mud now, with a bucket digging into the crook of her forearm, wet and bored and cold and tired.

"I'm going home," Kitty said.

"Just five more minutes."

"You said that twice already."

"Yes, well. It's an investment. We came all the way down here and we can't go back until we've made it pay. It's a golden opportunity . . ."

"It's sludge and worms," Kitty replied.

"You need to envision." Edmund squatted to prod at the mud again with his special stick. There was an oval of slime on his backside. Kitty had an urge to kick it.

"Well, I'm going even if you're not," she said. "It'll be dark soon anyway."

As she said this she realised Edmund would know that she didn't want to walk back up through the woods in the dark alone, and sure enough he turned to grin at her. He was infuriating. "How do you think that lot got where they are?" he asked her, jerking his thumb at the fine buildings which crested the other side of the gorge.

"I don't care."

"Well I do and I can tell you it wasn't from going home early. A proper merchant doesn't give up on his profits when they're already half made."

"I'm not a merchant. I'm cold and I'm covered in mud."

"That's exactly it. You can't be afraid of getting your hands dirty if you want to succeed in business. Just a few worms more and that will do. The tide is coming back in anyway."

"I'm going," she said, and although they both knew it wasn't true, she walked off along the curve of the river bank to make it seem like it might be. The glimmer had gone out of the water, now; it looked the same flat grey colour as the slime. Only it wasn't entirely flat because up there was something half afloat nudging the mud-bank a little way round the curve. Maybe it was something worth having. Kitty was filthy and sopping wet anyway, so she decided she might as well wade out to investigate, and that seemed a good idea right up until it turned into a bad idea, and by then it was too late, because by then she knew what the thing was, and even though it made her want to turn and run back to Edmund, her legs kept taking her towards it, daring it to change into a valuable sea-trunk or a rotten log or anything normal; it didn't have to be anything good any more, just so long as it wasn't a drowned body.

At first Kitty thought the darkness cloaking the corpse was the fault of the river or the approaching night, but by the time Edmund had reached her — he had heard her shouting although she hadn't heard herself — she realised it wasn't silt or the dusk that had turned the woman black. Edmund drew her away and told her to mind the buckets, which was maddening, since worms couldn't matter now. Then he astonished her further by dragging the body, inch by horrid inch, clear of the high water mark. When she asked him why he'd done that, he said that even though it was a blackamoor there might still be a reward.

CHAPTER
FIFTEEN

The springs on Carthy's coach were definitely shot. Even the worst of the town's hackney carriages gave a smoother ride. I had tried to persuade my employer to walk the short distance to the Dock Company's headquarters, but Carthy, whose attachment to his carriage is as unwavering as it is unfathomable, insisted otherwise. The man is cross-stitched with perverse streaks. Although the cobbles were relatively smooth, the coach gave them square edges. Carthy used the journey as an excuse to update me about Anne's "frankly phenomenal" progress with her reading; I signalled my awe with a grunt. By keeping my mouth shut, I hoped to stop my teeth from jolting loose in my head.

"What are you going to tell Orton?" I asked when the carriage finally jerked to a stop.

"Me? Nothing. I've done my share of the talking this morning." Carthy folded the step back on to the running board with ridiculous care. "You tell him what's what."

I ground my teeth, but said nothing. Although I hadn't had a chance to plan what I'd say, the uncertainty principle by which Carthy generally led meant I was prepared to feel unprepared.

We were shown into a room with tall, grand windows, whose grimy panes admitted little light. Our client, John Orton, was already seated behind a French-polished table. His face shone dully in its surface. Two heads. The facsimile was smoother than the original. Although in his early middle years, the real Orton was creased as an old man. When he rose to shake hands his palm felt papery. There was something the matter with his skin, I saw: it wasn't wrinkles so much as cracks that crazed Orton's brow and cheeks.

Before he'd finished greeting me, Orton was addressing my master. "Adam. A pleasure. You're in good health I trust?"

"I'm bearing up well enough. As, I hope . . . How are the . . . rocks?"

Orton gave what passed for a smile. "Multiplying. I was out collecting just this weekend. Down towards Dorset. These fossils are God's own fingerprints. They will afford us a view of life as far back as the flood."

Carthy's "Fascinating!" was warm enough to convince the Dock Company official to go on, but to my ear it rang hollow. Prod a man along a route he's already set upon travelling, however, and he'll continue well beyond the next milestone. Orton began expounding about sediment and alluvial deposits and natural history's own picture-book as the three of us took seats around the big table, and he continued to talk long enough for me to collect myself in advance of presenting our findings. A tongue of fire, tiny in the yawning mouth of a grand hearth, underscored the room's chill. It was warmer than this outside. Fossils: dry bones. There was an odd smell in this room, of lemon zest cut with something noisome. Finally, the man's droning stopped.

"So, how have you got on?" he asked Carthy after a pause, with what sounded like a note of resignation in his voice.

My master turned to me.

"Well, we've made progress . . ." I began. And on I went, carefully outlining the work we had done, the sound of my voice in my head measured and professional and, it appeared, of no interest at all to my client. As soon as I began speaking, Orton started picking at his fingernails, absently at first, but with increasing intent. He was soon ripping off bits of cuticle and flicking them under the table. The conviction drained from my voice. With a look of relief, Orton turned back to Carthy.

"And your conclusions?"

"Oh, Inigo's drawn those," Carthy said lightly. He nodded at me again. "Such as we've been able to make."

Although my master's flippant tone unsettled me further, I had no choice but to continue. Yet the discrepancies in the Western Trading Company's duty payments seemed suddenly petty as I spelled them out, and in the deadening quiet of the meeting room my deeper misgivings about the *Belsize* came across as more or less groundless. Orton just sat there scratching at his wrists. If the matter was of this little consequence to our client, then why was I allowing it to trouble me? Three faces stood reflected in the sheen of the table, ghosts swimming beneath ghosts. What in God's name was I doing here? There was a whole world of flesh and blood beyond this one. I had a sudden vision of Mary, the waitress from Thunderbolts, her rounded forearm and the swell of her hip. I was still giving my metronomic account of the matter, but what I wanted to do was shout an obscenity, kick a hole in the table, and walk out. If I was going to have such thoughts about a woman, then oughtn't Lilly to be the one to spring to mind? I stopped talking.

"Very interesting. Thoroughly . . . thorough. Thank you." Orton's palms, turned up on the tabletop, were a raw pink. "And you've nothing further to add, Adam?" he deferred to Carthy again.

"No. There's the matter of the Company's backers, which I can detail if you so wish . . ." Carthy's knowing look made my heart quicken. I did not want to have to concede Bright & Co.'s involvement. Out of the corner of my eye I saw the seat of an occasional chair beside the fireplace bulge and settle with the shape of a tortoiseshell cat. That was what the lemon zest was intended to mask, the smell of cat piss. Mercifully, Orton's lack of interest extended to those who had shares in the Western Trading Company. He waved away Carthy's suggestion with a flick of his flayed hands.

"A summary for the file, with your . . . findings set down, will suffice," he said quickly, and then, visibly more animated again, he began regaling Carthy with a

75

further account of his weekend's fossicking for rocks. Ammonites were the new old thing, he explained, his hands fluttering at one another with pleasure.

My temper wasn't improved by Carthy's insistence that we climb into his wretched coach again for the return journey. To avoid the appearance of fuming in silence, I eventually asked, "What was all that about?"

"I know!" Carthy shook his head. "Frittering his time away in the mud. I once made the mistake of telling him I'd collected shells as a boy. But that's a world away from a grown man, of his authority . . ."

"That's not what I'm talking about."

"No?" replied Carthy disingenuously.

"No. What's really going on?"

Carthy took a long look at the shop-fronts rattling past. "Hard to say. This job seemed like a perfect opportunity to make a difference. Heaven knows the mess the Dock Company presides over needs clearing up, for the good of the city. That's why Orton instructed us, I assumed. He's the new man there. I understood we were to present him with results he could act upon. There was no mention of the wretched fossils when he dropped off the documents. Evidently, I misjudged the man's intentions. He needs something on the file, but it certainly doesn't look like he's planning on waving it in anyone's face. Insurance of some sort, I'll wager that's what he's after. A note of our findings will give him leverage to shore up his position within the Company. It's a missed opportunity."

The coach had slowed up in the throng of Corn Street. A horse's head, hanging momentarily beside the open window, exploded in a sneeze: tendrils of snot swayed from its nostrils just inches from my face. I flinched; the apparition drifted from view.

"But it doesn't make any difference," Carthy went on. "Though Orton's softened for now, our brief is unchanged. You must finish your analysis and write it up and send it over for the man to file. Who knows, maybe the wind will shift again and he will enjoy a change of heart."

I nodded, placated by the note of confidence in Carthy's voice, even if what he was saying oppressed me further. That's the trouble with lawyering. Though it gives the appearance of being necessary, vital even, too often the work is adding braces to belted trousers, or is entirely for show. I hung on to the sill of the carriage as it slewed and clattered over a rutted stretch of road.

"Keep digging," Carthy muttered. "But carefully. Orton told me he uses a brush to uncover his precious fossils. We must be as subtle. Now's not the time for a spade."

CHAPTER
SIXTEEN

Noises filter in from the outside world, and the repetition of these noises creates patterns, and familiarity, and the creeping threat that this place will start to make sense. The same thing happened on the ship. Human resourcefulness and adaptability are a curse: despite everything, they will normalise hell.

So, the fact that there is a bucket with water here, and one for them to fill, because it is an improvement on the filth-flooded hold, becomes a privilege. The same is true of the straw. The cows at home sleep on a softer bed, but it is better than the dark planks she had grown used to during the first voyage, and when the man comes to spread a fresh sheaf on the ground she has to fight a sickening gratitude. Yesterday, after he had kicked clean straw around the cellar, he took a key from his pocket and unchained Idowu and took her away. There were no tears left in the sick girl, but Abeni and Oni held each other and sobbed for her, which changed nothing.

Oni thinks about the insult of this clean straw and gathers an armful and pushes it away as far as she can, and then she clears all the straw from within the circumference of her chain, exposing a half circle of bare dirt. You can taste the damp in it, the mould. She starts digging with her fingers.

She's not trying to escape, she's digging because the futility of it is an antidote to the fake normality.

She has no way of protecting herself when she's asleep. There's no such thing as a good dream. She can sleep through the happiest memories — a kingfisher arrowing into the mirrored lake-surface beside her father's canoe; the pink instep of her brother's foot held warm against her lips — and still wake up screaming. In some ways nightmares are easier. The rat gnawing at the base of her skull, the gag and rope and weight of him forcing her apart.

She's still scraping at the floor. They took Idowu away. She cannot allow herself to imagine where, or what has happened to the sick girl since. There are pebbles in the dirt which she digs free, and then further into the hole her fingers close over a knot that won't budge. She picks at the soil around it, uncovering a length of tree-root as thick as her wrist. That this root feeds a living tree is momentarily comforting. But though its roots share Oni's cell, the tree's leaves must reach up into the light. She pushes the earth back into the hole and drags a clump of straw across it with her heel.

Suddenly, there's the birdsong again, whose faint melodies are as terrifying as the smile of a snake.

CHAPTER
SEVENTEEN

The light was fading in Queen Square. Shadows cast by the plane trees stretched in long diagonals, streaks of tar thrown across a dirt floor. I paused outside Lilly's house. I brushed myself down and attempted to rearrange the flowers. A bouquet had seemed the right thing when I bought it from the flower-girl outside the Exchange at lunchtime, but the thing had a limp, doomed air about it now. I was looking forward to seeing Lilly again, of course. The twinge of uncertainty in my belly had nothing to do with my fiancée, and everything to do with my prospective father-in-law. The invitation I had accepted for this evening came from Heston Alexander himself. If I found myself talking nonsense to brush over the awkwardness between myself and Lilly's mother from time to time, my confusion before her father welled up into ridiculousness. I took a deep breath and set my jaw and raised my hand to the lion's head mounted high on the big front door . . . which opened before I had a chance to knock upon it.

The footman, Spenser, had either intuited my loitering on the steps or spotted me from a window. His bow was an inch or two deeper than necessary. A pianoforte was playing somewhere within. I followed the man further into the hall and allowed myself to be steered towards the music, into the drawing room.

"Here he is, let's ask him," Heston's voice boomed, before I was quite through the door. I had already determined to greet Mrs Alexander first, and pressed on despite her husband's interjection. She took my offering with a smile that told me I should have trusted my instincts and consigned the flowers to the waters of St Augustine's Reach.

"Why thank you, Inigo. Very kind."

I scrambled up the rope of Heston's question. "Ask me what, Sir? I'll do my best to answer."

"Of course you will." Mr Alexander leaned back in his seat and drummed his fingers on the expanse of fine cotton between the splayed lapels of his frock coat. "Say your good father began making mistakes. Taking bad decisions, giving voice to inappropriate utterances, issuing idiotic decrees. And say these mistakes had consequences for the whole family, and that they were born of a failure of his reason which everyone could see but nobody felt they could mention. Wouldn't you, as his son and heir, have a duty to intervene?"

Suspecting a trick, I bought time, nodding thoughtfully before crossing the room to kiss Lilly's hand. It seemed this had been wise when her father continued.

"Mind you, mistakes or no, the old man is still in charge. He holds the whip hand. You'd be challenging his authority, etcetera."

Lilly's younger sister, Abigail, had risen from her seat at the pianoforte. I took her hand, too. Addressing my response to the back of it seemed the safe thing to do. "I suppose," I said, "it would depend upon the extent of his failure of reason. It would be a matter of degree."

"Pah! The lawyer in you gave that answer. Swing both legs one side of the fence. Would you have a *duty* to intervene?"

Mrs Alexander was making no attempt to hide her pleasure at my discomfort; Abigail had already returned her attention to the sheet-music on the piano; an accomplished musician, she now began playing something I can best describe as explicitly saccharine. I turned to Lilly. Her smile of encouragement was girlish.

Heston Alexander himself came to my rescue. "I'll give you a clue. It's the King to whom I refer. Farmer George. From what I hear he no longer has the wit to steer a plough straight, much less an empire. And with the French threatening . . ."

"Of course. If the reports are true, the Prince must intervene on the nation's behalf," I said, conscious that this reply was as limp as the flowers now lying on the occasional table at Mrs Alexander's elbow.

Heston Alexander's fingers were still on his shirtfront, beating time to Abigail's playing. His mouth, a firm line set in the rampart of his face, gave nothing away. Though he lacks his wife's overt hostility, he still has a knack of making me feel I am off the pace. When I asked for Lilly's hand in marriage, he assented with a speed which suggested that the deal had been done before I formulated the question.

"Well said. Old George makes less sense than a box of bats these days, by all accounts. Young George should have himself declared Regent without further ado."

"Eighty years of Georges," said Abigail, pausing at the piano. "With another one still to come. You'd think they'd give a different name a turn."

This sparked a conversation between the two sisters about the name Lilly would give her new puppy, when it arrived, which subject, I realised glumly, aroused as little interest in me as did the state of the monarchy. I accepted a glass of punch and sipped at it politely as I took in the softness of Lilly's throat, the curve of her shoulder, and my eyes came to rest on the faint blue line in her upturned wrist. How could blood ever run blue? A streak of royalty. Heston Alexander was a Member of the Society of Merchant Venturers, like my father. Maybe he *did* know more about my prospects than I knew myself. The terms of my inheritance spelled out in Venturer-code over cigars. That would explain Heston's ready consent to the forthcoming nuptials. The bride-to-be was averring that a dog's name should be immediately recognisable as belonging to a dog, which explained why Buttons and Dash and Princess topped her list. You had to admire the smooth plane of her cheek. The angle of her sister's jaw was somehow more severe. That said, Abigail's advocacy was the more persuasive; I couldn't help agreeing with her suggestion there might at least be some humour in a dog called George.

We ate dinner in a room which Mrs Alexander had recently decorated in an oriental style. This seemed principally to involve lacquer. Lilly had helped her mother pick out the new furnishings: I did my best to signal appreciation. I thought I caught a glimpse of Heston winking at Abigail as I nodded approval at a black-wood lamp-stand, and their apparent collusion in a private joke, by placing me in league with Lilly and her mother, was oddly dispiriting. I found myself fiddling with the underside of the new dining table. There was some sort of ingenious mechanism beneath it which meant that the surface could be extended or contracted to suit the number of diners present at any given meal. My fingers brushed the teeth of a ratchet, found the gap between slats, tested the edge of a cogged wheel. I had a ridiculous urge to get down on my hands and knees to examine the device properly, but was drawn up by Heston Alexander's insistence that I describe, of all things, exactly what it was I was working upon. The man's eyes, set in his square face, had creased into smiling enthusiasm.

"A number of cases. Contractual disputes and so on. Some regulatory work involving the Dock Company. Nothing much of note."

"Come now. There must be some juice in it to keep you going. Mount the thing a credible defence!"

I was tempted to rise to this challenge, but suffered a sudden realisation that I had no real idea how far Mr Alexander's interests in the dock extended. In all probability he was up to his neck in the silt. I found myself flannelling.

"The work doesn't tell well at dinner, but rest assured there's interest in it close up."

"Lord above! Doesn't sound like much of an advertisement for the legal life. The cut and thrust of commerce is much more entertaining. That's where you should reconsider applying yourself. The sharp end!"

Was that it? Mr Alexander's tone was jocular, but jokes, like pearls, have a heart of grit. Did he imagine that I would eventually end up working for my family firm, or perhaps even take a position working with him? I smiled back genially. My fingers, beneath the table, had found their way into a sharp-edged recess between two cogs. I dug a knuckle into the gap.

Lilly was speaking. "Business, lawyering, they're both as dull as each other, aren't they? I can't see there's much fun to be had in a counting house. A playhouse or the recital rooms — those are the place to find entertainment. And I've got tickets for us all to go to a poetry recital tomorrow night!"

There was a false gaiety in Lilly's voice, yet it was less worrying in that instant than the fact that my finger, pushed into the table's winding mechanism, had somehow contrived to get . . . stuck. It would not wriggle free. I gave a tug, which caused the cutlery to shiver and the teeth of the device to dig painfully into my knuckle, but the finger would not budge.

"That's settled then," Heston Alexander boomed. "A family outing!"

Mercifully, the family's attention shifted from me as they discussed the arrangements for the theatre trip. As a boy I got my leg enmeshed in a set of wrought iron railings at Bright House. Panic, that was the problem. Clarissa had eventually freed me, as much with calm reassurances as by rotating my foot, calf and knee. I licked the palm of my free hand surreptitiously and greased the trapped knuckle under the table with spit, all the while nodding and giving the appearance of listening, though the conversation had moved on and, in truth, I had no idea what Abigail and her sister were talking about. It was no good. Maybe the ratchet had tightened a notch, or perhaps the cog I'd slid my finger past was in some manner . . . barbed? Lilly was breathlessly recounting the story of another dead woman, found stuck in the mud of the river, and the sound of that word . . . *stuck* . . . worked on me with a suddenness which caught me unawares. Before I could stop myself I yanked my hand back ferociously, causing the plates on the table to jump and wine to slop and my trapped finger to rip back free of the confounded pernicious device beneath the table's polished leaves.

Everybody stopped talking. Mrs Alexander reached out a hand to steady her glass. "My!" she said. "What on earth is the matter?"

I pressed my torn knuckle into the knot of my napkin. "Nothing. I'm sorry. A cramp."

"Might it have been the story of the woman murdered in the mud?" Abigail offered. "A spasm of sympathy, perhaps? I know how much the Clifton Killer has played on poor Lilly's nerves."

"Cramp," I murmured.

"But, but . . . she *wasn't* murdered," Lilly explained, happy to offer me consolation, but unable, it seemed, to erase entirely her disappointment with that anticlimactic fact. "They have the Clifton Killer" — here she shuddered theatrically — "locked up safely. It seems this unfortunate soul either fell into the river and drowned, or was caught unawares by the rising tide, or, most likely, through force of circumstance, was driven to . . . well . . . the article mentioned *felo de se* . . . by which I think they mean there's evidence to suggest the poor woman robbed herself of her own life."

"God forgive her!" said Mrs Alexander absently. She dabbed at the slopped wine, adding, "Shocking!" as she inspected the napkin.

The spillage, it seemed, concerned her more than the lost soul; she kept glancing from the stained cloth to her napkin as the meal wore itself out. We left the scene of one crime for another then, retreating en masse to listen to Abigail's syrupy piano-playing again.

CHAPTER
EIGHTEEN

Mary was working the morning shift. As an excuse to waylay her again, I asked for a copy of the latest edition of *Felix Farley's Bristol Journal* when I was halfway through my second cup of coffee. She fetched it and brought it down on the table in front of me with a thwack. The place was full; she was busy. Did that explain her confrontational air? I glanced up to see her looking me over, a red hand planted on the swell of her hip.

"Sorry to have troubled you."

"You didn't."

"Well, you have my thanks."

"Thank goodness. Can I get you anything else?"

"No."

"You're sure?"

Another customer called out from the café's darker recesses.

"I'm fine, for now," I said.

"Anything at all, you just ask." The waitress smiled, still surveying me levelly. As she turned away I was sure I heard her add, "Even a comb."

I watched her rounded skirt swish between the chair-backs, and was unable to resist the temptation to run my hand through my hair. The barber's, today, definitely.

I turned the pages of the paper and sipped my coffee. A house of ill-fame had been discovered in Marlborough Street. Its existence having been common knowledge for as long as I could remember, The Society for the Prevention and Suppression of Vice had apparently grown new teeth of late. What else? Yet another story about mad dogs plaguing the townspeople. Two children having died from the rabies this last week, there were further calls for a general culling of any unattended cur within the city limits. Cull away. Overleaf a chair-mender specialising in rush-bottomed something or other was touting for etcetera. His advertisement stood above the story of the discovery of a drowned woman in the river downstream of the Hot Well. I found myself reading the article. This was the case Lilly had spoken about so warmly last night. I ran my cut knuckle across my lips. A suspected suicide, as Lilly had said. No mention was made in the paper about a link — or lack of one — to the recent murder in Clifton. That had been Lilly's imaginative leap. But it mattered, somehow, all the same. I drained my already empty cup. The story made it clear that the drowned woman was as far from a Clifton lady as could be possible. She was a Negro. This, the writer seemed to imply, was justification enough for her having seen fit to do away with herself. Most likely the corpse belonged to a domestic servant, a one-time slave perhaps, shipped over from the Indies.

I shuddered and shut my eyes and pressed my torn knuckle to the softness of my lips again. I heard the wet thump of the cask hitting the stevedore aboard the *Belsize*, and the gravelly echo as it rolled across the deck, initials burnt into the wood of its lid. The Western Trading Company had dealt in slaves pre-abolition. There were no connections between these things, no logical links. I knew that.

I cast my eyes back over the story again. The body had been discovered by children playing on the banks of the Avon, a brother and sister from across the river in Long Ashton. It wasn't a big village. I left a tip generous enough to draw attention to itself next to my spent cup and sidestepped my way to the door. Gulls, more gulls, slashed about high above Carthy's rooftop across the street. I turned away from them and my office and headed to the docks. Work could wait.

CHAPTER
NINETEEN

As soon as the children were standing before me, I sensed that tracking them down had been a waste of time. The link I'd imagined between the suicide, the stamped cask, the *Belsize,* and my . . . tedious endeavours on behalf of the Dock Company, had broken. The boy did not pause from chewing the mashed end of a willow wand to return my greeting. He had an insolence about him. And the girl, though cherubic in appearance, had so far remained mute. What I'd hoped to glean from them seemed ridiculously remote. I thrust my hands into the pockets of my greatcoat and dug out the oranges anyway.

"Here."

"Just oranges?" said the boy.

His mother — if that's who she was; she seemed young for the job — immediately stuck her head out of the cottage door and hissed at him to mind his manners. He did not flinch, just slid both hands — and the fruit — behind his narrow back, as if suspecting the woman might snatch it.

"That's all I thought to bring," I explained. "What were you expecting?"

"The only reward worth having is one that goes clink."

"Reward?"

"For the dead blackamoor. We found it, and we didn't need to tell anyone."

"Tell anyone what?"

The boy's eyes narrowed. "What do you mean?"

I turned to the girl and asked her name. Kitty. She was still inspecting the orange I'd given her, and sucking on her plump lower lip. With her head bent forward I saw that her hair was a mat of curls streaked with sun and dirt. I thought of Anne Carthy's dreaded baths, and my own resolution to visit the barber, and was pricked with sympathy for the girl.

"I've got a brother who can fit an orange in his mouth whole," I told her.

She lifted her gaze to mine. "Really?"

"It's true. He started out more modestly, on hard-boiled eggs."

"That's not nice."

"No. And I wouldn't recommend that you try it. There are better things to be good at."

The boy was looking at his orange again. "I don't think he can eat it when it's in his mouth, can he? Chew it and such, I mean."

"No. I don't think he can."

"So there's no point in it."

"Which one of you actually found this body then?"

"We both did," the boy said.

"Both of you?" I repeated, looking at Kitty. She had begun biting at her lower lip again.

"And after you found it, what happened then?"

"I went to get Sammy. He's our uncle. I'm in business with him."

"You both did?"

Kitty was shaking her head.

"Just your brother went?"

Now she nodded.

"Somebody had to stay with it in case it floated away," the boy explained. He tossed the orange from one hand to the other. "What about apples. Could your brother manage one of them?"

"I think the stalk might be a problem."

I turned back to the girl, who was looking at me with a blank detachment which made her face ageless for a moment, so that I could see both the infant she had been and the woman she would become. I lowered myself to her level, squatting. "So you were with the body a long while, as the evening grew dark," I said gently. "And I'm sure that must have been horrid."

The girl gulped and nodded and the gesture felt to me like the first mark on a page, the mark which makes others possible, and I had a sudden hope that the thought I'd had may still return, and become sensible, with this girl's help.

"I imagine that you didn't want to look at it, but that you did, because you're a clever girl, and clever people are inquisitive."

"She didn't do anything to it!" said the boy. "She just guarded —"

"I know, and that was kind, kind to the dead woman, and sensible, because Kitty is a sensible girl. I can see that. I think she kept watch over the body very properly, just as you told her to, and I imagine that she looked at it carefully, just in case it would be helpful."

The girl's eyes had a taken on a translucent quality which I suspected presaged tears. I went on quickly. "And if she is able to help me" — I glanced at the boy — "if either of you are, then I'm sure I will manage a reward, and heaven knows, it may even clink. What I'm keen to find out, and what I'm sure Kitty can tell me, is this. Was there anything unusual about the woman's body? A mark on it, perhaps?"

The girl nodded.

"And you saw it, didn't you, Kitty? You looked closely?"

"There was lots of marks."

My spirits slumped. I pressed on regardless. "But was one of them perhaps special, like a word, or some lettering?"

The girl nodded again and sniffed. "Yes," she said, pointing to her thigh. "Here."

"Can you tell me what the lettering said?"

The girl gnawed at her lip again and looked to her brother, who stuck his chin out and said, "She can't read, Sir, and nor can I."

"No, of course not." Still squatting, I bounced impatiently upon my heels. The bellow of a distant cow gave way to the sound of the breeze swishing through treetops. "How foolish of me," I murmured at length.

"A crown," muttered Kitty.

My knees cracked as I stood up. Was the girl no better than her grasping brother? Still, what an ordeal to have gone through. "A crown indeed," I smiled. "You'll have to make do with a farthing each."

The girl shook her head. "No. The scar thing on her leg. It looked like a crown, and a tree thing, and a moon."

"What's that?" I knelt before Kitty again, a hand on the knob of her shoulder. I tossed a coin to her brother, who caught it, and I popped a second farthing into the pocket of her dress. Very gently, I said, "A crown, eh. With a tree and a moon. If we can just borrow that stick from your brother, and smooth out the dirt here, like so, do you imagine you could draw what you saw for me?"

CHAPTER
TWENTY

I made my way back through Leigh Woods, past the new quarries, open wounds in the flanks of the gorge, and dropped down to follow the river. Soon I was amongst the glass factories and iron foundries of Bedminster. Their haze stained the sky and lay thick upon my tongue. Finally I crossed the Avon, at low tide, a slit in the mud beneath the bridge, to enter Bristol proper.

As I walked, my boots turning grey and then reddish and then black with muck, Captain Addison was foremost in my mind. The Captain hadn't been straight with me. But he had not been the only man aboard the *Belsize*.

A world in miniature, that's what they called a ship. It was impossible to keep secrets in such a confined space. The decks were drum-skins reverberating with rumours; intrigue buzzed in the rigging. I turned the corner into Prince's Street. Home was a street away and I felt better for the walk. I would seek out some other of the ship's crew to interview.

But before I could turn into Thunderbolt Street, a presence materialised beside me and immediately whoever it was had gripped me harshly above the right elbow. I lifted my arm to remonstrate, whereupon my assailant, in an unnaturally low voice, growled, "Easy, now!" and shoved something sharp into the softness of my armpit. Out of the corner of my eye I saw that he was masked; a red neckerchief strained high across the bridge of his nose. Outrage gave way to fear, which flooded through me with nauseating suddenness. The man levered my arm back down to my side without lowering the knife, and marched me forward, his face now above and behind my shoulder, flat assurances coming at me in a gruff whisper, the two of us cinched together like a pair of monks in private conversation.

"What in the name of —?" I broke off as the knife-tip nipped me again. There was something awful in the man's restraint. *I'm not pressing hard* — it said — *yet*.

"Keep moving. There's nothing to be gained from stopping here."

"Where are you taking me?"

"It's for your own benefit. Get in."

We had approached a carriage waiting on the northwestern corner of Queen Square. I felt myself folded forwards and sideways at the knife's behest. The hand on my elbow slid up to guide me into the cab's recesses by means of pressure exerted upon the back of my neck. I pitched forwards on to my knees. Then the man was thrusting something over my lowered head. It was a sack. I felt myself struggle, but in truth I barely shuddered, the prospect of the knife being more than enough to snuff out my protest before I'd begun it in earnest.

97

"Good chap," said the voice. "Sensible."

The bag was made from thick hessian and admitted no light. In the darkness its rough texture was exaggerated, so that tree bark or glass paper seemed to be pressing against my brow and cheek. There was something else, something repellently *reassuring* about the sack. It had a smell so familiar and appealing that I could not at first place it. The carriage rattled from the paved street which ran around the square on to the uncertainty of a pitched road, and took off at a pace. Immediately I had no idea which way I was headed. The smell was warm and full and rounded. Coffee! A burning sensation worked in my throat.

"Take what you want! My billfold, pocket-watch. Just let me go. I beg you."

There was a burst of laughter. It sounded oddly underconfident. Then the growl came again. "Pull yourself together. I'm not here to take anything from you. On the contrary, my orders are to *give* you something."

"Fine. Give it to me. Then set me down. I'll breathe no word of this. I swear."

This plea was met with more staccato laughter, followed by, "Ever the optimist. Just sit pretty. All will be explained."

I gripped my elbows and hunched forward on the seat, which attempt to protect myself only increased the horrible sensation of vulnerability. The man still had hold of my arm, the knifepoint was still pressed into my side, though lightly now, perhaps to accommodate the jolting of the carriage as it churned the rutted streets.

Uphill. That didn't narrow things down by much: Bristol is all hills. On we dragged, to the sound of the road-noise and wind. The man did not speak again. In time the raw fear faded. It was replaced by a low panic which still rendered sensible thinking impossible, so that although I tried to imagine how best I might escape unharmed, I could not. Absurdities flitted about me instead. I wouldn't have time to attend the barber's today, not now. Why wasn't I more resolute about improving my drawing? And how could Lilly's wide-eyed smile be at once adorable and infuriating?

The coffee smell. I focussed on that. Maybe I imagined it, but there seemed to be something else behind the smell, the sharpness of strong alcohol. Christ! I coughed and shook my head and steeled myself by listening for the sound of the wheels grinding on.

CHAPTER
TWENTY-ONE

Up we went, up. The horse was blowing between the shafts, and the carriage rattled upon its axle, wooden-wheels slipping and biting and clattering over the broken road. Then we were slowing and twisting and heaving over what felt less like a road than earth and rocks. The man had a rough hold of my collar to steady me against the movement, which solicitude I could not help feeling as a kindness, even as I crouched there in the black shadow of the sack. Finally, the seat beneath my thighs bounced to a stop.

"Down you get."

The hand and the knife-tip steered me through the carriage door. I felt gingerly for the step. Beneath it my boot stumped into something wet. I squelched my way forward, the wind tugging at my coat-tails, and then there were planks beneath my feet and my footsteps acquired an echo which, taken together with the yawning stillness above me, told me that I had entered a building. I was manhandled to a staircase and prodded to climb it, feeling for each step. From the curve of the landing, I could tell the stairs belonged somewhere big. Up and up we went. Finally, I was jostled on to floorboards which flexed and clattered as I crossed them. They had not been nailed in place. Fearing a hole in the floor, I baulked, but the knife digging into the small of my back would brook no resistance. Rough wood snagged beneath my leather soles as I scuffed my way forwards.

"Good man. Steady. There's the spot."

The point of pressure at my back eased and I stopped shuffling. I could still sense the man looming behind me, and a fearful nothingness before me; though I locked my knees they were shaking unreliably, as were my hands. I clasped them together and clamped my teeth shut so hard that my ears rang.

"Look straight ahead. Don't turn around."

The man attempted to jerk the bag off my head, but his fingers took hold of a chunk of my hair along with the hessian. I winced and swung my head from side to side and the hand pulled and finally, as my eyes pricked full of tears, the bag came off.

I was standing on the edge of a precipice! I gasped and blinked and reached to steady myself against the stonework. There should have been a door here on to a balcony of some sort, but there was none. Just a ragged opening in the wall of a house perched high above the city, with a sheer drop down the front of the building on to broken stone and earth sixty, no, eighty feet below.

The voice growled in my ear again. "Don't look around, or my face will be the last thing you have the good fortune to see."

"What do you want from me?"

"Just look, and listen."

The view before me swam into focus. The whole city seemed to tumble away from the foot of this half-built shell of a building. Braced against the bare casement, I glanced left and right at the sweep of windowless, roofless terrace either side of where I stood. It looked like a wave of stone about to break upon the town. Though I'd never been inside it before, I understood now that I was standing inside the great unfinished crescent on the brink of Clifton Hill. The sky burned dull white for an instant as the sun tried to break through a seam in the canopy of cloud above me, then the wind swept shadows over the hill and the light turned grey again. Beneath the scudding cloudbank stood another, yellower layer of smoke which pulsed from the factories and tanneries and smelting houses and lay ragged and yellow in the basin of the city. From up here I could even make out a dirty slice of harbour stabbed full of masts, and, in the distance, monochrome hills gritted with sheep.

I flinched as the man laid a hand upon my shoulder again.

"Well?" he growled. "What strikes you in the scene? What do you . . . make of it all?"

"Strikes me? It's, it's, it . . ."

"Come on!"

"I don't know what you want me to say!"

"Say what you see!"

"It's . . . the city. It's Bristol. And beyond, the hills."

"The city and some hills. You can do better than that!" There was something almost comical about the rumbling depth of the man's voice. It seemed put on.

102

"For a man of your sensibilities, a *professional* man," he continued. "I expect something more evocative! This is the top of the world!"

"Clifton Hill then. And an almighty drop! Rubble, piles of stone, timbers, unfinished buildings. And beneath us the factories, and the smoke, the docks, and . . . For God's sake! What do you want from me?"

"What are your thoughts concerning the rubble?"

"I . . . don't . . . it's just rubble!"

"*Just* rubble! No, no, no. Think again! What does it signify? What's it for?"

"I've no idea. Building works I suppose."

"That's it." The knife pushed me further into the opening. "You suppose right. And that's why I have brought you here, to survey these half-cocked building works and to take in this scene."

The wind beat against my face. My feet were inches from the stone threshold. The man's demeanour seemed less threatening than it had in the carriage. But my knees were still trembling beneath the hem of my coat.

The man went on. "You see, this great half-cocked edifice is just part of the problem. Like so many other noble works, the spat with Bonaparte has condemned it to stand unfinished these how many years? War has sapped the city of funds. Without money everything grinds to a halt. I'll tell you a secret. Thieves come here at night to strip the shells of these houses of everything valuable: stone, tools, even roofing lead! But the owners have had enough. They have sprung mantraps in the basements! Men of action won't be stopped, you see.

103

The war has slowed them down, but with the end in sight they are stirring again. The city needs money. Men of action make it. They will complete these buildings, and set those factories to work, and keep our ships floated above the sucking silt. They are the force behind this city, you understand, the heart which pumps its sustaining blood."

A gull hanging in the wind above the great crescent now dropped a wing and veered sideways and away. It screamed in my face as it went.

"But what has this to do with me?"

"What the men of action want is for the benefit of the city, not just for themselves. Yet their ends are frustrated. By the war and by parliament, forces they have been all but powerless to resist. Now they find further . . . *petty* . . . obstacles in their way. Your meddling in the affairs of the dock is not welcomed." The voice had risen half a notch: "Not welcomed at all." The knife-tip dug into the small of my back, forcing me forward and on to the edge of balance; the barest push would have sent me toppling through the gap. "The last thing anyone wants is for you to investigate the rubble beneath us at close quarters. But . . ." fingertips bored through cloth and muscle, then jerked me back a step . . . "but I have been sent to warn you that this is your last chance."

I tensed from toe to jaw and rocked backwards on to my heels. My fists tightened to hammers. I was a half-beat from spinning round to assault this man, knife or no knife, and he knew it. His voice was hot against my ear again, very low again, insistent, and yes, sharp with spirits. "Don't fight, Inigo. You'll only make things worse."

I dared not breathe. I lowered my chin on to my chest and shut my eyes and heard the wind rise across the face of the building. My shoulders slumped, my hands hung open and the wind rose higher and then dropped again. In time footsteps behind me jarred the planks. I listened and listened and did not turn around until their report had disappeared.

CHAPTER
TWENTY-TWO

Dusk was turning the grey sky a dirty green before I set off for home. Even after I was certain the man had gone, I could not bring myself to move from the uneven floorboards. I felt peculiarly calm. Nothing that bad had happened. I'd thought it might, and had nearly brought disaster upon myself by fighting, but had held back. The man said there were mantraps sprung in these half-built mansions. Was that really the case? No matter, the danger had passed. Now I could sit and look at the view through this jagged gap without fear. Sky, hills, city, docks, trees, building works, rubble, sheer wall. The matchstick masts of some ship or other inching its way into port. I'd kept my head. I would not be painting the rubble with my own blood any time soon.

Such had been the intended lesson, surely, that I was master of my own destiny?

I lost the moving masts among the clutter of those others already moored in the harbour. Where had the new ship come from? What did her cargo comprise? What precious stuff, packed tight in her hold, would the stevedores soon be busy unloading? And how much of it would the ship's owners declare?

"Anchovies, alabaster, alum," I recited out loud. "Argol, arms, arsenic." I shook my head. What did I care?

I stared long and hard at the city bubbling beneath its cloud of grime. It was as full of scheming and scamming as the next place. Why risk everything, or *anything* even, battling against so commonplace a corruption? From up here you could see where the town ended and all else began. I had experienced so laughably little of the rest of the world. Though sharp, the knife had barely scratched me. Abducted! A melodramatic word. The memory of the fright served only to prove how thoroughly . . . intact . . . I was now.

Eventually, I stood up and shook out my limbs. Despite the long walk that morning and the fright of what had happened since, I felt light and abuzz and strong. I took deep breaths, savouring the fresh air. A church bell tolled in the distance. Its chimes did not resonate so much as evaporate above the city. I missed counting the hour, so checked my pocket-watch for the time and gave a start upon seeing that it read six o'clock. The poetry recital! If I paced it out, there would still be time to change my shirt and make it to the Alexanders' house within the hour.

CHAPTER
TWENTY-THREE

The poet was a woman. Her name was Edie Dyer. Upon making this discovery Mrs Alexander was all for turning around and going home, which reaction others seemed to have had as well, for visitors to the recital rooms were as yet thin on the ground. But the prospect of a spoiled evening so worked upon Lilly — her wide eyes set to quick-blinking, and the gloved fingers of her right hand fluttered before her mouth — that her father, Heston, overruled the proposed retreat immediately. "Man or woman, poetry's poetry," he explained to the audience members assembled in the foyer. This seemed magnanimous, but the shrug the merchant gave as he spoke betrayed his opinion that neither sex could redeem the activity from being, at heart, a waste of time.

Lilly recovered her composure admirably once the evening was no longer in doubt. She put her head together with Abigail, their eyes darting this way and that. My fiancée looked younger today. Something to do with being beyond the sanctuary of her own house, perhaps. I felt a surge of protectiveness and took a step in the girls' direction.

"Bombazine? Bum-be-seen rather!"

"And shouldn't someone explain that sleeves these days are trimmed and puffed?"

Lilly's laughter was a note higher than her sister's. I drew up short.

"A brooch and earrings that matched might not hamper her cause, either!"

"I think the poor thing is a little beyond that."

Following their gaze, I caught a glimpse of a slender young woman in an oddly old-fashioned, dark dress. She was quickly obscured behind moving backs. Before I could think of anything to add to their conversation, Lilly and Abigail had turned their attention to others amongst the guests, and I was left staring at my boots. They were dirty, dull despite the gleaming foyer lamps. I recalled the yawning drop that had stood before them earlier and my stomach turned over.

"You look pale, Inigo," said Mrs Alexander. "You're not feeling unwell, I hope?"

Something in her tone suggested that an affirmative response would not have disappointed her, and not just because it would have afforded an excuse for the party to go home.

"Thank you but no, I'm fine. Tired, perhaps. That's all."

"I always find the entertainments are more bearable on the back of a hard day's work," Heston Alexander said.

"Enjoyable rather than bearable, dear, I'm sure."

"Hmm? I suppose. What have you been up to that's driven the wind from your sails, then?"

"Oh, I don't think Inigo wants to relive his day now. Once was surely enough!"

I shot my mother-in-law-to-be an enquiring look, then wished I hadn't, for it registered in the wobble of her head. The woman liked nothing better than a chance to register a perceived sleight. She knew nothing of anything anyway. Lilly was still tittering with her sister — about another woman who was wearing kid gloves the wrong shade of yellow — behind me. Weariness welled up.

We stuttered through to the recital room, an expanse of red and gold burnished by lamplight. Concentric rings of plush chairs held a small stage at bay. I stood to one side and let the family jockey for position; Lilly eventually triumphed over her mother in her conspiracy to secure us seats together. This victory left me curiously flat until, as I sat down, Lilly took hold of my hand, and the warmth of her palm pressing through her silken glove stirred me to glance her way. She has the finest profile. A gentle chin, sweet lips, a pretty nose, and her skin, in this flickering light, was a coral pink. The chatter whispered itself silent like a breeze through meadow grass. I confined myself to a single pump of Lilly's hand, hard enough for the delicate bones within to flex and rub across one another. I felt her stiffen for an instant in her seat before I let go. A figure climbed on to the stage. Before Lilly and her sister had clashed heads in their urgency to whisper their recognition, I suspected what was coming: the poetess, Edie Dyer, was the thin woman in the black dress about whom they had been gossiping in the foyer. She was young, but appeared undaunted. A chair had been set on the stage. She picked it up mannishly and moved it into the shadows. There was something brazen about the woman, apparent not just in her unconventional dress but in the set of her bones. She was all angles, with a mile of gawky neck, and raw-looking wrists, and long fingers — no gloves. She took in the audience unhurriedly and without smiling, waiting for the final murmurings to die down, and pushed a strand of fallen hair — there was no way it could be termed a ringlet — away from her forehead before reading her first poem.

I listened.

I was drawn in and forgot myself.

Had I been asked to explain what the poems were about at the end of the reading I could not have done so, but word by word, line by line, verse by verse, they made sense. They were like dreams, realer than real in the moment before waking, then gone. The rustle of Mrs Alexander's skirts and Lilly's flower-water scent and the fact that my knees were skewed sideways to avoid the back of the seat in front of me, none of it had the power to distract me while the woman read. There was something oddly direct about the poems. The crags and buzzards and herdsmen and pastures and brooks in them were just crags and buzzards and herdsmen and pastures and brooks. Where were the satyrs? The heroes? The gods? By failing to invoke them and writing so . . . straight . . . the woman's verses were confrontational and mesmerising. Pain was hurtful; impoverishment was miserable; glimpsed hope was enough to make a heart soar. The woman's verses were infuriatingly good. It was well into the recital before I realised none of the lines rhymed.

At some point I had let go of Lilly's hand. I glanced at her to check how she was enjoying the reading and saw that she was already looking at me. Beyond Lilly, I made out the profiles of her sister and mother, both of whom were looking to the stage — Abigail with a wry smirk, Mrs Alexander disapprovingly, her mouth more than usually pursed. It appeared that past them Heston Alexander, whose chin had dropped to his chest, was asleep.

My walk out to Long Ashton, those scrawny children, my premonition about the washed-up body and the initials. The shock! A coffee sack thrust over my head. A carriage climbing a hill, building sites, the long, long drop. Dock duties and death. The sense I'd strayed somewhere I shouldn't have, and the revelation, once my misstep had been pointed out, that I was the sort to flee from consequences so swiftly. Was I driven by curiosity and nothing else? How easily my obligation to Carthy had been brushed aside. What mattered more, deep down, was Lilly's white throat and her tinkling silly laughter, and the coffee stain on Mary's apron and the heft of her hip beneath it. Coffee! Too much, and not enough sleep, and a father and brothers I could not reach, and now this complication of a girl in her widow-like dress with her awkwardness and assuredness and her words, words, words, which were somehow wrapping me up safe and belittling me at the same time.

112

The poet's recital ended. I was careful to keep my applause short. There was much waving and sidestepping and nodding in recognition from Mrs Alexander and her daughters as they worked their way through the other audience members and out into the foyer. Between them they seemed to know everyone. Heston followed behind with me, yawning and stretching and saying, "Marvellous, poetical," and clapping me on the back before adding, "though of course I can't claim to have a trained ear."

"The verses were original."

"Hmm? Absolutely. Certainly she gave me an appetite. Lord! I could eat, and dinner awaits!"

Heston attempted to steer his wife towards the door, but Mrs Alexander held firm on the carpet with a mincing smile, indicating that she and her daughters were in conversation with a man whose moustache, I noticed, was the colour of egg-yolk. Heston cast around for somebody of his own to accost, beckoning me as he homed in on Lloyd Sutherland, the new owner of the recital rooms no less, who was himself holding forth amongst a group which included ... the poetess. Before I knew what was happening, I found myself face to face with the woman. My prospective father-in-law appeared either to have forgotten her already, or considered her unworthy of including in his interruption; he opted instead to compliment the new owner on his purchase of so important a civic space, then asked him directly when he expected to see a return on his investment.

The poetess looked away with a feline lack of concern.

I shuffled from foot to foot.

Heston Alexander, perhaps sensing his faux pas, eventually offered his hand to the young woman and explained confidentially, "This young man is also prone to a bit of art, you know! Pictures, etcetera." His work done, he turned back to Sutherland and asked with what other entertainments he intended to improve the city.

I felt the colour rising in my cheeks.

"You paint?" the young woman murmured.

I offered my hand and managed a stilted, "Inigo Bright."

"What sort of paintings do you make, Mr Bright?"

"No. I don't paint. Mr Alexander was mistaken in referring to my doodlings as art. Simple ink drawings are my limit."

The woman laughed openly. Her eyes were too close together, her nose too big in her face. Yet the slash of mouth beneath it . . .

"What sort of quill do you prefer?"

"Quill?"

"Yes. For drawing. Don't pretend you're not troubled by the choice. It must matter more to an artist than it does to a writer, and I'm obsessive about these things. My father gave me a stock of hawk feathers last Christmas. I'm still using them. You can hold a finer point on a hawk's outer wing feather than is even possible with crow. The issue I have is that I'm left-handed. There are far fewer right-winged feathers

114

of any bird for sale, and I'm particular about curvature; the quill absolutely has to fit properly in my hand. I tried a swan's feather once, but found it overrated."

Was this in earnest? There was glitter in those close-set eyes. Unsure whether or not they were mocking me, I mumbled something about how gulls' wing-feathers were unusually straight, and possessed a longevity which few other quills could match.

"Seagulls. Really?"

"Yes, they're like goose, but better. They flex well, yet they're strong."

"Well. I'll try gull next then."

She was serious, no doubt about it; I heard myself offering to make a gift to the woman of one of my — Carthy's in fact — gull feather quills to try out.

"That's a kind offer. I'll take it up on one condition — that you show me how they have worked for you." Her eyes were still amusedly bright but their gaze was more penetrating than before. "Let me see some of these drawings you've made."

"I couldn't impose . . ."

Somebody had arrived at my side. It was Lilly. While I introduced my fiancée, the poetess looked her over as dispassionately as she had regarded her audience. A pause followed, in which I was unable to look squarely at either woman. Instead, I was distracted by the chandelier flickering above our heads. As I stared at it, one of its flames puttered out. The poetess eventually broke the silence. "Mr Bright was just agreeing to show me some of his art," she confided.

"Oh," said Lilly. She pressed her hands together and stuck out her chin. "I've seen a sample already. It's lovely. He has a . . . fine touch."

Immediately, I launched into a conversation about — of all things — the new science of gas lighting which I'd recently read about. More reliable than oil lamps, less smoke. I indicated the chandelier. Better than candles. Less easily blown out.

"How fascinating," said Edie.

"Yes," agreed Lilly uncertainly.

"Where shall I visit to inspect your work?" the poetess asked me. "And receive my gift, of course."

I mumbled Carthy's address, conscious that Lilly was wavering beside me. I offered her my arm. The shadow of a smile played on Edie's lips, but her eyes remained flatly serious. She thrust out her hand. To take it, I had to let go of Lilly again. I did so. The poetess's grip was cool and firm and the muscles in her thin forearm worked in the sliver of exposed wrist as she shook my hand. I backed away with Lilly. Gulls' feathers, gas lamps, gifts. I flinched again from the memory of myself.

CHAPTER
TWENTY-FOUR

Carthy did not favour Thunderbolts. He preferred to take tea in Corn Street instead, declaring the brew there more refined, the service more courteous, and the company altogether more edifying. I knew this was a ruse to allow me a bolt-hole away from my lodgings and workplace, both of which were, after all, set squarely beneath his roof. So when, the morning after Edie's reading, my coffee bowl leapt to the smack of a newspaper thumped down upon the table over which I was hunched, I looked up expecting to see Mary — who had grown altogether more *direct* with me of late — and not my employer's looming face. I had never seen those eyebrows as fiercely dipped, or his brow as furrowed.

"What did I do?"

"Read it!" Carthy fairly shouted.

I looked at the folded page of newsprint. Carthy had scratched a square in ink around a paragraph of text which, with its familiar tone of gleeful despair, proclaimed further corruption in the city. A lawyer, this time, stood accused of misappropriating client funds. It took a second before Carthy's name hit home, and my first impulse, on making the connection, was to laugh out loud.

"What is this?"

"It's no joke!"

"But —"

"I — *we* — stand accused just as it says. While you were out yesterday, I received the news first hand. Bullivant's boy delivered the letter in person."

Again I fought the urge to smile. "But . . . Bullivant! It's transparent. His grudge is common knowledge."

David Bullivant had invested in the *Hopewell,* a ship which sank while returning from the Indies that spring. The merchant's share in the lost vessel was uninsured; pressed for funds, he'd taken a gamble. In subsequently casting around for somebody to blame for this ill fortune, Bullivant had instructed Carthy to investigate the possibility of suing his partners. He alleged that they had been responsible for overloading the ship, but we could find no evidence of this. Not liking our advice, the man had refused to pay for it. Now, it seemed, he was claiming we'd stolen the money he'd advanced us on account.

Carthy dragged a three-legged stool out from under the table and sat down heavily. He knotted his fingers together forcefully enough to raise tendons in the backs of his hands.

"I prepared Bullivant's fee note myself," I explained. "He hasn't yet settled it. Should anyone take a moment to inspect the file, they will see that he stands in debt to Carthy and Co., not the other way around." My words

118

were ineffectual as flakes of snow swirling seawards. I went on regardless. "We informed him repeatedly —"

Carthy lowered his head. "No, no, no," he said.

"But —"

"Where were you yesterday?"

"Nobody will take this seriously!"

"Why were you not at work?"

"It's a stunt. He's been put up to it."

"Of course he's been put up to it! I know that!" Carthy's knuckles bulged. "Don't be so literal-minded, Inigo! I asked you a question."

To feel protective of my mentor was a reversal of Copernican profundity: I could not hoist its implications on board immediately. Better, instead, to concentrate on the injustice at hand than add further to Carthy's concerns. Taking responsibility in this way would be exactly what he would want. If Carthy knew I had been threatened he would not let the matter lie, and I had determined to do just that.

"Dead ends," I said. "I was chasing down the last leads in the Dock Company investigation. The books need balancing, monies are owed, we know as much. There's nothing untoward about the *Belsize,* not that I can see, at any rate. I was engaged in confirming that yesterday."

Carthy's hands had stopped working at one another. He looked away from me and said, "Really."

"Yes. And I imagine we should inform Mr Orton. He asked for a written report: I'll have you a draft today."

Mary now arrived at the table to take Carthy's order. She bent to wipe down the table before asking what he wanted to drink. Her hand was red, her forearm pink; the cloth worked hard circles around the fretted oak tabletop, and her hip brushed against my shoulder as she raised herself upright. She was suddenly infuriating. I barked, "Tea!" and waved away her nod at my empty cup. Her hip knocked my arm more forcefully when she spun to go. Carthy studied me as my thumb traced cloth-wiped circles across the black wood tabletop.

"So you're also of the opinion that this clumsy attempt to besmirch our name is connected to the case," he said.

I protested: "I didn't make such a connection."

"You should have. Because that's what this is."

"No. Bullivant is of no interest to Orton."

Carthy shook his head and pinched the bridge of his nose.

I went on. "I've not seen his name connected to the WTC."

Carthy's thumb and fingers spread out to grip and knead his temples. They then slid inwards again, running across the grain of his eyebrows, which bristled like cat fur stroked backwards. He appeared more resigned than angry, disappointed by a shallowness he'd perceived in me. This stung, but I could say nothing. I saw full well that the WTC might seek to undermine Carthy & Co. via an unconnected third party, but I didn't want to admit as much, because doing so would mean acknowledging the wider web of my concerns. I hung my head. Carthy would be outraged if he heard I had been accosted. Far from

120

retreating on the WTC and the *Belsize*, he'd raise a stink.

Carthy spoke patiently. "Of course he's not on the WTC's books, Inigo. An overt link is the last thing the Company's members would want. But — in this town especially — everything's intertwined. Tell me you understand that, please."

Mary arrived with Carthy's bowl of tea. The waitress was standing close to me again. When she bent forward with the milk jug, I could not help but notice the heaviness of her chest. That bare forearm, too, braced against the tabletop. She stood up and wiped her hand against her apron and I looked away. The babble of customers dropped for a moment; I fancied I could hear Mary exhale. I looked up to see her . . . looking back at me. Her tongue appeared to be pressed into her cheek. "Enough!" I growled. "For God's sake. We're talking here, Mary. Leave us be!" Without rushing, the waitress walked away. I concentrated on the window, trying to gather sensible thoughts. It had begun to rain outside; the frontage opposite the coffee house had darkened oppressively; it seemed the sky had lowered itself like a lid upon the rooftops. The two of us sat in silence in the gathering gloom. Of course I understood the intertwining Carthy was pointing to, and the real likely motive behind Bullivant's claim. Like the rain, spearing down now, greasing the cobbles, it was irrefutable. But as my chances of denying the connection receded, I found myself all the more compelled to stick to my guns.

"Bullivant's an ass. You know that better than anyone: it was your advice he refused to take. This assault is entirely within the ambit of the man's character, or lack of one. He's clutching at straws as he drowns."

"It's unlike you to speak to someone in that manner."

"I'm sorry?"

"You were rude to the serving girl. Why? It betrays something."

I felt an uncomfortable heat gather within my chest. I reached to my brow and looked down, attempting to shield my face from view as the warmth wound itself up my neck. I had to say something . . . anything . . . to regain my footing within the conversation.

"Rude? I was straightforward. We're talking. She was loitering. It's the truth!"

The look Carthy gave me, eyebrows furrowed, a forced smile, straddled incredulity and disappointment. "I see," Carthy repeated. "So your counsel would be to scale down the Dock Company investigation —"

"Which is what the client asked us to do!" I interrupted.

"— and debunk Bullivant's posturing as something entirely unconnected —"

"Squeal *conspiracy* instead and it will just appear that we have something to hide!"

Carthy drummed his fingers on the table. "I hear you," he said softly. "But no. The Dock Company investigation goes on. We must dig deeper. If you prefer to concentrate upon your other cases, I will see to the matter myself. But you will assist me in issuing defamation proceedings against Bullivant. We must contact the news-sheet with a rebuttal forthwith. We cannot sit still here; we must attack."

I rocked back on my stool hard enough to feel its joints creak. Outside, the rain was bouncing knee high now, raising a mist which helped veil the buildings just a few paces opposite. A similar fog had found its way between me and my mentor. It was apparent in the self-conscious manner with which Carthy was now inspecting his pocket-watch. Too closely; I sensed he was not really reading the time, but using the gesture to declare the conversation over.

Guilt swept through me. I rocked forward, but Carthy snapped the pocket-watch shut.

"So —" I began.

But Carthy immediately cut in. "I must return home. Anne . . . has a . . . performance which she . . . has asked me . . ." He waved a hand as if to imply that the details were unimportant, manifestly unconcerned whether or not I believed him, which made me all the more intent upon pretending that I did.

"Yes, yes. Little Anne," I said softly. "Her performance will transfix us all. I must not hold you back."

When I was a boy I accidentally injured Phantom, one of Father's lurchers. The dog was a favourite. He allowed it to sleep upstairs on the end of his bed. I was roughhousing with it on the landing one morning, and slipped in my bare-stockinged feet upon the polished floorboards, plunging myself and the lurcher down a flight of stairs. The dog broke my fall — and a back leg. My father nursed it back to health, but Phantom never quite trusted me again. It didn't run away from my approach, much less snap at me, but from that moment it exhibited an . . . increased awareness, visible in the occasional shiver which ran across its shoulders when it sensed I was close by, and in the way it tracked me around the room with a wary eye, and the eighth of an inch its haunches would drop in the instant before I stroked its back. I feared a similar gap had opened up between myself and Carthy, and determined to do all I could to broach it.

CHAPTER
TWENTY-FIVE

A note had arrived for me while we were in the coffee shop. It wasn't one of Lilly's; her cards are a distinctive peach colour, never mind their scent. My next thought was of the poetess, Edie Dyer. But no, the spidery handwriting belonged to my youngest brother, Sebastian.

Come home, the script read.

I set off without bothering to search for an umbrella, and slogged up the hill in the rain. My hair was matted with sweat by the time I made Bright House. My coat and hat were sodden, my boots filthy. I kicked them off at the door and left damp footprints across the tiles as I made my way to the music room. For a moment I stood outside the door listening. There was no pattern to my brother's playing; it was just so many notes strung together around pauses. I entered the room. I skirted the pianoforte and Sebastian looked up at me and smiled bleakly and did not stop playing, which irked me: had I rushed up the hill through the rain for no reason?

I spoke over the music. "Your note?"

"I . . ." he started. "I'm s-sorry. I didn't mean to c-cause you alarm."

125

I grabbed an upholstered chair from the fireside and dragged it to the piano stool. I sat down beside my brother. Sebastian is nearly five years my junior; when I turned twelve he was seven-and-a-half. At about that age his shyness and stuttering amounted to a pervasive twitchiness which was resistant to everything excepting my influence. When confronted by visitors to the house, Father's business associates, the Wiltshire branch of the family, anybody unfamiliar, Sebastian would immediately fidget himself beyond speech. Father construed this as rudeness: admonishment inevitably followed the spoiled visit. I discovered that if I stood behind Sebastian and held him still, a hand on each birdlike shoulder, thumbs pressed either side of his whipcord backbone, and whispered assurances, I could keep whatever it was that possessed my brother at bay. Little by little, Sebastian became more self-assured. The thumbs became unnecessary first, then the hands, finally the whispering; it was enough for me to stand close by to help Sebastian keep hold of himself. Music had a similarly calming influence; Sebastian gained in confidence through listening, more so when he learnt to play for himself. Now our conversation was underscored by the same rambling notes I'd heard on the way upstairs.

"What's happened? You wouldn't have written unless you had cause."

"I was hasty. It-it's nothing."

"Come on now. Tell me what's wrong."

"Your hair is wet."

"I enjoyed the stroll. Rain is no more than rain."

Sebastian's fingers swam lightly towards the higher notes.

"What's wrong? Is it Father? John?"

The music ran uninterrupted for a moment. Then Sebastian said, "Yes. John and Father and work. The problem attaches to Bright & Co. A business matter."

I kept my voice flat. "You want my help with a business problem."

The piano was very quiet, high notes straddling empty pauses.

"We have some concerns just now, that's right," Sebastian said. "A d-debt or six going bad. The French war is to blame; everybody's affected, the longer the thing d-drags on . . . every end a false horizon. We failed to win the Adams contract. And, to top that, hopes are f-fading for the *Penny-Ann*. She will be the third ship we've backed this year and l-lost."

"But the last time I was here John was saying he was confident of the Adams business."

"After dancing with the b-bear," Sebastian blinked. "I remember. But he was wrong. We lost out." Sebastian struck a high chord a little harder and went on. "John took it badly."

I could not help feeling half-pleased with this news; though I pretend otherwise, John's easy rapport with Father inspires jealousy in me. He would be appearing less perfect to the old man now.

"John has become too f-familiar with the bottle," Sebastian went on. "It makes him erratic. When Adams declined our offer, John took hold of him by the lapels

127

and laid him across one of the n-nails, in broad daylight, before one and all. He had to be dragged off."

Although this was shocking news, I knew it still wasn't the point. Sebastian went on.

"F-father was livid. He set upon John outside the counting house, berated him before the men. But he knows the failed deal is the least of our real concerns. The r-rest of the business is foundering. We've inadequate protection to weather this storm. Father's denying there's anything to worry about in the long term, but it's not true, not true."

"And you tell me all this because?"

"B-because?" Sebastian caught my eye for a moment. "Because I thought you would want to know."

All was not quite right here. I could sense Sebastian holding something back. The pale skin across his forehead appeared taut with some deeper concern. He doesn't care about business. His jagged movements and speech betokened a more personal collapse.

"I could talk to John, or Father, if you think it would help?" I suggested.

Sebastian's fingers shivered over the keys before finding another chord.

"N-no. It's not that. It's . . ." He shook his head as if trying to free an idea.

I bent close to Sebastian and in so doing saw the fine layer of dust covering the lid of the pianoforte. A realisation slid into place, clicking home like a well-oiled gun barrel snapping shut. "Is this about the Dock Company, Sebastian? The investigation I mentioned. *My* work?"

Beyond the dust-field stood a window through which I glimpsed the heavy moving sky.

"W-what? No."

I smiled, still certain I was on to something. "Good, because that has all fizzled out. It is not a thing anyone needs to worry about now."

Sebastian's fingers pressed down on the keys, cutting off what sounded like the beginnings of a groan with another chord. He overcame the tremor-blinking by closing his eyes and leaving them shut.

"Sebastian? What is it? I'm saying Carthy and Co., the Dock Company, too, has no interest in pursuing unpaid duties. Not now at least."

I stood up and moved behind the piano stool, took hold of my brother's shoulders, a knot of shivering in each hand. I pressed a thumb either side of the ridge of his backbone. He hung his head and played another, gentler, chord.

"I'm glad if that's the case," he said.

CHAPTER
TWENTY-SIX

The ship had moved. It no longer stood beneath the Merchant Venturer's crane. A new vessel now occupied that berth; smaller than the *Belsize*, it appeared to be cowering beneath the crane, which looked to me like a riding crop raised in threat above the ship's deck. I took off my hat and scratched my head through matted hair. The barber's, the barber's; I would get there yet. It had stopped raining but the sky, hanging hard over the quay and dock, seemed to press the stench of the place upon me. Rot and excrement pulsed damp on all sides

I walked along the Welsh Back in search of the *Belsize*. In this light all natural colour was tainted grey. Even the caged canaries for sale up by Bristol Bridge were a jaundiced yellow. The girl selling them caught my eye; she gave me a stained smile and planted a hand upon her hip as I sidestepped her cart.

"Have a little look," she said. "Just a peek."

I shook my head and moved on, but the woman stepped into my path, stretched out her back, and pointed to the canaries and goldfinches in their cage. "A friend in troubled times, a birdie is."

"I'm sure."

"They're no bother at all."

"No doubt, but I'm not interested."

"They live on thin air and a few seeds and sing something lovely every day. This one here has a marvellous tune in him. Like an angel."

The woman bent forward to point out the bird, the plumpness of her neck rolling into a double chin.

"I'm afraid I have no space for a songbird just now."

"They don't need no space! Just a spot for a cage."

"I don't have a cage."

"But I have one for you!" the woman said triumphantly, throwing back a cloth from her barrow's lower tray to reveal a jumble of woven wicker cylinders, each no bigger than a loaf of bread. "No more excuses; I can see from your face you need cheering up, and a bird is just the thing."

"I don't need cheering! And, no offence, but even if I did, I'm not sure a bird would have the power to help."

"Nonsense!" the woman laughed, her face flushing as she sensed incipient success. She danced around her cart, pulling a cage from the lower tier, releasing the door of the bigger one on the top shelf, and thrusting her hand in amongst flurrying wings. Her cheek, pressed against the bars of the cage, squashed ripe. "If it's not you that needs a friend, surely you'll give it to somebody else. They make a very amusing little present."

People were jostling by on either side of this conversation. The woman, all elbows and plump fingers, already had the canary tight in her first. She thrust the tiny bird head first into the box, where it scrabbled and fluttered in panic. I thought of Anne. A present for her would somehow help things between me and Carthy. I reached into my coat pocket for my purse and dug in it for the right coins.

When I looked up again a thickset Negro was skirting us with purposeful strides. Although the man had his head down against the weather, I recognised him immediately as the sailor who had helped me in my quayside confrontation, the day the *Belsize* docked. The woman had stuffed the miniature birdcage under my arm and was picking pennies from my palm. Her fingernails were filthy. I let the coins go. Then I followed the man off the bridge and into the Welsh Back. The sailor had a rolling, heavy-shouldered walk: I noticed how others on the quay stepped aside, like sheep splitting before a dog, or so much water parting around the hull of a ship. At King Street the sailor turned right and made his way straight to the door of a tumbledown inn, the Llandroger Trow.

I entered a few paces behind him.

CHAPTER
TWENTY-SEVEN

In honour of the low grey day outside, the inn's table lamps were aglow. A fire also licked at itself in the grate. Perhaps as a result of these generous touches, or simply because the inn stood so near the centre of things, the place was busy despite it being as yet mid-afternoon. As well as groups of merchants and sailors scattered around the tables, a clutch of men stood before the bar. I saw muddy breeches, a pair of split-heeled boots, and a sleeve hanging ripped like a broken wing. Labourers, freed early from a job. From the sounds of their raised voices they had been here a while.

The sailor had to make his way through their midst to reach the bar. Yet before he'd even uttered his first "pardon me", the atmosphere in the room shifted; whereas in the street outside the Negro's size had given him a right of way, in here it drew unwanted attention. Being big makes you a milestone by which smaller — and, often, drunken — men are compelled to navigate. The broken heels belonged to a wiry fellow who wore a short beard; as the sailor attempted to sidestep him this man planted his feet wide. The blackamoor checked and tried to slide the other way, but found his route barred. The man with the shot boots stiffened like a terrier.

"I fucking hate it when weight gets thrown around," he said.

The black sailor took a step backwards. I found myself right behind his shoulder. I recognised, in the way the sailor dropped his head and took an inch from his height at the knees, his attempt to defuse himself. It didn't work. The terrier man had his chin up, beard bristling like kicked embers.

"An apology will do it," he said, his eyes weaving back to his friends.

The sailor's silence was at once resigned and challenging. His back straightened. The inch he reclaimed in height seemed more like six in breadth. The workman, meanwhile, transferred his tankard clumsily from his left hand to his right. I saw the man's grip tighten on the handle. Without a doubt, he was about to swing it, contents and all, at the sailor. I stepped quickly to the Negro's side and threw my free arm around his shoulders.

"There you are!" I said.

The sailor flinched, glanced sideways, then stood firm.

"Out of the way, friends!" I slurred. I drew myself up, bird-basket tucked rakishly under an armpit, and felt the Negro's shoulders shift uncertainly beneath my hand. "This man owes me a drink. I must wring it from him at this bar! Ha!" Gripping a chunk of the sailor's coat, I surged forwards, pulling him with me. The terrier had no option but to step aside before the

134

advancing wall we made. The clutch of fellows behind him likewise gave way. "Cider for two," I growled at the publican as we thumped into the bar. I then spun around, swaying mock-drunkenly, grin in place, to fend off retaliation from the rear. None came. The labourers had turned away. They were laughing. At what, I couldn't see, but I supposed it might be their thwarted mate. In drink, aggression and humiliation are especially closely linked. Once the sailor had gathered up our tankards I steered him to an alcove, screened from the throng by the pub's centrepiece, an inglenook chimney breast.

"Thank you," the sailor said, sliding my drink towards me. "One apiece."

"You remember?"

"Yes, I do. Though I'd say I saved you from a greater harm than you did me. That fellow there —" he nodded beyond the fire "— would have gone down before a stiff wind. Your adversary, the shrewish stallholder, was tough as a Turk by comparison."

"I don't doubt you had the situation in hand, but still."

The Negro shrugged, his shoulders threatening the seams of his coat. He drew on his cider and winced and wiped his lips, muttering, "I should have held out for rum." Then he looked up at me and smiled. There was an appealing frankness in his countenance, and the deep calm I had sensed in him last time we met appeared bottomless yet.

"You sailed on the *Belsize*, didn't you?" I asked.

"I did."

"I saw you board her after you helped me on the quay."

"Joseph Blue," said the man, holding out his hand. I took it. Though I squeezed firmly, my palm felt soft against the sailor's calluses. "But nobody uses the Joseph part."

"Blue," I repeated. Then I introduced myself, continuing, "It's no coincidence that I came in here after you today. I saw you pass me in the street. I recognised you. I have an interest in your old ship. I followed you off the bridge and through these doors hoping to talk to you about her."

I saw . . . or suspected I saw . . . a cloud pass over Blue's face. His eyes narrowed, shadows beneath them turning purple. I gritted my teeth. I'd misjudged the man, should have been more circumspect, not blurted out my purpose straight. His frown of concern deepened as he scrutinised me. "Why are you carrying a bird box?" he said at last.

"Oh! This." I set the wicker case down on the table between us. "It's a gift."

"You bought me —"

"No, no, no. My master's daughter. It's for her."

Blue took another swig from his mug. "A funny way to advance yourself. It wouldn't have worked with the Captain."

"I've met your Captain Addison. I found him forthcoming. Eager to assist."

"Did you, now?"

"In truth, I did."

136

"Well, you're a luckier man than most. Those of us who sailed beneath him did all the assisting as was needed on board. Still, no seafaring man is the same creature on land as he is afloat."

"But we were afloat. He gave me a guided tour of the ship."

"In which case, he must have had his reasons. The owners leaned on him, I imagine. Back in port, he's no longer in charge, is he? Anyway, tied to the quay, you weren't exactly with the man *at sea*."

"No."

"And in any case, Addison finds the journey from ship to shore harder than most." Blue shook his head. "If you've only met the Captain since we put into port, you haven't really met him. Landfall has wrought a pitiful change upon the man."

"In what way?" I asked.

"He's lost his bearings. The last time I saw him, I had to help him to his lodgings."

I considered my cider. Its surface blinked at me when tipped towards the lamplight, but still I could not see the bottom of the tankard. Blue, draining his drink, now stood up abruptly. For a moment I suspected he was about to leave, but he merely went to fetch another round. The relief I felt upon his return made me realise how much I wanted the man's help. From its tiny cage on the tabletop, the songbird's chirruping was briefly audible.

"What's your interest in the *Belsize*?" Blue asked as he sat down.

I shifted forwards on my stool. "I'm not exactly sure. It's probably nothing more than clerical. I'm charged with chasing up dock duties, import fees and so on. Not just on this ship. I was hoping to find out a little more about what she was carrying."

Blue leaned forwards, too. Close up, I noticed his chin was flecked with stubble, some of it grey, and that two deep lines scored each cheek. The man's foreignness, and agelessness, suddenly struck home. On what basis was I hoping for his help? Yet I was, and my optimism pre-dated the warmth in my veins attributable to drink.

"Captain Addison gave up the ship's log, but I'm not sure it tells the whole story."

"No, you'd need more than sight of that to tell exactly what we dragged back from the Indies. You should have pressed the Captain himself. I've no idea what was in the hold, I'm afraid. My responsibilities lay above deck."

"I see." I sat back. Although I knew next to nothing of this man, there was something steady in his eyes, and in the way he held himself, something . . . contained. True to his word, he had returned with a round not of cider but rum. I took a mouthful and held it, teeth gritted, until the roof of my mouth was aglow, the back of my tongue numb.

"No," Blue went on. "You've got the wrong idea if you assume deck hands such as me would have known the ins and outs of what she was carrying. Even the purser would have been pushed to give you an inventory off the top of his head."

"I suppose so. And yet," I went on, "an inventory isn't quite what I'm after. More a sense of whether there was something unusual about the ship's cargo. Something noteworthy, which the books might not reveal."

The sailor's nod of confidence appeared a little magnified. Inside its wicker jail, the canary had taken a break from its piping lament. The immediate effects of a shot of rum, I considered, were not a million miles distant from strong coffee, taken very hot. Bite and optimism. The pub seemed to grow very quiet in the pause before Blue spoke.

"Ah, I see which way you're headed. But I'm not sure there's the wind to get you there. Waring is your man. The ship's surgeon. He was the only fellow — the Captain aside — with a *stake* in the ship. Interfering bugger, too. If there was anything of special value on board, he'd know about it. Whether he'd share the specifics with you is another matter, though."

"Waring, you say."

"The ship's quack."

"Where would I find him?"

The mountain range of Blue's shoulders lifted and fell. "No idea," he said, picking up his glass. But he paused before drinking. "Though it was him the Captain was raving about when I discovered him stumbling about the raggedy quarter of town. And if he's on the Captain's mind, I bet he'll know of the bastard's whereabouts."

"You think he'll tell me?"

"There's no love lost between them."

A pause followed this statement. With the songbird silent, and the labourers gone, the pub felt oddly quiet. Yet — I realised — there was nothing awkward about not speaking to this man. We finished our drinks. Finally, Blue offered to show me to Addison's lodgings south of the river. This generosity seemed so natural that I made no protest before accepting it.

CHAPTER
TWENTY-EIGHT

The man took Abeni away too. The poor girl screamed when he took her, a quick high hopeless squawk, like a chicken in the instant before its head is snapped back, though he didn't snap anything back at all. He was quite gentle with her. He undid the chain and led her out through the open door talking in a low whisper all the while. He talked like you talk to an ox, a cow, a horse.

This means Oni is alone.

You would think that the aloneness would make it worse, and it does for the first few moments, the moments after the door shuts, after the sound of his boots, dull on the hard earth, and echoing up the stairs fades. There's a new kind of panic then. It is water sucked into lungs. It is a knife slid hard under the skin. Oni wonders: will the aloneness be the thing to bring an end? Will it press down into her lungs hard enough to drive out the last air? Will it slice in far enough to let out the final drops of blood?

No.

Oni thinks: ever since they came and took us and put us all together, so many together that I couldn't feel where I ended and the next person began, I have really been alone.

On the ship there were those who tried to reach their own ends through the simple means of keeping their mouths shut to food and water. But the men had thought of that. They have the thumb thing, which twists until you eat. Oni once saw them use it on a woman who refused the pain. She would not cry out. So they tore her thumb off. But still she did not win. They shook their heads and sent for the mouth thing, which broke the woman's teeth as they fitted it, then forced her jaws apart, opened her up to the food. The first thing they made her swallow was her own thumb.

So Oni takes the bread when it is given and drinks water from the wooden cup. She does not wonder where they took Abeni, or where the girl is now.

CHAPTER
TWENTY-NINE

Buttoning my greatcoat, I followed the sailor to the door, and through it on to the quay. The rush of air and street noise hit me a fraction of a second before the first fist did. I saw Blue turn around in front of me. A shape slammed into the sailor and sheered away out of reach. Then something else slashed down. I ducked instinctively. The blow glanced off my head, shutting out all sound and striking a white-hot match before my eyes. I was still half ducking and half stumbling, beset by an absurd distraction: I must get rid of the birdcage, which was still clasped to my chest. Something hard broke across my upper back. My face was between my knees and my breath exploded wet on to the cobbles. The wicker case clattered away, the bird tumbling inside it, a flash of yellow, and my hands came up to shield my face just in time to prevent a further blow hitting home. Instead it bounced off my raised forearm.

Where the other knocks had stunned me, this one hurt. The pain was blade sharp and sparked rage.

Rocking backwards and upwards, I threw all my weight behind my left elbow, and felt it jar into something soft. I pivoted through the blow in time to see grey teeth knocked open in surprise, the black cave of a mouth behind them, a face dropping sideways. I drove my right fist into the falling face. Somebody grabbed my wrist and somebody else leaped upon my shoulders. In panic, I lunged sideways into the latticed window of the pub, crushing the man on my back into the panes. The man slid to the floor and sounds broke in again: a garbled yell, a crunch of glass. I looked down and drove the heel of my boot into the open mouth. Out of the corner of my eye I saw Blue clinched to a man in a long coat, apparently dancing with him, but the man's feet weren't touching the ground. Blue had him by the throat. The breath exploded from my chest again, and again, half gasp — half laughter. Somebody was running away and somebody else — the man with the iron-filing beard — still had me by the wrist. I allowed myself to be yanked clear of the broken pub-front and then I threw myself forward, my own momentum combining with the workman's, who was woefully slow, drunk and stumbling backwards. I swatted him into the road with an open palm and he went down and I kicked him hard in the chest. To my left I saw Blue hurl his assailant upwards and away, coat-tails split around his backside, and for a second they were a swallow's wings, and then they folded him, too, into the pavement. The way the man did nothing to break his fall drew me up short. I stood over iron-filings, poised to kick him again as he crawled away on his elbows and knees, but held back. My blood was slowing in my chest, beating to the same pulse as the stripe across my back. My arm was also throbbing and heavy with pain. The rest of the drunken gang had scattered, and iron-filings now staggered upright and began to lurch away. Only the broken-winged overcoat remained where he was, arms splayed awkwardly, cheek pressed into the slick cobbles, a wedge of tongue visible between his parted lips.

I looked from Blue to the fallen man and back again. Blue was stretching his neck as if to break an invisible yoke, and clutching his own shoulder. He caught my eye. Something passed between us. I felt it and was alarmed by it, then blotted it out.

The canary!

I twisted to find and pick up the bird, still twittering with panic in its cage, and was not surprised to feel my arm grabbed by the sailor as I stood up. I let myself be dragged away. My better instincts, to attend to the fallen man, and to confess to my part in smashing the pub's cobweb window, were as nothing compared to the urge to distance myself from the consequences. Together with Blue, I broke past the bystanders and quickened away down the quay.

CHAPTER
THIRTY

We did not slow down or speak until we had crossed the bridge again and left the main thoroughfare of Victoria Street. Further south, with the lanes tightening around us, I drew Blue to a halt. The Negro's eyes were gleaming. Though the dull stripe across my back was blooming into a proper hurt, and my left ear and temple had also begun to burn painfully, these things were inconsequential as compared with the deeper euphoria coursing through my veins. It wasn't the drink. As after my earlier escape from the stallholders, the near miss with the falling cask, and the moments held in the window-casement high above the city, I felt relief as a sort of reckless joy. This time, I'd not only been set upon, but had had the chance to fight back. I felt horribly pleased with the result.

And yet.

And yet, as Blue dusted himself down and growled his head clear, rueing the fight and making light of it in the same breath, I heard myself asking, "Why did they wait for us?"

"Why? I suspected they might. Our route to the bar was too easy."

"But it was just drunken posturing I walked in upon, nothing to justify such an attack."

"They determined to try for revenge at leisure."

"You think so? You're sure the quarrel didn't pre-date your entering the Trow?"

"What are you saying?"

"I'm not sure. It's just that they must have waited outside for more than fifteen minutes. Were they in fact waiting for you before you arrived?"

Blue shook his head, and asked, "Why would they be waiting for *me*?" He went on to suggest that I was perhaps suffering a delusion brought about by one of the blows I'd taken to the head.

But I had stopped listening after "*me*". Though I knew it could not be true, because Blue had been first into the pub, and the man with the broken boots had taken objection to him even before I showed up at the sailor's side, it suddenly seemed possible that the men had been lying in wait for me. Upon leaving the pub I had taken the first punch. My ear was still ringing. I dug a finger deep into its softness and the whining tone dropped an octave: it sounded like the moan of wind through a ship's rigging. Of course they hadn't wanted me. I'd recognised none of them. Just workmen, too far gone in an afternoon without work. They'd come off a building site; their soiled boots and dirty coats evidenced as much. And after we had brushed them aside they had obviously decided, no doubt befogged by drink, to lie in wait in search of . . . innocent . . . revenge.

The needling whine faltered, cut apart by the canary, still fast in its box, tucked under my arm, its twittering now a relief. There could be nothing sinister about such a botched attack. That was the point to hold on to. Whatever hurt had been intended, it had failed.

I shook my head. "You're right. They picked the wrong war! Two of us, and what, five of them? And they're the ones scattering for cover, or laid out to cure on the cobbles!"

Blue laughed at this, but his laughter petered out unconvincingly.

"He'll be all right, don't worry," I said.

"Yes."

Pinpricks of gauzy rain now found their way between the teetering house-fronts. I looked up. The sky above the rooftops was the colour of an old bruise, yellow-edged. Glimpsing even this hint of the sunset was destructive; when I looked back along the lane it appeared night had fallen that instant. I determined not to allow the fracas to divert me from my purpose in following Blue. The Captain's willingness to hand over the books had a simple explanation: they could not contain the whole of the ship's story. I would use the pretext of asking for Waring's address to hint at that allegation, intimate that I had proof, drop Carthy's name, and see how the Captain responded.

Blue had re-buttoned his coat and appeared to be waiting for me to make up my mind.

I obliged, asking, "Are your Captain's lodgings close by?"

CHAPTER
THIRTY-ONE

The boarding house stood at the end of a narrow passageway. I heard trickling water as I turned into its mouth. A stream — comprised mostly of sewage, by the smell of it — worked its way around the stoops and off towards the Avon. I trod carefully so as not to splash my boots. Following Blue, I made my way towards the only one of the crooked, tumbledown house-fronts displaying a light in its parlour window. It stood at the very end of the alley, where the dirt path splayed into a miniature courtyard.

The lamplight illuminated a bare, swept step, above which stood a front door. It shone as the owner of the house drew it inwards: fresh paint. The contrast with the surrounding dilapidation struck me as futile: a gold tooth in a mouth of blackened stumps. The landlady wore a tiny crucifix over her stained housecoat.

Shoulder to shoulder, Blue and I took up most of the cramped hall. I explained our purpose, the canary incongruous under my arm. Upon determining that we were not prospective lodgers, the woman's face fell. She had a strange hump of fat on the back of her neck, and kneaded at it while gesturing disconsolately at the stairs.

"Second floor," she said, her tone implying a silent, "if you must."

We clumped to the top landing. The higher it rose, the less the house pretended to cleanliness. The upper stairs were strewn with sawdust; on the landing it was mixed with straw. We paused before the door. The silence took a moment to catch up with us, as if the stairs we'd come up were unwilling to end their creaking complaint. But finally a stillness descended, which I broke with a gentle knock.

The quiet reasserted itself.

I knocked again.

This time the silence which followed became emphatic.

"He can't be here."

Blue said nothing, just stared at the door.

I knocked a third time, harder now, and cleared my throat. "Captain Addison."

The canary clicked in its cage.

Blue stepped forwards and gave the door a slap with an open palm.

I said, "Not in," and turned around to see the landlady arriving at the head of the stairs. Her having made it all the way up without triggering the creaky floorboards testified to the many years she must have spent prying into the affairs of her guests.

"He hasn't left the house today," she said, uninvited, but authoritatively.

"I can't raise him," I shrugged.

The landlady stepped to the door, rattling her keychain. When nothing stirred in response to her knocking, she slipped a key into the lock. One hand turned it, the other reached to knead the pad of flesh on the back of her neck. To interrupt a man in his late-afternoon nap boded ill: whenever I fall asleep during the day I come-to sluggish and angry. "It's no bother," I began to tell the landlady. "I'll leave a card and come back."

But the lock clacked open and the landlady turned the doorknob, calling out Addison's name again.

The door would not open. The landlady huffed and jerked at the handle ineffectually.

"Has he bolted it from within?" I asked.

At this the landlady growled, "Bolts *inside* doors? You've obviously not run a boarding house." She continued rattling the doorknob, and pushed at the door with her spare hand, levering it open no more than a quarter of an inch. "Something's —"

I motioned for her to step aside, then knelt down and put an eye to the keyhole. As I suspected, there was no clear view through it. When I gave the door a bump with my shoulder the darkness through the hole wobbled.

"There's something's blocking —" the landlady began again.

Blue now stepped to my side, set his shoulder against the door, and shoved violently. The door juddered open a handspan, something — heavy — scraping the floorboards inside as it did. The second time Blue barged forwards I threw my own weight against the lower panels too, and it crashed open with a splintering *bang*. A chest of drawers — which had been set

151

beneath the door handle — slammed over on to its back, upsetting the lamp placed on top of it. The light went out. Immediately the landlady bustled past me, muttering crossly about spilled oil.

Without the lamp there wasn't much light in the room.

But the glow from the landing was sufficient to unveil the shape of a man strung from the end of a rope.

CHAPTER
THIRTY-TWO

The next seconds were a quick-slow blur. I moved forwards into the room as if through treacle. The Captain's body — for it was definitely him, suspended from the rafters — seemed at once too small and yet somehow monumental, as if he were a scaled-down version of his former self, cut from wood or stone. In the half-light I fancied there was something *unstill* about the shape before me. It appeared to oscillate, shimmering disingenuously. And yet I knew this had to be an illusion: never had I seen anything so utterly in the thrall of the earth's gravitational pull.

Behind me, Blue: "How in the name of God?"

I wheeled round. The sailor appeared more amazed than horrified.

The landlady's lamp was flickering; that was why the corpse had appeared unstill. She was edging along the wall towards an alcove housing a window, which stood open. She stuck her head out into the night air and began sobbing. I went towards her — as much to retrieve the light as to offer comfort — and found myself looking past her at a cat, not ten feet away, which lay curled amongst the chimney pots. It blinked at us, stood up and wandered off across the roof. I patted the woman's shoulder ineffectually. She was bent heavily against the wooden sill, her chest heaving beneath the burden of that scoop of flesh between her shoulder blades.

Why did it matter that the window was open?

"Another lamp," I told her firmly, taking hold of the one she was carrying.

The woman nodded and took a deep breath and held it as she scuttled out of the room. "Get him down, down!" said Blue, his amazedness now apparently tinged with fear. I started towards him, but immediately stumbled in the half-light, tripping over the legs of a fallen chair. My head, I realised as I steadied myself, was pounding, each beat of my heart seemingly delivering another punch to my temple.

"Of course," I said to myself. "The chair . . . would have skittered out . . . from under . . . when he toppled."

"What?"

"But why is it all the way over here?"

"What on earth are you talking about?"

I bent down and slid the chair back a foot or so, on to the spot it would have occupied before I clattered into it. That was important. I turned to Blue to tell him something equally crucial, though quite what it was I couldn't yet articulate. There was a reflection of some sort beneath Blue's boot. As I swayed, the wetness turned from grey to warm yellow and back again, marrying up with the night-soil smell of the room. Which made sense. He'd have fouled himself in the act of . . .

Now Blue muttered, "We must get him down."

154

Not before I had made sense of the details. A pool of piss alive with reflected light, the slatted chair upended by the far window. The broken lamp and tumbled chest. A rope stretched taut, apparently searching for an escape through the rafters, but held back by the dead weight of Addison, his mouth a slack "O", those silver daggers in his beard now angled towards his own chest.

The landlady appeared again, galvanised. She raised her new lamp high and the shadows on the walls brightened. Not so Addison. Pallid hands poised indefinitely, grey sunken cheeks. Yet faced with this now irrefutable horror, the landlady quickly leapfrogged her shock to grapple instead with its ramifications for her business. She stood in the doorway, one hand pressing her crucifix into her chest, muttering: "Ruined. Ruined. Ruined."

"Take note of what you see," I said, as much to myself as the others.

"Down!" retorted Blue. He took hold of the body roughly. "Help me."

"No."

"Fetch a knife," Blue told the landlady. "Help me cut the rope."

The woman shifted from foot to foot, looking from Blue to me and back again. I saw the train of thought displayed in her face — if she followed Blue's instructions, might he not only get the horrible thing down but take it, and the trouble it represented, away?

I crossed the floorboards and gripped the sailor's forearm. "Lower the body. We must report this to the proper authorities."

Blue shook his head incredulously. His face was working, the muscles in his jaw bunching and releasing. It looked like he was fighting to stop his mouth from trembling.

I spoke quietly. "We must report what we've found here to Justice Wheeler, and keep the scene as it is until he has satisfied himself . . . Come on . . . easy . . ."

Slowly Blue released the Captain's body. As the rope — and neck — above them took the weight of Addison's body again, some complication within the corpse caused it to emit a noise very like a gasp. Both Blue and I started at the exhalation and looked up, but the rope and body were already cast in stone again. There was a crumpled corner of paper poking from the pocket of the man's breeches.

I knew I should leave it where it was.

To do otherwise would be to go against my own counsel.

But Blue, head down, had slow-walked around me and was now heading for the door, temporarily blocking the landlady from view, and in that instant, as I realised the chance would be over before it had begun, I found I had already pulled the paper free. I slid it surreptitiously inside my breast pocket. Instantly, I feared I'd made a mistake. Perhaps I should contrive to put the note back? No! Even if I managed to do so unseen that wasn't what I wanted at all! I had to know what it said. This wasn't just about curiosity winning out over caution. Waiting for the contents to be relayed in the pages of Felix Farley's news-sheet wasn't an option at all. Though this story would be of salacious interest for the Bristol gossips, it mattered to me. I was involved in it. The note's contents would simply be of more relevance to me, than to anybody else. In discovering the body, I'd gained the right to read it . . .

As ever, the urge for self-justification crabbed me sideways around my morals. I glanced up at Addison again, and the guilt I felt turned the Captain's hanging body into an exclamation mark of reproach.

I picked up the birdcage and ushered both Blue and the landlady out on to the landing, drawing the door shut behind us.

"You stay here," I told the sailor. "Guard the room against interference while I fetch Wheeler. Explain how we have moved nothing. Point out the open window, the position of the fallen chair."

Blue nodded. I put my lamp at his feet and guided the woman downstairs. "The Justice will want to question you. Best use the time between now and his arrival to collect yourself."

"Question me? But I've done nothing. He did that to himself, in my house . . . he's the one that's wronged me!"

"And the best way to mend your situation is to be as helpful as you can with the authorities. They'll want to know when you last saw Captain Addison alive and well, for instance."

"Yesterday morning. When I collected his breakfast tray. Though I've heard him since, stumbling about drunk or laying in bed groaning. But I couldn't have seen this coming! I thought he was sorting himself out."

I paused in the hall, a hand on the head of the newel post. The wood was worn; there was play in the joint between post and stair. I imagined Addison hauling himself upright on it, launching himself unsteadily up to his room.

"Sorting himself out? What gave you cause to think that?"

The woman narrowed her eyes and worked at her neck again. "The Captain was agitated, and the bottle had a grip on him. He was sick at heart, but only yesterday he had his doctor friend come and visit all the way from Bath! He was seeking help, I tell you. I'd have fetched some for him myself if he'd have asked."

There was a clock on the wall behind the woman's head. I had been staring at it as she spoke. Only now did I realise that it was broken: the pendulum wasn't moving and both the clock's brass hands were pointing straight up at the number twelve. Addison on the rope. I shuddered: the memory was more real than the thing itself. The little woman was still fidgeting, fizzing with anxiety. I explained that the authorities would no doubt want her to recall whether the Captain had had any other visitors during his stay. She explained that — to the best of her knowledge — he had not. That being the case, in the moments before I left to fetch Justice Wheeler, I helped the woman remember all she could about the Doctor from Bath.

CHAPTER
THIRTY-THREE

The words on the page read as follows:

Where I owe apologies, I offer them. From those willing to grant it, I beg Forgiveness. It is better I take this course than the other. C.A.

I stared at the script. It being dark outside, I'd had to wait until I came upon a lit shop before opening the Captain's note to read it, and in that brief delay the thing had become a flame pressed against my chest. Yet reading the message neither soothed my guilt nor quenched my curiosity. The only thing I was certain about was that this note was not what it seemed. And yet I couldn't quite put my finger on the oddness.

The handwriting was uneven, the ink smudged, the page itself crumpled.

That all made sense.

The document reflected — embodied even — a disordered mind.

And yet, looked at in a different light, the slash of words and ink conveyed something other than anguish. They suggested *haste*. That was it; the message looked as if it had been written in a rush.

I thought for a moment. Perhaps Addison had determined to kill himself and scribbled this down quickly so as not to give himself a chance of changing his mind? No, that didn't quite add up. If he'd feared a sudden weakening of will, he'd not have paused to write a final missive at all. It wasn't even as if the note conveyed anything of particular importance. His thoughts weren't addressed to anyone in particular. Vagueness was what made the note notable, in fact. Looked at straight, it appeared less a man's impassioned final words than a jerkily penned sham. I folded the piece of paper carefully back into the pocket of my greatcoat.

I would do the right thing. I had begun on the right track, after all. Fallen chest of drawers aside, the room was exactly as we'd found it. If ever a man was trustworthy, the epithet applied to Blue. You could see it in the way he held himself. And he clearly had a sense of allegiance to his unlucky Captain. So the sailor would definitely guard the room until the Justice arrived, and from then the matter would be in sensible hands. I was headed there now, Wheeler's house in Stratton Street; going straight there was the honourable thing to do.

I strode out, my pace fanning my sense of self-righteousness.

But what I really wanted to do was get beyond the Justice and back to Carthy's house. Availing myself of his help was suddenly more important than everything else. For with the discovery of Addison's death, I was irretrievably out of my depth. His dead weight, leaden upon the rope, changed everything. It gave substance to my suspicions. Never mind that I didn't understand quite how; that was where Carthy would come in. He would not expect me to soldier on alone now.

One of the Justice's children opened the house to me. She was carrying a cat which squirmed madly in her arms upon spotting the canary inside its cage. I had interrupted the Justice at his supper. The man appeared behind his daughter with his napkin still tucked into the collar of his shirt, his sleeves turned back for what his jowly, solid appearance suggested was, for him, the important business of eating. He wasn't pleased with my news. The cat must have scratched the girl at this point; she dropped it unceremoniously and aimed a kick at it which it evaded by leaping on to a pile of pallets to one side of the doorway. Girl and cat hissed at one another from a distance. Wheeler rolled his eyes and tore the napkin free, neither shocked nor surprised, and his brusqueness somehow made it easier for me to pass on a diluted version of the facts, as follows:

In routine pursuance of my duty I, together with one of the sailors from Addison's old ship, had that afternoon called upon Captain Addison at his lodgings, only to discover, together with the landlady of the premises, the unexpected news of the Captain's death.

Downplaying my role in the discovery in this way felt prudent. The Justice huffed and grumbled and sent for a lantern as he crammed himself into his

161

coat. I checked my pocket-watch and declared myself late. Wheeler knew where to find me if I could be of further assistance. For now, I trusted that my civic duty was done.

CHAPTER
THIRTY-FOUR

Besieged troops fight with renewed vigour ahead of the arrival of reinforcements, the prospect of help itself being enough to lift their heads. Despite the now sullen ache in my upper back, and the continuous ringing in my left ear, my decision to ask for Carthy's guidance buoyed me before I'd even reached Thunderbolt Street.

I crossed the imposing square and glanced at the Alexanders' high-fronted house, its windows boastful with lamplight. Lilly would be somewhere inside. I'd call on her again soon. In fact, I'd make a drawing for her . . . something as direct and honest as one of Edie Dyer's poems. Recalling the poetess at that moment irked me. I looked away from Lilly's house and shifted the birdcage from the crook of one arm to the other. At least I'd be rid of this . . . absurdity . . . soon. I rounded the final corner with long strides.

The door to Carthy's house stood open. Anne was sitting on the front step, bouncing a doll on her bare knee. Her father would be doubly annoyed. He didn't like her playing in the street unsupervised, and he insisted, in milder weather than this even, upon her wearing a coat outdoors. I squatted on the paving stones and reminded her as much.

163

Anne nodded and re-fixed her squint upon her doll.

Sorry that I had chastised her, I went on swiftly: "I have something for you."

The little girl's expression sharpened instantly, her attention switching to the basket under my arm. "What is it?"

I turned sideways so she couldn't see the bird. "I'm not sure how well this will go down with the authorities," I nodded over her head.

Anne's eyebrows dipped. "What is it?" she repeated.

"There's a chance you won't be allowed to keep it," I warned her. "Meaning I probably shouldn't have bought it in the first place . . ."

"Let me see."

I tumbled the basket forwards, a ham magician, and Anne took it and held it up, delighted.

"We'll have to get it a proper cage, I know," I went on. "Just let me do the talking if your parents object!"

Anne nodded, still squinting at the canary as it — gratifyingly — put on a twittering, flapping show. "Nobody will mind today," she said. "Not now Daddy has gone."

I began warning Anne that the bird would no doubt fly away if released from its cage outdoors, or within reach of an open window, and was about to elaborate when I simultaneously realised what Anne had said and heard a movement in the house behind her.

"Does it have a name?" Anne asked.

There were heavy feet coming down the stairs. A pair of women's boots, flashing beneath full skirts, stumped into view. A set of wringing hands appeared above

164

Anne's head. They connected themselves to a woman, Anne's aunt Beatrice. Her cheeks were flushed and her eyes, expectant as a bride's, were too large in her face.

"Oh, thank goodness!" she said.

"What is it?"

"Come in, come inside. Oh, thank goodness you're here."

"What's the matter?"

"Bedtime, Anne. Go upstairs."

"I've got a bird, but it doesn't have a name."

"Upstairs!"

Beatrice's sharp tone cut concern with excitement. She bustled ahead of me, energetic. Whatever was going on, there was something annoying about the way the woman appeared to be relishing her involvement in it. I could not stop myself from snapping at her. "Stop! What's happened?"

Beatrice paused and looked meaningfully — theatrically so — at Anne, unwilling to explain herself in front of the child. I put a hand on Anne's head. The softness of her hair was suddenly heartbreaking. I knelt before her again and said, "This little bird is very curious, Anne. Keep him safe in his basket, and take him up to see your bedroom. Explain where you keep things. Your shell collection, the conkers and so on. I'll be up in a minute."

The child nodded hard and skittered away upstairs.

I rounded upon Beatrice, backing her purposefully through the door into my office. "Where's Adam? Where's Mrs Carthy? What is going on?"

"Why, Mrs Carthy is taken to bed. That's the reason the maid sent for me. She's never been much use in a crisis. The shock . . . They didn't know where to find you. So the carriage was sent for me and —"

"An explanation!" I thundered.

The woman sucked in her cheeks and rolled her lower lip over her bottom teeth. She would not be hurried into spoiling her surprise. My heartbeat hushed in my ears.

"A note has arrived!" Beatrice said, finally. "A note about Mr Carthy. It says he has been taken for a prisoner. Kidnappers have him! And he says they will kill him unless you do exactly as they say."

"Where is this note?" I said coldly.

Beatrice produced a folded wedge of paper from her housecoat, triumphant as a magician: she would let nothing undermine the melodrama of her moment.

I took the paper from her without speaking, corralled her from my office, and shut the door behind her. Then I spread the note out on my blotter.

We have Adam Carthy. We will release him in exchange for all the documentation pertaining to our case, and a final undertaking to DESIST from further meddling. Deliver the papers to "the top of the world" at noon tomorrow. If you fail to do so, you will not see Mr Carthy alive again.

The blank threat of these words sent a shiver through me. But it was as nothing compared to what I confirmed by spreading out Addison's "suicide note" next to the demand. I'd thought as much from the jerky lettering on the front of the ransom note. The same jagged "f"s and "s"s. It was as if these sounds were hissing in my ear. Undoubtedly, both missives were penned by the same unhinged hand.

I didn't know what to do. I had never felt so alone. I slumped into the leather chair behind my desk, and recalled Carthy wheeling it into the office the day I qualified. Upstairs his daughter's footsteps skipped from left to right and right to left again. The heavier tread, of Beatrice, presumably, followed them. This was all my fault. I should have told Carthy I had been threatened, warned him. By trying to double-guess him I'd put him in danger.

The pattering footsteps upstairs drummed recrimination over my head. If anything happened to him . . . I could not complete the thought. What should I do? The question rolled round my head uselessly, evolving, eventually, into: What would Carthy want me to do?

That was easier to answer. He would not want me to give in. He would not want me to take the file up to the top of Clifton Hill as instructed, unless it was part of a wider plan. In any dispute, his reasoning was that a man put on the back foot should come out fighting.

But what did I have to fight with?

Well, the two messages on my blotter were a starting point. They were evidence of foul play. I could present them to Justice Wheeler and in so doing compel him to investigate Carthy's disappearance, as well as Addison's death. I'd have to explain how I came to be in possession of Addison's note, but so be it. It was evidence the Captain had not died at his own hand; Wheeler may well have reached that conclusion on the basis of what was in the room, anyway. Now he would have to.

I'd already shucked myself back into my coat; I buttoned it up forcefully, as if by doing so I could truss these addled, panicky thoughts into something solid. If I set off immediately, I'd stand a chance of intercepting the Justice back at Addison's lodgings.

Yet I had a duty to reassure Carthy's family before I set off. I took the stairs two at a time, then paused on the landing to force myself to breathe slowly. Beatrice jack-in-the-boxed from her easy chair when I entered Anne's nursery. I sidestepped her and knelt before the little girl.

"You know how your father likes to set us small challenges," I said. "Stories to find endings for, questions to answer ourselves?"

She nodded.

"Well, that's quite like what he's done today. He's gone somewhere to do with work, and it's my job to find out where it is and bring him home. Understand?"

"He likes puzzles," Anne said. "As well as treasure hunts."

"Exactly. And while he's gone, and I'm gone looking for him, I've got a job for you. You must work out a name for the canary, a good name, one you think your father will like."

Anne squinted at me thoughtfully and nodded.

"You work that out then," I repeated. "And I'll go and find him."

168

CHAPTER
THIRTY-FIVE

By now it was horribly dark. Even the glow from the windows appeared muted, rendered ineffectual by the combination of an evening mist and lowering smoke from the city's countless chimney pots, which together blotted all memory of sun, moon and stars alike. It was as if the air had turned black and greasy; it dug cold thumbs into my collar and ran wet fingers through my hair. I knew which way I was going, more or less, but reckoned I would make hopelessly slow progress if forced to feel my way through the rat-maze of streets in this cloying dark. A lamp-bearer would speed my progress. But there weren't any visible from Thunderbolt Street, or even in Queen Square. I had to cut down to the Welsh Back in order to pick up the only available light for hire and, as luck would have it, the lamp-bearer himself was a decrepit old man, so bow-legged, wheezy and round-shouldered that he appeared to be expending most of his energy in lugging the weight of his final breaths every step of the way, never mind the lantern. I asked whether I might not carry it for us, and so speed up our way, in response to which the man managed, through some peculiar combination of sniffing, coughing, and clearing his throat, to suggest I'd insulted him. He picked up the pace. We scuttled through the snot-slick streets, over the black river, and back into the city's rotten guts.

I noticed something else about the little lamp man as we stuttered back through the lanes. He kept looking round at me. At first I assumed he was checking my progress, but since I was hard upon his shoulder the whole way, that seemed a misreading: I was breathing in his ear. No, it became clear he wasn't looking at me, so much as past me, almost as if in search of some . . . pursuer. I said nothing, but fell subject to the fear that we were perhaps being followed. When I turned to check for myself though, I could of course see nothing beyond the meagre glow cast by our lantern, nor could I hear footsteps. The lanes were all but deserted at this hour; if anybody had really been following us, their progress would have written itself in echoes, would it not?

We ferreted our way through the lanes as fast as the little man's lungs would allow, and in the time it took us to reach Holt Court, my faith in the course I'd set out upon began to dwindle. Disclosing the handwritten notes to Justice Wheeler would mean explaining how I'd come to have them both, which was tantamount to admitting . . . what? That I'd tampered with a crime scene? Stolen evidence? Conspired to pervert the course of justice? Construed unfavourably, such accusations could prove at the very least problematical . . . perhaps even terminal . . . to my career.

My career? Ha! For an instant I saw the thing as it was, a pebble upon a beach. What did my fledgling ambition matter set against a man strung up from the rafters and Carthy abducted, apparently by the same hand? But even as I saw, in a flash, the true scale of things, I was standing before the boarding house door, my understanding foundering upon the stoop, leaving me fearful of revealing Addison's note to the Justice.

I knocked.

There was no immediate answer.

I knocked again, then listened for the sound of footsteps clumping down the stairs within the house. Nothing. Yet as I leaned towards the door it swung open abruptly, revealing the landlady, whose powers of moving around the house inaudibly now left us a foot too close to one another. I stood back. Behind her, on the half landing, sat the sailor, Blue. From down here he appeared shrunken.

"Well?" the landlady said.

"The Justice. Wheeler. I need to see him. If you'll excuse . . ." I made to go past her.

She lowered her head but held her ground, the hump of fat between her shoulders now giving her a bailiff's solidity.

"He's not here."

I rocked on the threshold. "But he must be. I gave him the address a good two hours ago. Something must have delayed him."

"No, he's been and gone."

"What? Already?"

Blue had advanced downstairs. "It's true," he said, placing a hand on the newel post, which rocked uncertainly in its socket. "He was barely here ten minutes —"

"It didn't take a man of his experience long to determine the obvious," the landlady cut in, a triumphant note in her voice. "Disposing of a suicide is the undertaker's concern, not a matter for the Justice."

Blue shook his head, looking at me from under his brows. "I explained your concerns —"

"But the Justice Wheeler wasn't impressed —"

"He said, if I was disposed to complicate so open and shut a tragedy, to *make a meal of it*, those were his words, then I'd be throwing myself into the pot ahead of the dead Captain."

"He said *what*?"

"His meaning was plain. Since I, or we, found the man dead, he said, we'd naturally be the first subjects of an investigation."

"This is ridiculous!"

"No, he was highly serious," the landlady asserted. She'd grown defiant since the Justice's visit. I ignored her and spoke to Blue.

"Did he not look at the room, the furniture, the open window?"

"He did. I pointed such things out to him as you instructed. It made no difference. He merely drew the window shut and righted the chair, and then he had me cut the Captain's body free and lay him out on the bunk to await the undertaker."

"The coroner surely? Somebody to examine the . . ." I trailed off. There was something sorrowful in Blue's demeanour. He'd as good as been threatened by

Wheeler, warned away, yet he was still here, awaiting the undertaker out of loyalty to his dead Captain. The landlady was kneading complacently at the back of her neck again; there was something sinister in her newfound composure. Who was going to pay for the undertaker's services? Not her, I was sure of it. If anything, the look on her face suggested she'd lost a farthing and found sixpence.

I paused, hand on chin, doing my best to give an impression of thoughtfulness. Then I nodded at the landlady, fought out a conciliatory smile, and turned to address Blue. I suggested that the Justice was no doubt correct, that his professional eye must, indeed, have made sharper sense of the tragedy, which had so disturbed us all. Then I bade the sailor come with me. A frown cut purple lines in the darkness of his forehead. He opened his mouth to tell me, no doubt, that he had a duty to Addison still, but I headed him off with some nonsense about how we owed a greater debt to his remaining crew members, including the Captain's good friend Doctor Waring. We must inform them of the sad news. Though the prospect of starting out on such a chore after nightfall was little short of absurd, the big man caught my meaning and stepped forward. For a second I thought the landlady, unwilling to be left in the house alone with a corpse, might try to prevent us leaving, but when Blue moves he does so with something of a ship's momentum, and the lady, clutching at her crucifix, thought better than to bar his way.

CHAPTER
THIRTY-SIX

The bow-legged lamp-bearer had vanished; when the door shut behind us Blue and I were enveloped in near darkness. We inched our way back down the alley, but I still managed to stumble into the noisome gully and splash unknown filth up the inside of my left leg. I heard myself growl out loud, and then felt the solidity of Blue's hand upon my shoulder.

"Steady as you go," he said.

These simple words, and the dark, and the weight of events, conspired to pull me up short, my lungs tight in my chest. I sensed that despite it all I'd just had a lucky escape, been saved from myself, from making matters infinitely worse. Of course Wheeler would be in their thrall. They — the Venturers, the Dock Company, Bristol's merchants — were the powers that be. Even if he'd dismissed this case out of personal lethargy — and that was, of course, more likely than some deeper conspiracy — sooner or later they'd get to him and call him away from any awkward investigation-making. The two notes, the fact of their being written by the same pen, they were like playing cards: in revealing them to Wheeler I would have shown my hand, and lost.

Shoulder bumping shoulder, Blue and I made slow progress back into town. We exchanged no words. Not until Bristol Bridge, upon which the sailor stopped. The relative openness of the scene cast the stone and the sky and buildings either side of the river in lighter shades of black. The water itself stretching away beneath us was pricked with dots of light whose infrequency only served to emphasise the unreflecting surface of the rest.

"Here's where our ways part," Blue said.

My feet felt suddenly sore within my boots. I hugged my coat to myself and shifted from heel to heel. "Of course. Well, thank you for —"

"But . . . Waring," the sailor cut me off. "I heard the woman tell you he'd come from Bath. If you like, I'll help you find him there. You'll still be wanting his account of our cargo, and regardless of that he needs to hear what's happened." He lowered his voice for these last words, I fancied, before raising it again to give the address of his own lodgings.

I repeated this last back to him gratefully.

We stood for a moment. The wind had picked up. It shivered the surface of the river and drew a low moan from the bridge.

"Why did you come back?" asked Blue.

"I'd raised the Justice. I wanted to follow up with him."

"No. There was something else."

"I wanted to make sure the Justice investigated the case properly. I wanted him to be in possession of all the facts."

The sailor paused before replying.

175

"There was a look upon your face, when the woman told you that he had left, which said something else."

Though the wind tugged at us both, his quiet voice had a depth which made his words solid as the stones beneath our feet. It took an effort of will not to reply with the whole truth, but for now I simply could not.

"Soon," I said. "I'll call upon your help, and when I do I'll be in a position to add detail to the picture."

"As you wish."

CHAPTER
THIRTY-SEVEN

If they wanted the case file, there had to be something
in it worth having. On arriving home, by which I mean
Carthy's home, a fact made all the more emphatic by
his absence, I first checked that Anne had been put to
bed. She had, and she was asleep, her mouth open,
snoring delicately: the way children sleep is the most
convincing argument I know for the existence of God.
Ignoring the chattering of her aunt, I asked after Anne's
mother; she, too, was in bed, pinned down by nervous
exhaustion. I shut my office door behind me and
prepared to spend the night sorting through the Dock
Company document crates.

It was a daunting task. I decided to narrow my
endeavours. I set the Western Trading Company files
aside from the others: these had to be where the cause
for concern lay. I separated the various documents out
according to type. Bills of lading, contracts, schedules
of works, duty declarations, receipts from merchants far
and wide, accounts . . . detailing investments in
individual voyages, as well as summaries through time,
even tables of expenditure on repairs to ships.
Somewhere in all of this was something they didn't
want anyone to see. Not knowing what it was . . . was

infuriating. I fell back on one of the first lessons Carthy taught me: when attempting to get to grips with complicated facts, sort them chronologically. I worked long into the night ordering the documents and then longer still making a list of what had happened when, and how it could be proven by reference to the evidence. Once under way, I have to admit there was something heartening about the exercise. It was at least manageable. The sound of my quill upon the pages of the ledger, the compact sureness of the letters and figures flowing from its crosscut tip, reassured me, temporarily masking the brutish truth, that I still had no idea of the significance of my annotations, or the wider, devilish plot they should be revealing. But as the slice of window pane above the shutters turned pale, and the first footsteps outside underscored the truth of the new day, I did have an account of the Western Trading Company's doings before me in black and white. And although the lack of sleep, and lack of coffee, and the disorientating horror of the past few days' events had worked to unsettle my stomach and make my scalp itch, I felt a sort of solace issuing from what I'd achieved.

Carthy would have wanted me to make this note.

He would want to refer to it upon being set free.

There were still six hours or so before noon, and at noon I would fulfil the demand left by his kidnappers. Outwardly at least. The ledger I'd written in constituted damaging evidence of "failing to desist" if discovered. I had more or less reached the end of practical thought, but had a sudden recollection, of myself and Carthy hauling livestock upstairs two years beforehand, and knew instantly where I could hide the book. Treading softly to Anne's landing, I cracked her door and checked she was still asleep. Her rocking horse stood in the corner. I tiptoed to it and, putting my shoulder against its flank, tilted the pedestal upwards a hand-span or so. The heavy base — cast in back-breaking metal — is hollow. I slid the ledger inside and lowered the horse, its tail shivering gently, to the floor. Instantly, I was overcome with fatigue. I stumbled downstairs and collapsed upon my own bunk. As I fell asleep, I fancied I could hear the canary I'd given Anne tweeting at me through the floorboards.

CHAPTER
THIRTY-EIGHT

I slept for no more than a couple of hours and woke with the giddy, jarred sensation of a man who has struck his head upon a beam. No time was afforded me to gather my wits. I had barely doused myself with cold water, and was half-heartedly attempting to claw my hair into something approaching an acceptable state, when the women of the house were upon me. They had been talking. By which I came to understand that Aunt Beatrice had whipped Mrs Carthy into further paroxysms of panic.

I ignored the Aunt and told Mrs Carthy directly that the matter was in hand.

"But the terrible threats!" Beatrice exclaimed.

I did my best not to respond to this, yet found I was blinking despite myself.

"Yes," said Mrs Carthy, more quietly. "The note."

I tried to give an understanding nod, but the effect, I fear, was mechanical: I felt wooden as a marionette.

"As I say, I have the matter . . . including the demands made in the note . . . in hand. We'd all be best advised to carry on as normal for this morning."

Mrs Carthy shivered as I said this. It was the manifestation of her stoical attempt to pull herself

180

together. Her sister, by contrast, felt it necessary to slump down upon a chair gasping.

"Anne's reading," I went on. "Adam would not want her to miss a morning's practice. You should occupy yourselves with that."

"Of course," Mrs Carthy said.

"Very good. I must get on."

Carthy's wife advanced towards me and gripped both my forearms and squeezed them; the gesture suggested I was fooling nobody, and yet still I felt compelled to continue.

"I must prepare myself for the meeting," I repeated. "If you'll excuse me. All will be well ... I'm ... confident of ..."

There was no need to deliver this stillborn sentiment. Mrs Carthy was already ushering Beatrice from the room. I recognised in the way she did not meet my eye as she left that she intended to spare me further embarrassment, and this in turn was an expression of faith in me, that I might prevail, despite myself. The click of the door-latch made my knees feel weak.

But I forced myself to do as I had promised and reassembled the WTC files slowly, taking care to double check I had not missed anything in my nocturnal study of the contents. Save for a note detailing an investment, made by the ship's surgeon, Doctor Waring, in the voyage of the *Belsize*, which was unremarkable enough, nothing stood out. These documents were what they wanted, but I still didn't know why. It had begun to drizzle outside. Before I set off on the long hike up Clifton Hill, I wrapped the folders in an oilskin cloth to protect them, and lastly thought to do the same for myself by way of a hat. It helped against the rain, but as I set out the hat was powerless to prevent the hot sensation of six eyes boring into me from the upstairs window of the house. Anne's were hottest of all.

Up I went, up. My last trip to Clifton had been at the point of a knife; this one felt less pleasant. I took my anger out on the incline of Park Street, buried my uncertainty with long strides, turned fear into a pair of aching lungs. Soon I was among the half-built hulks of ostentation that are the new borough's speciality, with the biggest folly of all, that unbroken wave of stone that is the great crescent, rising in my sights.

I made my way to the rear of this edifice and located the house. The lane was a mess of ruts, heaped earth, and puddles. I checked my pocket-watch: a quarter to twelve. The fifteen minutes were an ocean ahead of me; I clawed through them like a drowning man, and yet I did not, deep down, want to arrive at the other shore. Nobody came or went whilst I waited. I suspected this must mean they were inside already. Although it made no difference to who held the upper hand, the fact undermined me further, and I walked the final steps to the back of the house as if they were a pirate's plank.

The door swung open at my touch. I stepped into the gloom. It crossed my mind to call out, but I feared my voice would give more than my arrival away. Instead, I trod heavily across the loose floorboards and fairly stomped up the staircase, all the while clutching the parcel of wretched documents to my chest. There was a stillness in the stairwell. When I advanced to the threshold of the topmost room, it had deepened to an underwater roar. In fact, it was just the wind across the eyeless window sockets. By now I could no longer resist the urge to announce myself, and fairly bellowed my name and greeting.

There was no response.

I called out again and received no answer.

I advanced into the centre of the room and looked around me. Alcove to un-plastered alcove, open chimney breast to gaping window, it was empty, empty and unchanged; the grey flat light and rushing sky visible through the window casement were exactly the same as when I'd last stood there. Was I here ahead of them, after all? Where should I put myself within this room to wait? There was nothing to sit down upon but the floorboards, and yet, standing up, I felt vulnerable, as if, whichever way I faced, I could not head off the dagger's threat at my back.

I waited.

I eyed the door.

I waited, and my gaze shifted around the room.

The wind across the face of the building was driving rain in through the window hole. Unable to stay put any longer, I edged towards it, drawn ineluctably to the spot where I'd stood before. I put a hand on the rough brickwork either side of the aperture and looked down again at the smear of city tumbling up from the docks to the rubble-strewn footings beneath me. The rain was falling in swathes, curtains of gauzy grey, torn and re-stitched by seagulls. I opened my face to its coldness for a second, then dipped my hat-brim. Off to my right and a long way down two men were barrowing something or other through some scrub. I strained to follow their progress, and then there was a noise in the building behind me, a banging, and I was spinning on my heels, framed by the void, to face the door.

What had I heard? The slam of wood on stone, or stone on metal, or a heel striking the floor? The wind rose behind me again. I strained to hear, but could make out nothing more.

Looking back into the room, however, with the light now coming from behind me, it appeared altered. In particular, I noticed a shadow this side of the gaping fireplace hole, a darkness that seemed to be dripping down the lath and plaster wall. I edged towards it. A stain, which could have been some intrusion of rain, perhaps, though it seemed darker than that, mud-brown against the grey of the plaster, an imprint of something left wet against the wall. The floorboards which abutted it were discoloured as well. I squatted down upon them. The dryness in my mouth, an ashy quality to it now, had advanced down my throat. There were dents in the floorboard. Half moon crescents, flat shadows within them. Something had been driven into the wood here, repeatedly, hard.

I rocked forwards on to my knees. The files, wrapped in their oilskin bandage, slid from my hands on to the floor. A memory, swift as the jab of a gull's beak, flitted before me, of planks, and stains, and the sound of a

184

gale, and the floor suddenly felt unstable beneath me, as if the whole building was shifting in the wind.

Nobody was coming to meet me here. I did not have to check my pocket-watch to know half an hour had elapsed since noon. The note had told me to deliver the documents here and *desist* if I wanted to see Adam Carthy alive again. I stood up and set my parcel square in the middle of the room. That fulfilled the first part of the demand at least. I turned my collar up around my ears and ducked back down the stairs.

CHAPTER
THIRTY-NINE

The man comes for Oni.

It is night. She is asleep, wrapped in the frayed blanket, her head cushioned by her forearms. Then she is awake and aware that he is in the underground room, lamp held high, watching her.

The man holds a golden hoop. There are keys on the end of it. He angles them towards the lamp and chooses one, then slips it into the padlock. The fetter comes undone. He lifts it off her leg gently, like a doctor taking off a bandage. But the sensation has gone from that part of her leg. She cannot feel his solicitous touch. When the man offers her his hand it is as if she has just fallen, and he has stopped to help her up.

Somewhere upstairs, the sound again. It is a deaf bird's song.

She stands. She is as tall as he is. She cannot look at him directly. He starts to whisper, just as he whispered to Abeni, fake reassurances. Then he takes a bag from inside his coat and fumbles it open and puts it over her head. She does not move. She makes no noise. The sack smells strange. Something spiced, crushed bark, embers. Its foreignness makes no difference.

She lets the man lead her from the room. There is no point in resisting him. Where would she run to? She knows she cannot escape. Pretending otherwise is as pointless as imagining herself capable of flight, or breathing underwater, a bird or fish.

Oni sees: flowing water, darkening sand. Her feet advancing, one after the other, into the coolness. The water inching up, a gentle tugging circle around each ankle, calf, knee. The ribbed floor of the river puffing and shifting between her toes, the river reaching her backside, her hips, her waist. She remembers it: the weight of herself giving in. Up it rose, covering her chest, her shoulders, her chin.

But then she feels a hand on her arm. He is leading her. The ground turns cold and then wet, pushing up between her toes. Her mouth opens in surprise and the bag is rough against her lips. The man grips her arm tighter, bringing her to a halt. Then he's steering her up into a cart, a closed-in cart. It rocks back and sideways and they are moving. She can hear the animal breathing, its feet striking the ground, and the wind, and the man whispering, but now there's something different in his voice. He is whispering to steady himself, she realises. She moves her head within the sack and it works. The scratching blocks his noise out.

Everything comes to a stop. She is steered out, steps down, and is led forward inside somewhere new and up, up wooden stairs, which go on and on, and it's not just the not knowing caused by the sack, it's the longest set of stairs she's ever trodden. Eventually they stop. There's wind over silence. Oni thinks: is this it? Will it happen here?

Or will there be another man, like the last time, ready to take her somewhere else?

No.

When the sack comes off it is just her and him in a room leaping with shadows as he sets his lamp on the wooden ground. He stands up. She sees it, then, sees his intentions written upon his face, and for a second everything switches place. He is insignificant in his obviousness, and she looms above him. Then, in a blink, she is powerless again. He pulls the blanket from her shoulders; it pools around her dirty feet.

He gestures at her. Take your clothes off. She cannot. He reaches inside his coat again and brings out a knife. He points at her rags with a casual flicking motion of the knife's tip, then drops it to his side. Her shadow upon the wall leers at her as she complies.

He takes hold of her, but she's in the water again, weightless, stepping deeper. She sends ripples across the reflected sky as he unbuckles his belt but she can't see or feel him through the blessed, benumbing cold. Her eyes are shut tight against it. He's moving and breathing hard and it goes on but she's not there. The water has closed over her head. She cannot think.

Eventually he stops.

There's just the sound of the wind.

Until he starts breathing again, very slowly, sips of air, controlling himself with difficulty. And finally the wind forces its way into her lungs as well, in a great rushing gasp that makes him turn away. He doesn't look as she covers herself. He's focussing on the blade. She's mesmerised by it, too. The vicious hope in the thing. This is it. When he finally faces her she can see he is sick, sick with guilt, sick with shame, sick to the heart. And she is the cause of it. It's her fault. She draws herself up again, daring him not to do it. I have made you feel this way. The knife is trembling in his hand. His knuckles are purple. He must do it, he must. She knows only a handful of his words, and uses one now. She lifts her chin, exposes the length of her neck.

"Please," she says.

He blinks.

He advances, stands before her. For too long. No, no, no. He slides the knife away. She has no idea what he's saying but his meaning is plain. He points at the blanket, indicates she should pick it up.

"A keeper," he says. "For now."

CHAPTER
FORTY

I cut down towards Brandon Hill on my way into town. Thunderbolt Street was in my sights, but somehow I found myself veering towards Bright House. Though I did not admit as much to myself, I wanted help, approval that I was doing the right thing.

The front door was locked, so I let myself into the boot room at the side of the house. I called out a greeting but received no answer. I was therefore surprised, on advancing into the main hallway, to see my brother, John, slumped upon a chair there. He was staring at the grandfather clock as if he'd never seen such a thing before, much less this one, which had stood in the hallway all his life. I knelt before him and he turned his head toward me slowly and sighed, and I immediately discerned the pinch of hard spirits upon his breath. He seemed almost not to know me at first. Then his recognition and greeting were ridiculously forceful.

"Oh, oh! Inigo! Marvellous!" We stood up. He hugged me; I thought of his encounter with the dancing bear. No sooner had I returned his embrace, however, than his knees seemed to give beneath us, and I found myself supporting his weight. John is a big, heavy fellow. It was all I could do to steer him back on to the chair, which scraped sideways on the flagstones.

The noise must have disturbed Sebastian; next thing I knew my youngest brother was coming down the stairs. He seemed less surprised to find John in this state than he was anxious that our father should not. He raised his eyes at me in greeting and said, "To his room. Q-quick. Between us we can manage."

I did not argue. I helped lever John upright again. Working together, each of us with a shoulder under one of his arms, we manhandled him up to the first floor landing. Once there, he seemed to regain some sense of himself, and shucked us both off. I noticed he was wearing no shoes, and only one stocking. It was disturbing to see him like this, and yet a thread of satisfaction ran through my concern. John would appear more fallible to our father now. He swayed on the faded rug.

"Bed," said Sebastian.

I steered John towards his bedroom, opened the door. "What cause have you for such celebrations? At this hour of the day?"

He shook his head. "Ha!"

I looked at Sebastian. "Is business really this bad?"

John's laughter redoubled. "The big bad wolf of commerce," he nodded, swaying at the foot of his bed.

"Our troubles haven't gone a-away," murmured Sebastian. He guided John to sit down and said, more loudly and more slowly, "But it's not all John's doing."

John seemed to find this amusing, too. He laughed and shook his head and rolled on to his side.

"I doubt drink will improve the balance sheet," I said. "At least not taken yourself. You're better off plying customers — or the competition."

This attempt at levity seemed to work, inasmuch as John laughed harder still. But when I looked back at Sebastian, I regretted my poor taste. He reached a trembling hand to his brow.

"He'll sleep it off," I said, and together Sebastian and I withdrew.

I had barely shut John's door behind us, before the scattering of paws upon stone downstairs announced Father's arrival. He was without his stick, and limping, and viewed from over the banister, there was something about the shifting of his shoulders as he progressed to the foot of the stairs that was unapproachable. I was therefore surprised, when he looked up, to see a broad smile upon his face.

"Welcome home, Inigo!"

We descended to meet him.

"You're looking hale," I told him.

"Early nights, and time in the saddle. I've been out hunting!"

"As ever, it agrees with you."

"Eh? Course it does. It would agree with you, too, if ever you chose to accompany me."

This took me aback. It was unusual, so inclusive an offer coming from Father. Compared to John's ashen complexion, his was boisterously red; the outdoors appeared to have flushed him into garrulousness. Why could I not thank him for this unexpected kindness? I don't know. The best I could do was mumble, "One day, one day."

"Well, suit yourself."

"I'm glad business isn't standing in the way of your enjoyment," I heard myself say.

"Business? No. My only distraction just now is an empty belly. By the end of the ride I could have eaten the horse. Have you taken your lunch yet?"

Sebastian was shifting from foot to foot beside me.

"It's just that John seems troubled by the firm's predicament."

Father became still. "Is he now? Is he?"

"It seems he's taking —"

"And this is a concern of yours now, the business?"

"It's John I'm concerned about."

"Quite right." Again Father flashed me his newfound, countryside grin. "Well, between the three of us," he winked at Sebastian here, "I think John's overreacting. The firm has sailed stormier seas than these. Of course, he must still be frustrated at his failure to bring in the Adams business, but such a mistake is forgivable. I'll have a word with him, don't worry."

The light in Father's eyes had turned glittery and deceptive; ice crystals are no warmer for being caught by the morning sun. One of the lurchers was turning circles between us. I bent to run my fingers through the rain-beaded fur between its ears. There was no way for me to broach the subject of my predicament. Whatever

I said, however he replied, we'd both know deep down he felt no sympathy for me.

"Some kind words from you will galvanise John, I'm sure," I told Father. "He stands in need of your help."

CHAPTER
FORTY-ONE

I excused myself from lunch with the half-truth of work as a pretext and staggered back out into the day. Even the rain had given up. The sky still hung heavy, though, an opaque grey, like milk spoiled with mud. They would be letting Carthy go by now, they had to be. He was probably already back at the house, meeting Anne's canary, cursing me for having given it to her.

But just in case he wasn't home yet, I jinked into the Thunderbolts to give the situation some more time to come right. From a seat in the window I'd be able to watch the front of the house, so I chose a dark corner in the rear of the shop instead. That way I would not be plagued by the sight of nobody arriving. One bowl of coffee became two, and then a third, which Mary kindly laced with rum, which dampened my surprise when she slid heavily into the seat beside me, announced that her shift had come to an end, and placed a hand upon my leg.

"There's a strange look about you today," she went on.

Very slowly I replied, "I'm engaged to be married."

"So you are."

Her hand slid up my thigh. She leaned into the table. "Maybe that's what's put you out of sorts."

195

"Not exactly."

The waitress's hand had moved higher still. Emboldened, she whispered a direct invitation. And it wasn't the rum, or the coffee, or Adam Carthy's disappearance, or the dead Captain hanging from his rope, or my having been held out of a window, and attacked in the street, or even the combined, disorientating effect of those separate factors, so much as the conviction of the girl, the sight of her teeth wet behind her lips, and the delicate red spreading up the side of her thick neck, which made me accept her offer without blinking. I left behind her, followed her through the everyday street, skirting the fresh horse-dung and nodding at the boy who sells whelks on the corner and noting the brilliant burnished feathers of the headless pheasants hanging outside the butcher's, tracking Mary to her nearby lodgings, as I had promised I would. In those moments Lilly was as remote from me as a star in the night sky, and as I made my way up the stairs to Mary's bed-sitting room, the star was snuffed out.

CHAPTER
FORTY-TWO

Later the girl held me and rocked me and before the
guilt crashed in I shut my eyes and I fell: through the
open window, the air, the filthy docks, the silt at their
heart, the rotten centre of the earth, and lay buried
there for I know not how long. Then, smells. The heavy
honey-and-sweat hair-smell of a pillow, grey up close,
and ash, ash spilling out of an unswept grate. I licked
my lips and tasted salt. My shirtfront was undone. I
levered myself upright and it fell open, revealing the
oily pallor of my chest. There was a smudge of some
sort across my midriff; I rubbed at it and flinched. A
bruise, one of the collection I'd received outside the
Llandrodger Trow . . . just the day beforehand, less
than twenty-four hours ago. Already that version of me
seemed distant. A glass stood on the bedside table, with
a hopeless rose stem in it. What had I done? Mary was
awake beside me, with her face turned to the wall. I sat
up on the edge of the cot, every joint creaking, every
bruise aching, and got dressed.

"I have my own sweetheart," Mary began.

"He needn't fear . . . I won't . . ."

"And yours has nothing to concern herself with either."

"I appreciate . . ."

197

"Yes, yes." She rolled up on to an elbow, dishevelled, grinning. I couldn't work out whether her bravado was frightening or heartbreaking. "You can run along now. I'll be seeing you soon no doubt. No use us not pretending!"

I touched her shoulder and her smile widened and I forgot my hat on my way out of the door. There was no question of going back for it. It was late in the afternoon. I stumped my way out into the mire again, a man who had paused to visit relatives and drink coffee and take a strumpet to bed, unsure of whether his patron, confident and closest friend, at the mercy of their joint enemy, was yet alive or dead.

CHAPTER
FORTY-THREE

I knew before I let myself into the Carthy household that he had not returned. The door stood blank before me, pulsed reproach at my touch, swung shut with a sullen bang. There was an incongruous smell inside: airing laundry, fresh scones. I descended to the kitchen and found Anne and her mother with their sleeves rolled, pounding dough. Little Anne's cheeks were pink with exertion. It took a moment for them to look up.

Hope soured to despondency as Mrs Carthy and I each realised that the other had no good news. She turned back to the dough-mix with both fists. Anne mistook this surge of energy for some sort of game and aped her mother, jabbing at her dough-ball with splayed fingers. Then Beatrice burst into the room behind me and made everything instantly, leadenly, worse.

"He's not with you?"

"Good afternoon, Beatrice."

"And yet you promised you would bring him back!"

I turned to little Anne and said, "Which batch of scones is this, then?"

"I'm not sure. The third, I think, or the fourth. We're going to sell them."

"Good idea. Your father will be proud."

I turned to the two women. "I have fulfilled our half of the bargain. It can only be a matter of time before Adam is back with us, ready to eat his share of the spoils."

Anne clapped excitedly and soundlessly: sticky dough. She turned to her mother and repeated, "That's good then, isn't it?"

Mrs Carthy nodded and smiled at her daughter with a brittleness which made me swallow hard.

"But *how* can you be so sure, Inigo?" Beatrice insisted. "Have you received some communication or other, giving assurances? Because if you have not, then I suspect our reasons to be hopeful are running out."

I glared at the woman, knowing she was right.

She blinked consternation back at me and went on. "In which case, if you've nothing sensible in the alternative, we should take Adam's disappearance to the proper authorities. An investigation must be launched by those with power!"

I felt my shoulders tense and had to hold back an urge to force the woman bodily from my sight. "Trust me. Involving others would only make the situation worse."

"Well!" she huffed. "I can't for the life of me fathom why."

Mrs Carthy, I noted, was wiping her face with the back of her wrist. Stray flour, tears? I could not be sure. Her wrist was plump and homely and induced a stab of guilt in me.

"I know what Father will say when he returns," Anne said absently.

"What's that?" asked her mother.

The little girl didn't answer at once. We three adults all watched her fingers hooking and twisting at the pale dough on the counter top, a miniature sea eagle tearing the belly out of a fish.

"He'll ask Inigo why he still hasn't attended to his funny hair. It looks like he's just got out of bed, all sticking out at angles, but it's nearly tea time already." She giggled triumphantly and pulled the dough-fish apart.

"A gale outside. I've lost my hat," I managed to say. Some things, the wind for example, and the embarrassment-inducing-embarrassment of blushing, are impossible to fight against. Others are not. I would not do nothing so long as there was something . . . anything . . . I could do. Orton. He had set us on this infernal path in the first place. I would force him to point out a way through this impasse. I took a deep breath and steeled myself to mollify Beatrice, determined not to rise to her bait. "No. Before we risk the involvement of a third party," I said softly, "there are yet one or two avenues I must pursue." I turned towards the door, adding, "I say this in the knowledge that it is what Adam would want me to do."

CHAPTER
FORTY-FOUR

I hurried back out into the street and set off at a trot, determined to make it to the Dock Company offices before Orton left for the day; from the little I knew of the man, he was prone to shirk work in favour of fiddling with his fossils. Rounding the corner of Marsh Street, I rushed headlong into a pair of squabbling gulls. They rose as one, still joined by the scrap they were battling over, four blue-white wings whumping about my ears as I bowled through them. For all the apparent panic, their flapping seemed half-hearted, suggesting I was an inconvenience rather than a threat. I hurried on my way.

As it was, I only just made it in time. The porter who answered my knock raised an accusing eyebrow and told me he doubted whether Mr Orton would be able to squeeze me in. I pressed the urgency of my visit upon him in the shape of a coin, which worked. He gave another little bow and led me through to wait in the same meeting room in which Carthy and I had had the pleasure of Orton's desiccated company on our previous visit. The Dock Company official joined me a few minutes later, his coat pointedly buttoned.

"Blight, wasn't it?" he said, without offering me his hand.

"Inigo Bright."

"Of course. Well, I was just —"

"Adam Carthy has been abducted," I said simply.

Then I took hold of one of the legion of chairs surrounding the vast polished lake of the table, pulled it out, and sat down uninvited. The cat-piss smell of the room was stronger than before; they had not had time to mask it with spices.

"Abducted," I repeated.

Orton sat down reluctantly. He placed his hands on the polished surface between us. They appeared, even in this dull, shadowless light, to have been scalded. His fingers interlocked and then began picking at one another, and in so doing they gave away more than the man's face. And yet, now that I dwelt upon it, I could see that the same dry rash had spread above the line of his collar, too. Like paper laid across embers, his skin appeared to be cracking, scorching, holing itself from within.

"What do you mean? Where's he been taken?"

"If we knew that . . . I'm here in the expectation that you will be able to answer that question."

"Me?"

"Yes. His disappearance has to do with your case. Somebody objected to it, and decided to voice that objection by terrorising him."

"What case?"

I stared at the man.

"There was a note, left at Carthy's offices, which cited the matter we were working on for you as the root cause of his abduction."

"But the matter we instructed you on . . . ended. I terminated our instructions, as you know."

He pushed himself back from the table in a half-hearted attempt at suggesting the meeting was over, but did not stand up.

"You suggested we pause in our endeavours on your behalf. Scale down. That was the phrase, if I recall."

"No, no, no! I said no such thing! I told Adam he must stop!" The man was collapsing in front of me. "You have no idea," he went on, "no notion of what it is you've stirred up. And neither do I, and that's the whole point! Christ, man! Why did you not listen? Why did you not cease when I instructed you to do so? And he's been taken, has he? They've got to him. This means it's only a matter of time . . ."

The wrinkles of concern across Orton's brow looked as if they had been cut there with a blunt knife. His hands! They were like a pair of fighting ferrets now. Had there been any blood in the man, it would surely have been running at me across the table. I almost felt sorry for him. And yet, he was still culpable. I leaned forwards across the table and fairly shouted at him.

"Who in the name of God are *they*? What have *they* done? What's in their records to damn them? Those cursed files, which you so casually passed our way! Why did you lose interest in the case so soon after instructing us upon it? Who got to you? What did they threaten? You should have told us the whole truth. Who is behind all this? Tell me! *Who?*"

Orton was shaking his head, as if by doing so he might physically evade my questions, or butt them away. I wanted to tear him in two. Before I could stop myself I had one knee on the polished tabletop and was lunging at him. The ferrets were slow to react. I grabbed a fistful of fingers and hauled them towards me across the expanse. Orton came trailing in their wake. Next to the peeled rawness of his hands mine looked as if it had been hewn from mahogany.

"Tell me the truth," I growled, twisting his fingers until I was sure they were about to break.

"I cannot!" he whimpered. "I know no more than you do. Beyond . . . the *Belsize* . . . I know nothing for sure!" The whites of his eyes were the colour of rancid milk. They were curdling before me with unmanly fear.

I stared at Orton and hissed, "Then guess!"

CHAPTER
FORTY-FIVE

Threatening the man was pointless, of course. It shook no useful information from him. But it was circuitously instructive nevertheless. Orton's silence meant one of two things: either he really did have nothing further to tell me, or any fear he felt before me was as nothing compared to the deeper dread which our mutual enemy had instilled in him.

On balance I suspected the latter was most likely.

Instructive did not mean heartening.

I returned to Thunderbolt Street beneath an inky early evening sky; what light remained snuck in upon the scene cross-hatched. The sensation I'd had before, of being followed, stole over me again; in Wine Street I felt so observed I could not resist the urge to turn around and check for eyes in the gloom. None were discernible. A sketchbook image flashed to mind: upturned eye-whites, gleaming at me through a grate.

Beatrice intercepted me before I'd crossed the hall. Her flushed cheeks spoke of a continuing excitement. Weariness passed through me, heavy as nausea: Carthy still had not returned. I hadn't dared to hope otherwise, yet this woman's jostling and jiggling still managed to crush something inside of me.

"Another note!" she exclaimed. "Like the last one, slipped through the door!" She handed me a long brown envelope, continuing, "Only this one is addressed to you."

"Thank you."

Her obviousness continued. "There's something in it!"

"I can feel that, as well as I can read my name."

"Well? What does it say? Open it!"

"I will," I said, and turned into my office to do so.

False hope being worse than none at all, I stared balefully at this new envelope, defying it to raise my spirits. When I did try to open the flap, the letter had worked upon my fingers to produce in them the sensation of having endured a gloveless journey through snow. I tore at the paper, the envelope ripped apart, and a flurry of . . . feathers . . . tumbled to the floor.

Quills, to be exact.

The note inside read: *I will be keen to hear how you find these hawk quills, when you have a chance to try them out, and I look forward to working with your gull points, in time. Let me know when it's convenient to call in person. E.D.*

I had quite forgotten the poetess, yet I am ashamed to say that for the second time that day Carthy's predicament was blotted out by thoughts of a woman other than my fiancée. The handwriting was as bold as the message it conveyed. Gawky almost, slashing angles and plunging tails. It brought the poetess's raw fingers and aquiline nose to mind. E.D. Using her initials like that was at once distancing and . . . familiar. I gathered the quills up, and fought an absurd urge to test one there and then. The Merchant Venturers' crane, that's what I would have drawn, stark and upright and trailing its great hook. But I did not have the chance to uncork my ink, because Beatrice had become audible outside my office door, her huffing quickly blossoming into, "It really won't do". I set the quills carefully in a drawer. The poetess's note emboldened me. *Desist* the ransom note had ordered. But they had not kept to their side of the bargain; I had handed over their precious documents, but they had not given me back my mentor. That being the case, why should I do as they say? I framed this question not out of petulance, but coolly. What guarantee did I have that Carthy would return unharmed now? None. I could not simply sit back and hope. I let Beatrice into my room, even patting her shoulder as she bustled past me.

"Well? What did it say?"

"It was from a friend."

"But it . . . can't have been. A friend would surely have announced himself."

"And yet," I paused to consider. "It was useful. My friend has given me encouragement to take the next step."

"The Justice then," Beatrice said, her frown tipping into a told-you-so smirk.

"No."

"Why ever not? Such obstinacy is . . . absurd."

I sat back on the edge of my bureau and crossed my arms. "When you lose a thing, and have looked everywhere for it to no avail, where should you refocus your search?"

"What new perversity is this?"

"As a little girl I'm sure your mother taught you this lesson."

"Have you lost your mind, Mr Bright? What has my mother to do with anything?"

"One should go back to the beginning, look again in the spot where your search first began. True?"

"I shall suggest that Mrs Carthy contacts the authorities if you persist with this frippery," said Beatrice.

"Adam himself pointed to a ship called the *Belsize* as the root of this case. Meaning it is where he would want me to look."

"I will go to the Justice myself if I have to," she replied.

"No, you won't. You'll stay here and offer comfort," I said, as kindly as I could. "Mr Carthy's life is in danger. You must trust me. By involving the authorities you will only succeed in putting him in greater peril."

CHAPTER
FORTY-SIX

I was at Blue's lodgings early the following morning. Very early: Thunderbolts had not yet opened; I counted just one ferryboat at work in the dock, and there was as yet a pinkness in the sky which brought cuticles and seashells to mind. I half expected to find that the sailor still hadn't risen from bed. But he was up and dressed and, when his landlady announced that he had a visitor by name, he replied "Good" in such a matter-of-fact tone that I almost suspected he had been sitting waiting for me to arrive.

"To Bath, then," he said once we had shaken hands.

"Yes."

"The quack shouldn't be too hard to find. Rumour had it on board that it was his last voyage. He'd been salting his takings away, and was set to invest in his own practice. If that's true, then Bath would make sense. There's no end of sick folk there for the waters. Better than just sick, in fact. Sick and rich. Waring's not the sort to have wasted time."

"Meaning?"

"Meaning he'll have been taking premises, advertising his so-called services, putting himself about in all the right circles."

210

"You don't sound fond of the man."

Blue shrugged his sideboard-wide shoulders. "You be the judge."

In Redcliffe we found a stagecoach, destined for Bath that morning, with seats yet available. Though he was young, the left side of the driver's face was set in a rictus frown, and his left arm also appeared frozen. Half a driver does not inspire confidence. Yet he was battling on to make himself understood, and when I handed him a note his one-handed method of magicking change from his purse into my palm was mesmerising. The sensible side of his face smiled. We took our seats.

And shortly afterwards the stage took off along the interminable Bath road. Though the two cities are as close together as any others in the kingdom, each insists on looking at the other through the wrong end of a telescope. The road connecting them plays its part in this, co-opting every rut, runnel and pothole to keep the adversaries apart. Our fellow passengers included a young mother whose baby took to wailing with a mechanical intensity before we'd set off. The stagecoach's motion over the appalling road amounted to a cavorting, reeling, buffeting progress. It was a case of hanging on to the doorframe to avoid being juddered apart.

We passed a newly ploughed field in which labourers were occupied collecting stones. A mineral smell, cut with decay, rose on the breeze. The sight of the men, stooped, drawn out in a line, working their way infinitesimally up the lay of the field to where it struck the sky: they could toil for a thousand years and never finish what they'd begun! The turned earth had attracted birds. A spattering of crows off up to the left were strutting and pecking arrogance at the raggedy red earth. They looked like black sparks. Then, out of the brightening sky, gulls swung down. They wheeled lazily above the field and speared into the crows, assassins amongst muggers, spurring the crows to flap up and away like litter blown down a lane. There were caws of protest; the gulls shrieked defiance in return; and the baby's wailing, a steady drilling insistence, underscored it all.

It wasn't yet noon, but the other of our fellow passengers, a short fat man with a leather case clutched protectively on his lap, now dug inside his coat for a silver hip flask. He unscrewed the cap.

"You look like I feel," he said.

I declined the offered flask with thanks, but he thrust it at me again.

"You need fortifying. I understand. This journey always depresses my spirits too. Bath. A silver spoon sticking out of every arse . . ."

"Why are you making the trip?" I asked.

He tapped his nose and took a swig from his flask. When I refused it again he cranked the cap back on viciously without offering it to Blue. "Because people foolish enough to poke silver up their britches will spend it soon enough." He patted his case conspiratorially and said, "Needs must."

It was obvious the man wanted me to ask him what was in the portmanteau, and — his rudeness to Blue aside — this blatancy made me determined to resist humouring him.

So I returned my gaze to the window, to see that we were approaching two men on horseback coming the other way. The lead horse shied as we passed, its hooves skittering into a bright-surfaced puddle, which exploded in flowers and tendrils of red mud. The rider regained control. I shut my eyes and steeled myself for what was to come.

CHAPTER
FORTY-SEVEN

We split up on our arrival. By making separate enquiries we would cover more ground before reconvening to share what, if anything, we'd managed to find out.

Accosting strangers is the sort of work I shy away from; if I've a streak of salesman in me, it's buried deep. I fortified myself with coffee, which I took standing by the coffee shop window. The Bath crowds ambled past with the same lack of intent that the walkers up Ladies' Mile back home in Bristol display. But this was the city centre. Nobody here, it seemed, had anything pressing to do. The men walked with their hands clasped behind their backs; the ladies held the fingers of one hand in the other before them at waist height. After ten minutes of this I was battling the urge to rush outside and yell "swing your arms!" at all and sundry.

Then I spied the same little flask-wielding man with whom we'd shared carriage-space, scuttling along the walkway, his grip upon his portmanteau unchanged and ridiculous, and it struck me that if a man such as he could hawk his wares in this city of loafers, I, too, should feel no compunction about troubling them for little more than the time of day.

Bath has more than its share of trinket-shops. I ducked into one, reasoning that gossip would be quickest to circulate amongst the purveyors of pointlessness. The shop was busy: I had to wait ten minutes to interrupt the proprietor, who was doing a thundering trade in lace whatnots, Toby jugs, bits of coloured glass, shells, etcetera. Little Anne would have loved the place, but the shopkeeper was of no use to me. Neither did I have any luck in the Fiddler's Arms next door, and nor had the florist heard of a new doctor's arrival in town. The woman there was chopping rose stems on a big wooden block stained green with plant juice. She slapped it in excitement at my news, reasoning, I don't doubt, that more doctors would mean more patients, who warrant visiting, by visitors bearing flowers.

Dead ends notwithstanding, I found it progressively easier to waylay and question these strangers. The trick, it seemed to me, was in projecting the right balance of authority cut with respectfulness. Order a man about and you may as well stop his mouth up yourself; simper and he'll brush you aside. Ask him his advice, however, in a straightforward tone, and he'll soon spill his innards.

Yet it wasn't until I took the obvious step of visiting the bathhouse that I obtained my first lead. After all, the whole point of the city, as with our own Hot Well in Bristol, has to do with the alleged healing powers of its warm springs; up until then, I realised, I'd been asking cream of all the farmyard animals save the cow.

They're odd places, bathhouses. Where else does fashion purposely rub shoulders with disease? Imagine choosing to take tea, meet friends, go courting even, in a hospital! Yet that's more or less how the hot-spring clientele choose to spend their time. I had to pause while a woman clutching two canes wheezed past the doorman. Every time she coughed, her head shook so violently that a halo of powder puffed itself free of her hair. As I waited, two foppish men not long out of school trousers tittered straight past me up the lemon-stone steps. They did not seem to notice the dying woman. Or rather they treated her with a familiarity suggesting that were she lucky enough to live until the evening, they'd no doubt be dining on an adjacent table.

Waiting proved worthwhile. The master of ceremonies was willing to offer advice once I'd addressed him as such. A new doctor was indeed in the process of setting up in town. He had come from a ship, and would thus face an uphill battle in persuading the gentlefolk of his worthiness to address finer illnesses. John Street was where this man had rented premises, apparently. No doubt he'd be pleased to welcome me; he could not yet have had many other visitors.

I met Blue in the Six Stars, as planned. The place specialised in a strange, cloudy sort of ale, which the landlady, who no doubt had a share in the brewery, pressed upon us. It had a potato-mould aftertaste, which I fought off with a cold slice of game pie. Bolting this meal did nothing to diminish its impact: I had not realised how hungry I was until I cleared the plate.

As it was, Blue had also ascertained the whereabouts of Doctor Waring's premises. It may have been my full stomach, or the fact that the afternoon sun had broken through the clouds, burnishing the stone mullions beside our table, or it may just have been the beer, but I felt compelled in that moment to take Blue into my confidence fully. He should know the true import of our search before continuing it. A cart rocked past our window, the long spokes of its rear wheels scissoring through the warm light. I explained Carthy's disappearance, the ransom note, Orton's strange reticence, and my conviction that the *Belsize* was to blame.

It struck me, when I'd finished, that in painting Blue's ship in such an unpleasant light, I was in a way slighting the man.

"Of course. I'm talking about some aspect of its cargo. Something Addison and his ship's inner circle would have been privy to. I'm not suggesting that you would know . . ."

The Negro shifted in his seat, a slow ominous movement that rendered my words ineffectual. I ceased talking. At length he looked up and said, "Waring," very quietly.

"What of him?"

"He invested."

"You've mentioned as much. And I've seen a note of it in the Company's file."

"Well, it's those with a share in the voyage who ultimately care what a ship carries."

"I hope you're right."

I could tell from the sawing motion of Blue's shoulders against the fretted wooden splats of the bench-back that he was uncomfortable, that there was something more he wanted to say. I kept quiet. In the right circumstances, Carthy has always maintained, silence has the power of a Spanish Inquisitor: at length Blue gave in to his urge to break it.

"There was a storeroom, constructed for the journey's last leg. A space between decks. They fashioned it during the refit, after the storm. You see . . ." The big man shucked his shoulders again uncomfortably. "But none of that is important. Only the Captain himself, and Waring, held sway over the new store. They presided over it. They held the keys."

A pressure in the back of my neck squeaked its way through my jaw: the millstone grip of ground teeth. "Well," I said. "What was in it? And . . ." I could not hold back the further question. "And why have you not told me until now?"

The bench-back creaked as Blue leaned against it. Partly silhouetted by the window, his face was doubly dark, yet a new, yellowish flash was present in the man's eyes when he turned them upon me. I realised anew his foreignness, and bolstered myself against it, drawing myself up in my chair.

"Because I don't know for sure," Blue went on. "And what little I do know, which I'm telling you now, I forswore to keep secret."

218

"The Captain is hardly in a position to enforce orders now," I said, and instantly regretted the heat in my voice: the Negro's eyes narrowed imperceptibly, the yellow fire there dimming to an appraising pity.

"No," he said softly. "It's not his censure that concerns me."

CHAPTER
FORTY-EIGHT

John Street was a narrow, inauspicious thoroughfare, just shy of the centre of town. Either Waring's investment hadn't lived up to expectations or he was a cautious man, starting small. It was obvious which house he'd taken for his premises: the windows were still blanked out with wax paper and the wrought iron contraption above the door was as yet unencumbered with a hanging sign. Though the frontage was adorned with the yellowy stone ubiquitous to the city, it needed attention. A series of stains ran from the guttering and windowsills of the upper storey down to the pavement. It looked as if the building had broken out in a sweat.

The front door stood open. To admit tradesmen, no doubt: if the outside was anything to go by, the Doctor's treatment rooms would need tarting up, too. Blue rang the bell. He seemed uncharacteristically nervous. When nobody descended to greet us, I leaned into the hall, knocked on the door and called out a hello. There was no answer.

I called out again, more loudly.

Still no response.

I inched over the threshold and drew breath to call out more loudly still, but at that moment a muffled

220

thud upstairs stopped me short. Perhaps the Doctor was unpacking. I was about to mutter something to Blue about the necessity, in a city of such fashion, to equip a doctor's surgery with gilt mirrors, grandfather clocks and chaises-longues, when the sailor lunged forwards unexpectedly and hammered up the uncarpeted, wooden steps. I followed quickly. The walls of the stairwell, covered in a lilac print paper, flashed by.

In the time it took me to reach the head of the stairs, Blue was already disappearing into the room at the back of the house. Perhaps he'd heard something in there. I was about to go in after him when I noticed, on the wallpaper directly in front of me, the daub of a handprint. It was like the marks Anne makes when Carthy has her paint with water on the courtyard flagstones. Only this hand was bigger, and the shape wasn't painted with water, but with blood. There was a smear of it further along the wall, too. It had not yet dried to the dark brown mud colour, but was still the shocking orange of a nosebleed caught in a handkerchief.

I heard Blue saying, "What the?" in the room at the back of the house even as I approached the door at the other end of the corridor, at the front. It wasn't shut. I reached for the handle but it, too, was stained red, and I when I saw this, I flinched from touching it. But Blue was immediately back out on the landing, and my inaction felt foolish.

I shouldered open the door.

There was a man on his side in the corner of the room. He was lolling against the skirting board, clutching something to his chest, and his progress to that spot, from the doorway in which I stood across the painted floorboards, was spelled out in a ragged trail of red. Evidently he had crawled. Never had I seen so much blood: it didn't seem possible that one man might spill that amount and still live. Yet this man was alive. He was blinking. The thing he was holding was grey and glistening and alive too, and suddenly I understood what it was and felt the bile rise up my throat. I went towards the man. He did not appear to take in the fact of my presence. He was preoccupied clutching at his spilled entrails and trying to breathe through lungs filled with blood. Ginger whiskers, bright as the stain. It was Doctor Waring. He looked at me, and then, with his eyes widening, at Blue. His body shivered uncontrollably. Our arrival there offered him no solace.

CHAPTER
FORTY-NINE

I knelt beside the Doctor and pulled him upright against the wall. I wanted to help him, but I didn't know where to start. The wetness soaked through my breeches immediately: red knees, a red shin. He was the doctor. He would know what to do, but I didn't. His orange whiskers were slick with blood. He coughed weakly and there was more of it in his throat, leaking down his chin. I wanted to stop up his mouth. And his guts, oily in his hands: I wanted to cram them back inside his trunk. So much blood. His shirt was sodden with it, agape from waist to chin, but . . . the buttons were still done up. The cloth had been slashed, as had the skin beneath it, and the softness of his belly, his innards hoiked out through the hole. What devil would do such a thing? Each chop and suck of breath was weaker than the last.

And yet for now, just, he was still alive.

"Who did this to you?"

The man blinked past me, over my shoulder, and began shaking his head violently. I turned round to see Blue. His face was a mask of shock.

"Help me here," I said.

"At the back of the house," he said. "There's a window that has been put through. Whoever it was, they got away."

"Fetch help!"

The head-shaking had turned to a shuddering which racked the man's frame. I thought for a moment that it may have been prompted by Blue's appearance; it almost seemed as if Waring, in this desperate state, still found it within himself to be frightened of the sailor. Indeed, as Blue came towards us the shudder turned to a spasm. Then the Doctor's grip on himself slackened, and his hands slipped into his lap, and I found myself taking hold of one of them, despite the blood. Though I couldn't help the man, I might still comfort him.

Chop and suck. Chop and suck.

Beside me, Blue, quietly: "What's the point?"

Chop. And suck.

I could see the sailor was right. Nevertheless, I gripped the Doctor's hand, and held his gaze while it softened, the amazement in his expression dissolving. Slowly. He took long minutes to die. Finally, just as I thought it was over, I felt him gathering one last breath, and harbouring it, and shaping it to use with intent. Though his eyes were mere slits, they took on an improbable, all-seeing cast in that instant. He studied my face. I squeezed encouragement into his hand. Then he looked to Blue and let out that final breath in a wet whisper. His words were difficult to catch, and I was powerless to reply.

"You're kind," he said. "Forgive me."

CHAPTER
FIFTY

I knelt before the dead Doctor. I reached inside my coat for a handkerchief and rubbed at my palm, but could not entirely erase the pink smear. Blue hadn't spoken or moved. I turned around. He looked thoughtful, which was impressively . . . collected . . . of him, given that we'd just watched a man die. There was nothing of the consternation he'd exhibited on discovering Addison. Instead, he was scratching the corner of his mouth with a fingernail. The nail was pearl white and square cut. Held up to his face like that, the hand looked monumental. Purple black stubble dusted the grey black of his skin.

There was a pause.

Then Waring's body slid gently sideways and the arm he'd been clutching across his torn midriff fell to the floor. Something metal clattered dully on the boards. My knees peeled sticky outsized thumbprints from the wetness as I rocked back up on to my feet. I skirted the body and bent down again to inspect the metal object, which was still connected to the doctor's fingers. I had never seen such a tool before. It was like a cross between a pair of scissors and pliers. The blades, cracked open, looked fiendish. My first thought on seeing this ugly contraption was that perhaps the Doctor had done this terrible harm *to himself*. No. It wasn't possible. He'd been trying to defend himself, surely, against an attacker armed with another weapon.

Blue pulled me away from the body and into the room at the rear of the house, through which, he said, the Doctor's killer must had fled. Sure enough, the sash window had been smashed. The sailor told me again how he'd heard footsteps from the alley: he was sure we'd arrived just as the killer was leaving. Here was some more evidence, he said, kneeling to point out spots of blood at the foot of the wall. As he pushed himself up again, he winced, sucking air over his teeth. He'd cut the base of his own thumb on a splinter of glass at the foot of the wall: shards from the window, it appeared, had tumbled inside as well as on to the outer sill. This was confusing. It meant the window could have been broken either to gain entry or exit. When I said as much, the Negro, wrapping his neckerchief around his sliced palm, pointed to the trail of blood across the swirling Turkish carpet.

"Whoever it was, I reckon Waring nicked him with his shears."

"This blood could be the Doctor's, though. The attack may have taken place in this room. Maybe Waring was set upon in here and subsequently staggered to the front room."

The Negro shrugged. "Maybe."

We stood in silence a moment. I tried not to stare at the bloodstain on the floor. The Doctor's attacker had struck after we arrived in Bath. *After* or *because*? I returned my gaze to the sailor.

"What was the *Belsize* carrying, Blue?"

He said nothing.

"What secret bound those beyond them to Addison and Waring, that they should both pay for it like this?"

"I don't know."

"But you were going to tell me something. In the pub. What was it? What were you going to say?"

"I'd say there's every reason to keep quiet. The Captain is dead. So is the Doctor. My tie to the ship is cut. I've no reason to get caught up in the likes of this now."

"But you already are caught up in it," I said softly. I looked down at my stained trousers. "We're covered in it. Both of us are."

CHAPTER
FIFTY-ONE

Justice Pearce was a gaunt man with a wide smile, better befitting a social visit than a murder investigation.

"The Doctor's body is upstairs," I explained. "I don't know what the boy has told you, but, well . . . you should prepare yourself. The scene is macabre."

"Rest easy. This isn't my first corpse." The Justice tugged on his frock coat, rejigging himself. Then he smiled again and said, "Inigo, wasn't it? I'm not sure what your line of work is, young man, but in mine we get our fair share of excitements! I doubt this will top them."

The man's blitheness worked upon me. It seemed manufactured, corrupt. Pearce strode up the stairs. My first inkling that there was a seriousness behind his chipper façade came when I saw him run his hand over the banisters as he ascended. It appeared he was counting them. I led him to view the broken window. Then, with Blue silent at my side all the while, I showed the Justice through to the room at the front of the house, in which Waring's body lay. Pearce's eyes took in the corpse swiftly, then skipped off around the blood-soaked room, glib as his footwork, before

228

returning to the poor Doctor again. His spilled entrails were still glistening. They looked like something those children might have dug up, fresh from the Avon mud.

"So," the Justice said at length.

"Abominable, isn't it," I replied weakly.

"You came visiting, you say, to find your host in this terrible state."

"As I explained, he was still alive when we arrived."

"Yes, yes. The door was ajar. Etcetera."

I described again the order of events: Blue had discovered the window; I found the Doctor first.

"I see," the Justice said absently. "But you journeyed to Bath together. The visit was a joint one."

"We split up to discover the whereabouts of the Doctor's new premises," I said. "And then, yes, we reconvened and arrived here at the house together."

The Justice waved the specifics aside with a lightness apparently designed to persuade us that the exact details were unimportant, but in doing so he conveyed the opposite impression to me: I understood instead that he was testing whether it would serve to drive a wedge between Blue and me.

"What did you do when you found the victim, then?" Pearce jerked on the lapels of his coat again, making a show of getting back to the point.

I told him of our futile attempts to comfort the dying man, yet what had seemed so obvious at the time — that he was beyond assisting — now appeared glaringly presumptuous. We hadn't sought help. My voice sounded thin in my head, reedy with guilt. The Justice was nodding and puffing out his cheeks consolingly, but

I suspected, deep down, that if he was drawing any conclusions from what I was saying they were unsympathetic to our cause. He let my explanation eat itself up, then squatted down next to the corpse. He bent low over the wound. It appeared he was surveying a flower bed or cake decoration, not a man's insides.

Eventually he bobbed back up. "Good!" he said. "So, to sum up, I'm to understand that the two of you came looking for the Doctor. That was your intent. You came together, then split up, then you were together and apart and together again, until finally you found him. And when you did he was alive. Alive but torn down the middle, as he is now. Dying. You watched him die, by which I mean witnessed it, comforting him, helping him face his end."

I could feel Blue stiffening in his boots beside me as the Justice trotted out his insinuations. We had raised the alarm, I insisted, yet this seemed irrelevant to Pearce, whose pink-blinking eyes said he'd already made up his mind. He pulled a rumpled polka-dot handkerchief from an inside pocket, retrieved the gruesome scissor-shears from the Doctor's blackening lake, and calmly wiped the murder weapon down. I found myself explaining — in terms so nebulous I instantly regretted it — the business-nature of our visit. The Justice clipped the blades open and shut a few times, waiting for me to dry up again.

"I knew a sailor who owned a tool not dissimilar to this pair of . . . things . . . once," he said cheerfully. "The hooked-stiletto end he found useful for jabbing open knots in rope, apparently, and the shearing action had something to do with sail-cloth. What profession did you gentlemen say you engage in again?"

I glanced sideways and saw what I can best describe as resignation in Blue's expression. So as to avoid him spelling out that he was a sailor, I found myself not responding to the Justice's question myself. "They struck me as perhaps relevant to a surgeon's work," I said quietly, instead. "Perhaps Waring gathered them up from among his medical kit to use in self-defence."

At this Pearce puffed out his hollow cheeks again. "Perhaps," he said. "And perhaps not. It's a theory I'm happy to pitch into the pot. But the mix is going to take some stirring. And you gentlemen, I'm afraid, are going to have to bear with me, by which . . ." he bared the tips of yellow teeth in a grin ". . . by which I mean assist with the investigation, just until we've got this . . . unfortunate business . . . sorted out."

CHAPTER
FIFTY-TWO

By which I mean assist meant no such thing of course. While we stood talking upstairs I'd been dimly aware of noises outside: the thud and clack of hooves, men's voices gruff above the town hubbub. It turned out that the Justice had sent for deputies. We followed him out into the light and there they were, two mounted, two on foot, all four wearing greatcoats fastened with wide leather belts, giving them a hackneyed military look.

"Good. My men are ready to receive you," Pearce said, rubbing his hands together. By which he meant take us into custody.

Movement beside me made me glance Blue's way again. His neck and jaw were rigid. For a horrible moment I suspected he was going to lash out, or make a dash for it, and in the next instant I feared I might do the latter myself. By detaining me this man could make my already untenable situation infinitely worse: I should therefore run. But the temptation was fleeting, a bird flashing close past a window-pane. If I ran and was caught, "infinitely worse" wouldn't be the start of it.

One of the mounted men had a beard, thick as ivy covering a tree-stump. The two on foot both carried staves. Justice Pearce must have called for them on his way here, before he'd even met us. Perhaps they were just a precaution. Pearce himself was still feigning solicitousness, beckoning and inviting, the carrot to his sidekicks' sticks. I walked towards him and Blue followed and somehow there was a horse either side of us, and a man front and back. Within this flesh-and-bone cordon we were led to the Justice's offices, a grave, stone-built town house not ten minutes' walk away.

But once we were inside, Pearce's pretence of civility evaporated. He instructed his men to lead us into what he called the trunk room. Its walls were of un-plastered brick; its single window was high in the wall and cut with bars. He was going to lock us in here! I turned in the doorway, panic rising, only to see the Justice's scrawny back retreating down the hall.

I called out to him. "You asked for our line of work. Well, I'm a lawyer. I'm investigating a matter connected . . ."

He paused and looked over his shoulder at me. "In which case you'll no doubt be willing to wait here while I set about ensuring due process is done."

Through teeth clamped tight in an attempt to compose myself, I said, "Quite so. But you must permit me to do more than just wait: let me send word back to Bristol. My associates may be able to help shed some light upon this horrific turn of events."

He knew what I was really after, I'm sure, but couldn't refuse a request put in those terms. Muttering, "For what it's worth, then," he instructed the bearded henchman to take up my offer as he departed.

CHAPTER
FIFTY-THREE

They left us a long time. The shadow cast by the window lengthened down the brickwork and drifted across the dusty floor. There being no furniture in the room, the dust is where we sat, me with my arms round my knees, Blue squatting, cradling the cannonball of his lowered head in starfish hands. I could not see his expression, and so did not speak to begin with, fearful that if I began to talk, I'd end up admitting to our powerlessness, and so worsen it. But, eventually, the silence became too much to bear and I found myself reassuring us emptily that I'd summoned help which would, in time, arrive.

By help I meant Sebastian. In Carthy's absence, he was the only person to whom I could turn, and the distinction between the two of them — Carthy with his clout, as against timid Sebastian — undermined me even as I voiced my faith in the latter. Blue cut me off.

"Your kind," he said.

"Kindness hasn't much to do with it. We're both stuck —"

"No. Not *you're* kind — *your* kind. 'Your kind, forgive me.' That's what Waring said as he was dying.

That's what the Captain's death, and Waring's, this whole godforsaken mess, is about."

To witness Blue trembling was like seeing a boulder shiver.

"I don't follow."

"He meant my kind, my people. The Negro race."

"But . . . why would he ask forgiveness from them?"

"The cargo you've been asking about was alive. It comprised extra passengers."

"Passengers?"

"Yes. Live goods. *Unwilling* passengers."

The shape of it came clear.

"Shipped from Africa to the West Indies, as before. We sailed the full triangle, middle passage included, not just out and back. Which explains the duration of our voyage. The extra months had nothing to do with any storm damage, as you were told, though it's true the ship was refitted in Barbados, its extra decks — of slave quarters — stripped out. That's what accounted for the green timbers in the hold which Captain Addison was so keen to explain."

I let this sink in, then said, "But still . . . she's not the first ship to have worked the trade illegally, since its abolition, I'm sure. And in Waring's case, well, as ship's surgeon he must surely have concerned himself with the relief of suffering, during the voyage. I can see the man having guilty qualms about his involvement. It's been outlawed for a reason, after all. But still, until two years ago there was no illegality to be ashamed of. Why would Waring, a doctor, seek forgiveness with his last breath?"

235

Blue glanced up at me from beneath his lowered brow and breathed out heavily through both nostrils. "You have not sailed on a slaver," he said simply.

"No."

"*The relief of suffering* is not a phrase bandied about on board."

"No. I didn't mean to suggest that . . ." I felt like a schoolboy, floundering to justify myself. "My family has . . . or had . . . connections to the trade. An historical involvement. I do know something of what it's about."

"The city was built upon it. Everyone has *some* idea. I thought I had, make no mistake. My father made the journey himself after all. Between decks, at fourteen years of age. He spoke of the ordeal rarely, but I believed I understood . . ."

Blue trailed off, rocked forward on to the balls of his feet, spread his fingers wide and planted them before him in the dirt. He looked suddenly animal, steadying himself like that on all fours.

"I understood nothing. We were not told of the *Belsize*'s true intent until we'd already put to sea. When Addison first gathered us round, there was little surprise among the men, and no room to object. News of the extra wages helped. Anyone with any *qualms* was invited to leave the ship at Tangiers. Nobody did. We reinforced the crew as we took on the cargo, extra hands being a necessary deterrent to unrest, and trimmed our number back on reaching the Indies, where the slaves were sold. Abolition has worked wonders on the prices. Apparently they're worth three times as much on the black market as they were five years ago."

I let him talk on, circling his subject, inspecting my fingers for fear of putting him off his stride with scrutiny. Finally he landed upon the Doctor again.

"It was Waring's job to protect the value of the investment. That's the surgeon's role on a slaver, to inspect the merchandise as it's bought and keep it in good condition, as best as possible at least, for sale. In that way it does serve him to stave off sickness on the slaves' behalf, you're right. But his responsibility is to the cargo as a whole, not to individual souls. Waring's genius . . . well . . . he had it that preventing the spread of sickness was preferable to administering cures. He'd been successful with this theory before, apparently, and he put it to work on the *Belsize*, to good effect. Most slavers lose a quarter, some over a half, of the souls they ship, but of the five hundred and twenty-two we carried, all made it to the Indies save seventy-nine."

"Seventy-nine died," I repeated.

"Yes." Blue drew his forefinger and thumb together across his brow and the bridge of his nose, digging them into his eyelids along the way. He went on.

"Dysentery. Or rather the threat of it. To curtail the spread of the disease the good doctor had upwards of fifty slaves thrown overboard upon the first sign of their falling ill. He carried out inspections. *To stem the tide of sickness*, he had us understand, *nip any epidemic in the bud*. If a body appeared to be wasting, the legs befouled and so on, Waring would administer water and wait to see whether the subject kept it down. Those who didn't he jettisoned, for the good of the flock. Many were children. Evidently they are most prone to the disease."

I said nothing. A panicky sensation, the canary's wings beating inside its cage, rose within me.

"The mothers", said Blue, "go mad." He repeated the pinch and drag movement of his fingers, then planted his hand again, held himself steady on all fours. "One of them, I recall, upon seeing her sick child pitched over the rail, attempted to leap after it. When restrained, she took her own life. She bit through her wrists, spat out lumps of herself and bled to death in plain view, on deck."

The wings were flapping about my head now. I stood up and paced the length of the room, trying in vain to escape them. A church bell sounded in the distance, ripples of normality fading outside, high overhead. I approached the door and shouldered it hard, causing it to judder in its socket, which only served to demonstrate its solidity.

"But . . . what does it matter? The ship was trading illegally. It carried a consignment of slaves to the Indies, with all the outlawed horror that entails. How does that account for what happened to Addison and Waring?"

Blue looked at me balefully and said nothing.

"Why raise it now, then? If it's not relevant, why mention it? And for that matter, if the cargo *does* have to do with the murders, why did you not broach the subject with me before now? Why wait until this point in time, when we're stuck here, powerless, to bring it up?"

Blue shook his head, then answered.

"I do not want to die, so until now I've held my tongue."

"But when we found Addison hanged? I still don't see it. What could he do to you then?"

"At sea, the Captain is God. His is the last word. But on land . . . there are owners above him."

"And Waring?"

"The Doctor invested," said Blue simply.

This didn't add up. If there had been whisperings of a ship plying the old trade, Thunderbolts would have been full of it, never mind the Bristol papers, but I'd heard nothing. And although the seriousness of the crime went some way towards explaining the pressure put upon Carthy and me to desist from picking over the *Belsize*'s paperwork, I'd seen nothing in the file capable of evidencing such an accusation. Accounting discrepancies cover a multitude of sins — we had not come close to pinning them on one of this magnitude. I held my tongue. The light in our mean room, having taken on something of the quality of Avon silt, was thickening further as the afternoon lengthened into evening. It seemed I'd have more than enough time to think the thing through. Blue planted his back against the brickwork, drawing his jacket tight round his barrel chest. He had begun to shiver. I offered him my greatcoat but he refused to take it.

CHAPTER
FIFTY-FOUR

I'm not sure what hour of the night it was when they returned, but it had long been dark, and the blackness and deathly quiet and fading shock had conspired to produce in me the stupor of a waking doze. I sprang up at the metal on metal grating of the lock, only to discover that my legs had cramped beneath me.

Justice Pearce's face, dark as offal, swam before me, and he was grinning and nodding, mock-jolly again.

"Progress!" he said. "A question here, a bit of chat there, the good luck of a witness or two, willing to talk."

"What do you mean?"

"Don't look so frightened. It's not you the finger is pointing towards, for now." The Justice puffed out his cheeks, turned to Blue, and went on matter-of-factly, "Though I'm sorry to say things are looking less promising for you."

Blue glowered at him.

"I'm afraid a man of your . . . countenance, well, he stands out. Makes it a sight harder to get away with things, I imagine."

"We discovered this crime together," I said as evenly as I could. "And then we reported it to you."

"So you say."

"What are you insinuating?"

"How well do you know this Negro?" Pearce asked equably.

I looked at Blue. His eyes were cast low, his arms hung heavy at his sides. The flickering lamplight caught the backs of his hands as they curled and uncurled, raising veins. I looked back at Pearce and said, "Well enough."

"I wouldn't be so sure about that," smiled Pearce. "But then, who is to say?" He grew mock-thoughtful. "Even those closest to us are full of surprises. It's impossible to know for sure what makes another man tick." He rounded on me, grin in place. "But in this particular case there's no need to plumb the profundities. It's enough to point out that you have no idea what this man here was doing between half past twelve and one o'clock today."

"We arrived at the Doctor's house together."

"So you say."

"I say so because it is so. Do you doubt my word?"

"I'll be happy to doubt your word as and when I see fit, but for now there's no need. It doesn't matter. What matters is the word of one . . . Mrs Gregory, who says she saw a man fitting his description" (he nodded at Blue) "outside the house in question long before the two of you turned up on your errand. Her word is important, as is that of Mr James Cowper, who says the same."

Blue's eyes were still fixed on his boots. I took a deep breath to remonstrate further, but it was as if I had sucked in a lungful of water, not air. Who was to know that this accusation about the sailor's whereabouts wasn't true? Not me. I could come up with nothing sensible to say, just so much spluttering.

"And then there's the further complication", Justice Pearce went on, "of the unfortunate episode back in Bristol. You failed to mention it, but . . . a night's hard riding, the opportunity to catch up with my colleague and good friend, your own Justice Wheeler, and we turned that nasty business up, too. To be first on the scene of one violent death in a week is unfortunate, but two . . ."

Pearce, his cheeks puffed taut, breathed out through tight lips in wonderment. There was something about the man, his taunting way. I'd never seen a face at once so benign and yet so inviting to punch.

"And the connections, once probed, have just grown stronger!" he marvelled. "I'll be honest in admitting I don't quite understand your own involvement in this matter, Mr Bright, *yet*, but your friend here has been cooped up in a leaky ship for nigh on two years with *both* victims! Taking orders from one, and at the other's ministering mercy. If I can't find a malicious motive, a reason to exact horrible revenge and so forth, in all of that time at sea, well I don't deserve this rewarding job, do I?"

The Justice cracked a knuckle, then another, complacent as a man popping drumsticks from a roasted chicken.

"The long and the short of it is that we need to take this fellow", he cocked his thumb at Blue, "for questioning."

242

Behind him, the man with the beard yawned. Framed by the black mass of his bristles, the inside of his mouth appeared a shocking blood-red. He huffed hard enough to flex the thick stave he was leaning upon, grinding its end into the packed dust of the floor.

"Inigo." Blue's voice was low as a priest's. "You need to —"

"Mr Bright needs to wait here patiently until we find a reason to let him go," Pearce said gently, motioning at the beard to take hold of Blue.

"The ship, Inigo," Blue continued in a murmur. "The cargo." The bearded guard, stave across his chest, had advanced towards the sailor, who showed his palms peaceably as, eyes on me, he allowed himself to be backed from the room. "The cargo," Blue repeated. "That's the root of this." He paused in the doorway. "And not just on the outward leg. There was a *grudge* in the hold coming home, too."

CHAPTER
FIFTY-FIVE

Being incarcerated alone was much worse than my time locked up with Blue. The waking sleep I'd managed when he'd been alongside me did not return after Pearce took him away. Now the darkness was of such an intensity that it made my eyes ache, so I sat in the corner and kept them shut and listened for the church bells, hoping their occasional chiming would pull me through the night. But there was scant comfort to be had there: even straining, I could barely make out the bells' distant clamour; some shift in the atmosphere outside had robbed them of their last resonance, so that their striking was that of a muffled pianoforte key tapped at a great distance.

Why hadn't Blue remonstrated with the Justice? He'd said nothing to defend himself. Where had he been when we split up to locate the Doctor? Did I imagine the disturbance upstairs on our joint arrival? Had he planted the seed of it as we stood on the stoop? Why hadn't he told me of the *Belsize*'s dirty slaving secret upon our discovering Addison? If there'd been a crime against *his kind* did it not make sense, as Justice Pearce had unknowingly suggested, that Blue himself may have sought to right the wrong he'd unwittingly helped perpetrate?

No, no, no. I would not fall prey to the inevitable prejudice against the man. We'd spilt blood together. I'm a good enough judge of character, and the sailor was no murderer. His composure, the very set of his spine, told me enough to know that . . .

I was staring blindly at the coal-smoke darkness again, and my eyes were stinging. There was a clue in all this blackness. The illegal transportation of Negroes, the polished onyx of Blue's knuckles, and . . . and . . . the blackamoor-woman's corpse, the purported suicide discovered by young Kitty and her enterprising brother. But there was something else as well. I reached for it tentatively, a tongue probing the memory of a toothache, and found it, a gap between rotten molars. The first corpse, the one discovered by the workman, Ivan Brook. *Charred*, the report in Felix Farley had read. It was alleged he'd burnt his victim beyond identification. A burned corpse: black.

Dawn does not break. Like scum pushed into the river's gullet by the incoming tide, oily with advancing wavelets, it creeps up gradually. My panic was likewise incremental; by the time my hand cast a shadow on the wall I was sick with it, fearful for my very life. In this day and age, no matter what stock you come from, custody is a limbo from which prisoners are wont to . . . disappear.

Even so, the first thing I felt, later that morning, on hearing my father's voice echoing in the hallway, could best be described as amazed anxiety rather than relief.

What was he doing here? I hauled myself from the floor, shook the woodenness from my limbs, dusted myself down. I couldn't hear exactly what he was saying, but there was no hint of anger in his tone. If anything, it sounded like levity. After a pause, the lock's innards rolled over themselves again and Justice Pearce stood in the doorway. He beamed at me. What was left of his hair he had greased with pomade this morning, and he smelled of bacon.

"Well, Mr Bright, I can't say I was expecting cavalry of this sort to ride to your rescue, you admitting to lawyering pretensions and so on, but there we have it. Argumentation I could have withstood, but Papa has come with the best sort of help. Altogether more persuasive! He's put up the surety we require to let you go free for the time being. Lucky you, your father is a generous man."

He led me through to the front of the house. The place appeared much less austere, comfortable almost, in reverse. Potted geraniums stood on a windowsill in the hallway, and I saw a pair of curtains held back with ribbons. An image of Lilly's hair, burnished with sunlight, flashed before me, immediately followed by the thought of Mary's naked waist solid between my hands, and the resulting shudder of guilt rendered me still less prepared to stand before my father.

But there he was, leaning on his stick, his back to the doorway he must have known I would come through. He turned upon hearing us, finished picking at a tooth with his free hand, inspected whatever it was he had

246

freed from it, then wiped his fingers upon his breeches and summoned a smile.

"What's wrong with drunk and disorderly, Inigo? A bit of boisterousness. Some breaching of the peace. I'd prepared myself long ago to retrieve one of you — though if forced to guess, I'd have plumped for John — from a night in the cells!"

"Is Sebastian with you?"

"But this, this, is altogether less seemly. I don't doubt but there's a perfectly sensible explanation for your involvement." Here he shot Pearce a look from eyes sunk deep beneath the rock-face of his brow. "And yet it still won't do. You shouldn't have allowed yourself to become mixed up in business of this nature at all. As I was explaining to the Justice here, one would have expected a member of your profession to be altogether more . . . circumspect."

He marvelled at me. His journey had raised the weather in his cheeks. It was as if he had returned from a day's hunting to find me — still a boy — caught in the act of stealing a rock-cake.

"Sebastian was indisposed. Fortunately for you, he passed on your . . . request for help."

"I did not want to trouble you."

"No, no. I don't doubt it."

"But my friend." (The word had a juvenile overtone — yet neither *accomplice* nor *colleague* would do instead.) "Joseph Blue. Also wrongly — mistakenly accused. Justice Pearce has explained our mutual involvement, yes? You've persuaded him to release Mr Blue, too?"

My father picked his teeth again while Pearce tugged at his lapels, puffed up with more punchable self-satisfaction.

"Give a starving man a loaf and you expect a 'thank you,' Inigo. Not: 'I want two.' "

"The fact is, Mr Bright," Pearce told me pleasantly, "I've already got shot of the Negro. He's on his way back to Bristol, headed for the embrace of your own Justice Wheeler. Our murder here has convinced him to take a closer look at Mr Blue's last encounter with his dead Captain. Anderson, was it?" Here, he tapped his nose. "My counsel would be to put a bit of clear water between yourself and that black. I don't know where you found him, but he's in a world of trouble now and", he glanced at my father, "I'd hate his guilt to rub off on you, by association."

"Is this some form of joke?" I began, and the heat rising in my chest broke from me in a snort of laughter. But as I opened my mouth to continue, my father cut me off in the voice he uses for commanding the dogs. "Enough!" Instantly, he snapped back into feigned good humour. "Let us be on our way before the good Justice here suffers a change of heart."

The two of them exchanged a nodding smile. They even had the same metal-heeled walk: a gunshot tattoo accompanied our progress across the flagstone hall.

248

CHAPTER
FIFTY-SIX

My father had brought his own carriage. It stood spattered to the door handles with grey mud. Never mind the horses, Webb, at the reins, looked exhausted; they'd obviously set off early and ridden hard. Even so, the coachman managed to wink at me as I climbed into my seat. I'd overdone a night out, he seemed to think, warranting a sort of patronising respect rather than admonishment.

We wound out of Bath's prissy heart and picked up the Bristol road. To begin with, I was too angry to speak. But I was also exhausted, and the rutted road shook the heat from me by increments, leaving me hollowed out. It had been raining overnight. The ploughed landscape we rattled through was cut with black waves. They smelled of wet canvas and rotting timbers . . . and . . . it was everywhere, the damned ship, even the inevitable screech of gulls slashing low over the furrows reminded me of the horrible thing.

"You know what the *Belsize* was trading, don't you?"

My father had been feigning sleep. Now he opened his eyes. "What's that?"

"You know what your ship carried to the Indies?"

"*My* ship?"

"The *Belsize*."

"We haven't owned ships for ten years, Inigo. You know that. We take a stake in voyages, we invest."

"It amounts to the same thing. You knew what you were taking a stake in."

"The same thing? There's a world of difference between owning your own fleet and backing individual ships. Responsibility, for one. And authority over proceedings. Manning the ship, etcetera."

"The ship carried slaves."

"And then there's the share on return an investor can expect. Less risk than an owner, but less profit, as you understand."

"Somebody is killing people to keep the secret. Those who knew. The ship's surgeon. Its captain."

My father blinked at me incredulously. "Killing people? Because of a . . . trade infringement? That sounds far-fetched."

"But that's what this is about. Murder. You saved me from being accused of it outright myself, though it seems the sailor Blue now stands charged alone in my stead."

"Slaves, you say? On the *Belsize*?" Again he shook his head.

"You expect me to believe you didn't know?"

"Indeed I did not know! If I'd suspected such a plan was afoot I'd have objected to it on any number of grounds. You'll recall our firm was one of the first out of the trade. It's no longer profitable. Liverpool has had the edge on us in that respect for donkey's years."

"And yet you invested in it."

"Inigo. I can't blame you. The nature of our business is still clearly . . . opaque to you. So let me spell it out. My share in the Western Trading Company venture is slim. It is but one of Bright & Co.'s concerns. And we're only involved as a means of *minimising* our exposure to risk. The WTC takes stakes in trading vessels. It had but a proportionate say in the running of that ship. If what you are saying is true — and let's for a moment assume that it is — then the brute fact that I was unaware of it remains unaltered. I'm as astonished — as *exercised* indeed — as the next man to hear of this."

More furrows jolted past, compressed beneath empty sky.

"Mr Carthy has gone," I stated.

"Gone where?"

"I don't know."

"Well, I'm sure he'll pitch up again soon enough." My father ran his thumbnail between his two front teeth.

"He has been abducted. There was a note."

He picked at his teeth again and narrowed his eyes in puzzlement. "A note from whom?"

"I don't know."

"You're sure it isn't some sort of a hoax? You know how fond that man is of a practical joke."

I watched him carefully and did not reply.

"It's his method, isn't it? To launch you into deep water and watch your progress from the safety of the shore."

Again I said nothing, but my silence spoke loudly enough.

"Abducted, you say. Goodness."

The coach hit a vicious rut and we were both jerked from our seats. My father hit his elbow upon the woodwork. He rubbed at the hurt after we had gathered ourselves up and something about the gesture made him look frail and fallible all of a sudden. He had been up all night. He had journeyed to Bath and done whatever it took to ensure my freedom. I had not offered him a word of thanks.

The irrationality of my indisposition towards him struck me full in the face then. What had he ever done to deserve it? Despite the difficulty of losing my mother, he had raised me, creating a new family for us both, and allowing me alone to do as I please. John and Sebastian were circumscribed by their duty to the business, yet when I'd objected to becoming involved, Father had paid Carthy to take me on. When I'd announced my marriage plans, he'd offered to help with the wedding. I was still welcome at his table, in line to inherit a share of his wealth, and as soon as he'd heard I was in trouble, he'd dropped everything to rescue me. I'd cooked up my consternation at his involvement with the Western Trading Company out of what? Figures on a balance sheet. Yet he'd been the investor conscientious enough to rectify shortfalls in the Company's payments of duties. Even if he had known of the slaving, it meant little: there had been nothing illegal about it until recently; he had been raised on the trade; I could hardly blame him for failing to blanch at

252

the news that he had been an unwitting partner in so novel a crime. And, in any event, I had seen nothing — either on the file or in his face — to suggest that he did know anything was afoot with the *Belsize*.

In fact, Blue aside, the only person who expressed concerns about the ship was Carthy, and he'd been altogether unforthcoming about what exactly his concerns were. Somebody had got wind of our work for the Dock Company, and that somebody evidently objected to our involvement, but beyond that I knew nothing of the details. Like the screech and grind of the carriage — its axles were in need of grease — it was all just so much noise.

"Might Mr Carthy's absence have to do with the recent news story? Bullivant's complaint and so forth."

I shook my head, and yet . . . could I be sure? The handwriting on the notes had appeared similar, but . . . the carriage bucked and slewed again, jostling the two of us together, and beyond the certainty of that collision, shoulder to shoulder with my father, at once bruising and reassuringly solid, I knew nothing in that instant, *nothing*.

I swallowed. My Adam's apple worked thick in my throat. I turned away.

"Son," said my father. Perhaps the physical contact broke down a barrier within him, too; I'm not sure. But as I watched the hedgerow jag past I felt his hand upon my shoulder again. It slid round to squeeze the back of my neck, and he bent his face towards the side of my head so that I could feel his breath, warm upon my cheek.

"You need a haircut."

CHAPTER
FIFTY-SEVEN

The temperature dropped that afternoon and the wind rose. A biting cold skewered us within the carriage. By the time we made it back to Bristol, it was needling my joints. The exposed skin on my cheeks, forehead and the backs of my hands felt taut and raw.

Without asking my opinion on the matter, my father had us driven straight to Bright House, where the fire in his study was already lit. We'd exchanged no further words for the remainder of the journey. A familiar curtain of reticence had descended to hold us apart, yet anticipation coloured it: I knew he had something else to say.

He stood to one side of the fireplace, and I stood at the other, leaning on the marble surround, warm beneath my palm. Father sent for a bottle of rum and two glasses and, again without asking, he poured a generous measure for us both.

"Only so much warmth to be had from without," he said, handing me a glass.

I took a sip. The rum bloomed abrasively in my chest.

Father followed suit, then lifted his glass. "Success," he said.

254

This seeming an absurd toast in the context, I merely nodded.

"I have admired your tenacity a long while, Inigo. I like the fact you decided not to take my advice over the Dock Company issue, your resolve in choosing to pursue your case come what may."

I sensed a "but" coming, and held my tongue, and here it came.

"But . . . the ins and outs of that particular matter aside . . . I worry that you are pitting your talents in the wrong direction." He winced back another sip of rum. "There are two sorts of folk in this world, according to my experience. Those in control, and those held down. Success is as much about choosing the right game to play as it is about winning it."

There was something unsettling about listening to this wisdom, not because I disagreed, but because of the oddly solicitous tone with which Father was delivering it. The speech felt premeditated, and the idea of him thinking in advance what to say to convince me — of what, exactly, I didn't yet know — was as cloying as it was touching. I would have felt more comfortable faced with told-you-so scorn: practice had taught me how to push back against that.

"In this city, now as before, the game to be in is trade. Lawyering is worthy, as is doctoring, or any other of the professions. But the whip hand, here in Bristol, goes to business."

I watched his face, glowing now, balloon and shrink in the bottom of his glass as he raised and lowered it again.

"Neither Sebastian nor John have your strengths. I haven't always seen it that way, I know, but I do now. The pressure of this difficult patch has made things clear. The upset has made John . . ." he picked his words out of his raised glass . . . "overly reliant on this stuff. And Sebastian's . . . sensitivities seem to have got the better of him again. You, by contrast, have held firm in your own adversity. As a result I'm asking you to reconsider your position. Come back to work for our common good. Bright & Co. needs you."

Warmth spread through my chest, and it wasn't the drink; I could not stem a sense of satisfaction at having risen above John in Father's estimation. But the feeling didn't last long. Something was not right, not right at all. Given that he'd just had to rescue me from bungling powerlessness, referring now, of all times, to previously unseen "strengths" made little sense. Added to which, there was a beseeching quality to this overture. My father was looking at me now with filmy eyes. That could indeed have been a result of the rum, but I suspected it had to do with something else. He smiled and dipped his brow, nodding. Waiting for my answer. *Hanging* upon it.

"Why would you not use your influence to ensure the release of Blue?"

Father stopped nodding. His face was blank.

"Joseph Blue. The sailor I stood falsely accused alongside."

"The Negro?"

"Yes."

There was bafflement in his eyes. "I know nothing about the man. How could I possibly vouch for him?"

"I did."

"Yes, but. Have you not heard my offer?"

"I vouched for him."

"Inigo," my father said, and in that one word, my name, said in that flat tone, was a lifetime's dominance. *I'm in charge until my last breath*, he might as well have said.

"I'm grateful to you, Father, both for what you've done this morning and for this . . . compliment. But I have a new career. My duty is to Adam Carthy and this case. I must return to Thunderbolt Street to see whether he has been released. And then I need to take steps myself to prove the sailor's innocence."

Very carefully, my father placed his unfinished glass of rum on the leather top of his desk. He screwed it one way and then the other. "I had not realised the extent of your faith in this man, Blue," he said. "What do you know about him?"

"He did not kill the *Belsize*'s captain, or Doctor Waring."

"So you say. But beyond that?"

I put my glass down next to my father's.

"You forget", he said quietly, "that I have experience of dealing with blacks. You cannot trust them, much less know their true intentions."

Outside, the wind was stripping leaves from the birch tree. I stared at them, streaks of dirty-silver. No matter how many tore past, the tree seemed undiminished. It had an endless supply. In the aftermath of the drink, I felt my exhaustion afresh.

"And if this ship", my father went on, "was indeed carrying slaves, then you have to admit that he or his kind are among those most likely to bear a grudge. That's their common character, a sense of obstinate aggrievedness."

"As I say, I need to return to Carthy's house."

He took a step towards me and grasped my wrist. I pulled away, but there was iron in his grip.

"Think on my offer, Inigo. Your tenacity has stood you in good stead until now, but push this matter any further and I will not be able to help you. By joining the firm you will be saving face, not quitting."

"I thank you, but no. For now, I cannot."

His face was close enough for me to see the moisture glittering within the pores of his skin. I heard the grinding of his teeth before he said, "There's the matter of your wedding to consider. It presents an opportunity to unite the Bright and Alexander cause. But if you refuse me now . . ."

Unmistakably, this *if* was the precursor to a threat. But he pulled up short of explaining himself, and released my forearm, and patted my shoulder, and forced a smile.

"The offer still stands," he repeated. "Think about it."

CHAPTER
FIFTY-EIGHT

The man comes for Oni again.

She dreams of the three-legged lion which terrorised the village when she was a girl. It first broke through at night and stole a goat. Nobody saw or heard it but it left tracks, three massive paw prints, the gap between them longer than a man's stride. A hunting party followed the trail, which disappeared in rocky ground. For a whole season the lion did not return. The village lost interest. But then it did come back and this time it stole a child. It walked into a hut and dragged a seven-year-old boy from where he lay. Hunters followed its trail again, back to the rock ledges. They found what was left of the boy's body — a foot, the head — but the lion had vanished.

The elders raised a thorn cordon around the village and set a watch which saw nothing from full moon to full moon.

Then the lion came back and killed one of the watchmen at his post — the ground beneath his mat was sticky with blood — and again dragged the body away without being caught. The elders demanded a doubling of the guard, but the volunteers were scared and inattentive.

As fear overran the village, the lion grew bolder. It killed another child the following week, and two days after that took an old man from his sickbed in daylight still capable of casting

259

a shadow. A day later it returned to the village and killed a young woman carrying water, but this time the killing was different because the lion did not carry its victim away. Her torn body was discovered fifty paces from the well.

In her dream Oni knows the lion is coming for her next. She is unafraid. The lion makes sense. It was wounded once and reduced to killing people and its addiction to the taste of human flesh has grown. Oni dreams it will be caught, as it was eventually caught in reality, and strung up from a pole by its three huge paws, the withered hind leg hanging wing-like at its side. The difference is that in the dream this won't happen until the lion has taken her from her bed into the night.

CHAPTER
FIFTY-NINE

The house no longer bore the false-hope smell of laundry and scones. I knew as I stood in the hallway removing my coat that Carthy still hadn't returned. Mercifully, Aunt Beatrice wasn't there either. Adam's wife and young Anne were in the parlour together, but separately engaged: Anne was drawing and her mother was making alterations to a dress. Or at least she was pretending to do so. She had removed the garment's arms, which lay outstretched at her feet. The bodice was crumpled in her lap. She made to get up as I entered, but slumped back down on registering my expression and said nothing. Anne, meanwhile, clapped her hands and began babbling at once. Something to do with the natural habitat of canaries and the drawing she was making to replicate it. I sat down on the floor next to her and we discussed how accurately to depict a coconut tree. I suggested it might have the broad leaves of a walnut, and she set about translating that into scribbles.

There was a chill in the room. I banked up the fire. With my back to Mrs Carthy it was easier to suggest that I was still making investigations and expected to turn up answers yet.

But I could not remain there long. I felt guilty. I had not asked to become involved in this case. That was Carthy's doing. And yet the black heart of the thing seemed to beat within me now. I had poisoned this house and endangered its occupants; my presence now was just making things worse. I told Anne she should incorporate the coconut tree landscape into a map of her canary's imagined island, and crossed the street to Thunderbolts. Coffee would help me take stock.

With one hand fighting its way through the tangle of my hair, and the other brushing down the front of my coat, I crossed the threshold intent upon spotting the waitress before she saw me.

Yet it wasn't Mary who caught my eye upon entering Thunderbolts, but the poetess, Edie Dyer. She was sitting at a table reading a news-sheet, alone. She looked up as I entered and her face split into a genuine smile, the first such that I had seen in days. She stood and cocked the paper at me, indicating that I should join her, and at that precise moment, as I was lurching woodenly towards her, Mary intercepted me.

She stood close enough for me to catch her honey and sweat smell above the coffee. I blinked and saw grey pillowslips. She, too, was smiling, but wryly.

"I keep telling you. It's no use pawing at hair like yours. Curls that thick have too much spring." Her gaze worked its way down my chest and for a moment I suspected she might reach out and touch me in plain view of everyone.

"A bowl of coffee, please, Mary, as usual," I said, and made to pass her.

262

She stepped sideways with me and our thighs collided and she smiled as she let me go.

I therefore arrived at Edie's table flushed hot under the collar and, at first, unable to concentrate upon what she was saying. It was all I could do to respond, when she stopped speaking, with an apology for not having sent thanks for the packet of quills she sent me.

She looked at me curiously.

"Of course. Have you tried them?"

Something in me wanted to lie: it felt bad saying I hadn't.

"I'm looking forward to doing so. But I've been distracted."

"What by?"

Her directness took me aback. There was something in the combination of her sharp openness which made it hard for me to dissemble. "A case I'm working on has taken an unexpected turn."

"What's it about?"

I studied her face. The contradiction between the tautness of its harsh angles and that wide mouth. "Murder," I said.

She swallowed, blinked, and said, "Goodness."

"It wasn't to begin with. At the outset I was checking import duties, which was boring yet manageable. I wish that is how it had remained. But it has not." I looked at my fingertips and repeated simply, "It is about dead people now."

"Not *this* poor soul, I trust?" she said, smoothing the news-sheet down on the tabletop.

I bent to read the item she was pointing at, but my view was blotted out by a bowl of coffee which slopped upon the paper as Mary plonked it down.

"Oh dear," the waitress said. "I am sorry."

I picked up the bowl and set it down next to the paper. "That's all right, Mary."

She didn't leave. Instead she leaned across me to dab at the spillage. I felt like a traitor, pressing back into my seat to avoid contact with her free arm. It brushed against me nevertheless. She stood up, stared levelly at Edie, and said, "How is Miss Lilly, Inigo?"

"She's well, thank you."

"The wedding preparations are not taxing her too much?"

"No."

"That's good to hear. Send her my best wishes." She gave me the same wry look and brushed her hip against me again as she turned away. When I glanced back up at Edie her smile had broadened — there's no other way to put it — to an amused grin. She *knew*.

I looked back down at the now blotchy news-sheet. There, at the top of the page, stood the story Edie had been referring to. It told of a recently discovered dead body. My first thought was Addison. Perhaps Justice Wheeler had come to his senses and determined that the Captain had not committed suicide. But the first line of the report made it clear that the body in question had been discovered in undergrowth on Brandon Hill, and dread immediately wormed oily in the pit of my stomach.

Not Carthy, please, no.

264

I forced myself to read on, and had to restrain myself from slapping the tabletop in relief on reaching the word *woman*. On I read. The unfortunate's corpse had been discovered just the day before, in a clump of blackberry bushes, by an elderly lady out walking her dog. It was wrapped in a sack which the dog had torn free, and when the owner saw what was beneath it she had suffered a fainting fit. A passing stranger had helped her up. Rats, apparently, were thought responsible for at least some of the disfigurement to the dead woman's face. Justice Wheeler was reported as having "no exact idea" of how long the corpse had lain there undetected. Nobody had reported a missing person, after all. Perhaps, the article speculated, this death had to do with the terrible suicide of the other black woman found recently drowned in the Avon Gorge.

Other *black* woman?

The reporter had seen fit to omit this detail until the second column! He went on to report the Justice's speculation that the woman may have been a vagabond. In all probability she had sought shelter within the bushes, her sack an inadequate covering, and died of cold. But no, the broad-minded detective conceded, it wasn't possible to rule out foul play in this instance. He would be keeping an open mind.

I took a mouthful of coffee, swilled it burning over my tongue, gulped the heat down whole.

"Sickening, isn't it?" said Edie simply.

"Yes it is."

"But nothing to do with your case I'm sure."

I caught the poetess's penetrating gaze and held it a fraction too long. There was something shrewd in those close-set eyes which forced me to see the thing clearly myself. Though she had no notion of it, this death, this *murder*, had to be connected. They all did.

What was it Blue had said before he left our cell? That there was "*a grudge in the hold coming home, too*". The *Belsize* had carried a cargo of blacks across the Atlantic and sold them into slavery in the Indies. I had taken Blue to mean that somebody — himself perhaps — had objected to the clandestine slaving, and brought their grudge home to avenge. But just because the ship had been refitted — as Addison had been so keen to show me — for her homeward leg, during which she'd carried an innocuous cargo of sugar and rum, did not mean that she had brought nothing else home with her as well. Two unknown black women had been found dead in the city since she docked. A third *charred* corpse had been discovered as well. Were the poor women on board? Had the *Belsize* conveyed slaves — however few — to these shores, too?

"The honest answer," I said, and I noticed that my fingertips were trembling, so pressed them into the oiled tabletop to keep them still, "is that I do not know. I have lost true north. The case has so shocked me that I am disorientated. Those closest to me are also, it seems, drawn in. I no longer know where the thing begins and ends; I never did, in truth, but I certainly don't any more. And . . . I am unsure of what to do."

266

The poetess leaned forward and covered the rigid backs of my hands with her own fingers. They were cool and bony and she pressed down firmly with them, just as I was pressing down on the table. Gradually, she released the pressure.

She said, "I don't trust people who pretend they always know what to do."

I glanced back down at the news-sheet.

"The shocking thing about this is that you can tell nobody minds much about it," she said. "They're not even interested in finding out why she died."

"She was black."

"So?"

I looked up at her. The question seemed genuine, which I found suddenly annoying.

"The city has spent two hundred years trading blacks. Just because that's supposed to have stopped hasn't elevated the Negro race much above livestock in many people's eyes. They aren't predisposed to mourn them any more than they're set up to grieve for the cow which gave them their roast beef."

She smiled at me again, and when she did so the teeth at the sides of her mouth revealed themselves whitely. "But some of us have never considered there was much of a difference between them and us," she said. "Have we?"

I drained my coffee, felt grit from the crushed beans swill over the back of my tongue, and shrugged.

"So why is it that you care about the Negroes, Inigo?"

"I don't, particularly."

"Yes, you do. I would go as far as to say you have an affinity for them, and that it was that aspect of this story," she tapped the paper again, "which so moved you."

"You'd be mistaken. If my family has had any undue affinity for the race, it's because selling them has lined our pockets."

"I wasn't asking after your family."

"No. But I spent the first years of my life in the Indies. Though I left when I was a child, they will have left their mark."

"I don't doubt that. The question is what sort of mark they'll have left. You're uncomfortable on the subject. And this particular news story upsets you. You say you are lost within your case. It has to do with murder. There have been no other suspicious deaths reported, so I'm guessing that it's the other black woman you're talking about. This Justice fellow may be denying there's anything afoot, claiming it's all suicides and frozen vagabonds, but you've already concluded otherwise. And the fact that they're blacks makes the matter worse for you, and it's that which —"

"Please!" I said, with sufficient force to make heads turn round. I waited for the hubbub to reassert itself before continuing. "I'm sorry. The truth in what you're saying doesn't change anything. I still don't know what to *do*. There are other factors which further complicate the thing, trust me. Matters even you are unable to guess at, despite your . . . preternatural . . . gift for divining the source of my troubles."

268

"There's nothing preternatural about it. I'm observing and drawing conclusions. Given the impasse you've reached in your case you might want to fall back upon the same technique. With patience you can trace even the most tangled vine back to its roots."

CHAPTER
SIXTY

The wind had risen again. I crossed Queen Square with the plane trees flashing the silvery undersides of their leaves above me, and those the gale had already torn free spinning about my feet. A vaulted cathedral sky ran with towering and prophetic clouds, their edges beginning to pulse sunset purple. Down at the harbour, still jumpy with the combined effect of strong coffee and Edie Dyer, I took stock. The wind was dragging its teeth across the broken surface of the water, jagged and brown. Even this breeze wasn't enough to dispel the stench of bedsores turned green.

Gulls, more gulls, lashed past slantwise. Black-tipped, grey wingbacks, and yet, seen from beneath, streaks of brilliant white.

I could see no alternative, so cut back through town to Stratton Street and hammered on Justice Wheeler's door. There was a glint in his eye when he saw it was me. It suggested that he'd been expecting my visit, looking forward to it even. He ushered me into an office with bare floorboards and whitewashed walls, in which a vast and empty desk confronted four spindly chairs. They looked guilty, rickety with admonishment.

Wheeler made a great show of arranging himself behind that desk and inviting me to sit down as he planted his elbows on the expanse before him. No paper, no inkstand, no quills. He'd never done a stroke of paperwork in his life, I realised, and I did not know whether to fear that fact or draw strength from it.

"I've come about Joseph Blue."

"Yes," he said, cracking his meaty fingers.

"You must release him. He has done nothing wrong."

"Hasn't he?" The corners of Wheeler's lips betrayed his impulse to smile.

"No, he has not. I've explained to you how he discovered Captain Addison's body with me. My word must count for something. As you know I am an officer of the court, here in Bristol. You must heed that!"

He nodded, and somehow his nod managed to convey the exact opposite of agreement. "Yes, yes, your word is important. That's why I paid attention to it. You suggested there might be something untoward about Captain Addison's death and I took note of your suspicion. There *was* something rum about it. As there was with the other one, that fellow Doctor Whatsisname, in Bath. And between us, Justice Pearce and myself, we have identified and contained the culprit."

"You're not listening. Blue didn't do it. He's as innocent of these crimes as you and me."

The moment I said this I regretted the opportunity it gave Wheeler to raise an eyebrow and inspect his knuckles. He said nothing for a long while. I'd made his point for him: press the issue and he'd drag me into the

271

fray, too. I looked around the room. There was no filing cabinet. A bookcase in the corner had slumped sideways into obtuse angles, its shelves grey with dust.

"Please," I said levelly. "There was a note. Purportedly from Addison, declaring his suicidal intent. I took it from his coat pocket at the scene."

"You meddled with the evidence? You're admitting it?"

"Yes. I thought the note more necessary for our purposes than yours. It purports to be from Addison, his final words."

"You're saying it was suicide now?"

"No, no, no. It's complicated. Here." I took the two pieces of paper from my pocket — the one I'd found on Addison and the one announcing Carthy's abduction — and spread them on the empty desk. "My master, Adam Carthy, has been taken for a hostage by the very people who killed Addison. You see? The same hand. Both events have to do with the same case. Whoever attempted to frame Addison for his own murder also stole Mr Carthy away. Blue was with me at Addison's precisely when my master went missing. He's not responsible for either wrong. He cannot be."

I watched the man's face intently. He glanced at the papers spread out before him, but only fleetingly. His gaze slid sideways away from the evidence as if he were repelled by what he saw. No, not repelled, intimidated. He huffed and stood up and backed away from his desk.

"I'll have these ditties scrutinised," he said. "But they add nothing. Anyone could have written them. The

272

sailor; your absconding employer; even you! They make no difference to the facts as I see them."

My mouth tasted brackish. "Of course they make a difference," I said as levelly as I could.

But Wheeler just grinned. "No, they don't. For you see, Mr Blue has confessed."

"What?"

"To the murders of his fellow shipmates." The Justice could not prevent his voice from rising in triumph. "He has claimed the deeds as his own!"

"That's ridiculous. Impossible."

"I too serve the court, Mr Bright." Wheeler ran his fingers across the grain of his jowls, pausing for effect. "Does my word not also deserve respect?"

"Listen. The deaths of Addison and Waring have not occurred in isolation. They are part of something larger, I'm sure of it. The other bodies, recently reported, of the women — found in Clifton, on mudflats in the gorge, and at Brandon Hill — were also connected with the ship."

"You know this how? Where's your evidence?"

"They're all black for a start . . ."

Wheeler shook his head slowly, savouring his incredulousness. "Two of them were," he pronounced. "Who's to say about the first?"

"Manacles," I said. "The report mentioned that the first woman was chained foot to foot."

"There's no accounting for perversion."

"She was trafficked here on the *Belsize*. I know it! The children in Long Ashton said the second woman had been branded. She had the Company's initials burnt into her leg!"

Now the Justice began pacing the width of the room.

"This has been your game, eh. Tampering with evidence. Spurious private investigations! Well, you've been pissing into a headwind, my boy. Ivan Brook was caught red-handed. The second woman threw herself to her death. And the third froze or starved or a combination of both. I don't much mind. Whores, no-hopers, vagabonds. Nothing to do with our eminent ship's surgeon and the sea captain."

"But the *Belsize* is exactly the connection. The ship!"

Wheeler walked from left to right and back again. He paused by the sagging bookshelves and turned on his metal-tipped heel and stumped back to the other wall, on which there hung a notice board and a length of varnished wood spiked with hooks. The notice board was empty. The hooks were hung with keys. He looked like an actor buying time so as to remember his lines. I had a premonition that he had been speaking words written by another hand, and now found himself having to ad lib. But when he raised his eyes to mine again there was no lack of conviction in them.

"If these last two women, the ones we know to be Negroes, did have to do with this ship, the one Doctor Waring and Captain Addison arrived on, both those estimable men being now dead, at Mr Blue's hand, and him being a sailor on the ship as well, and a blackamoor to boot, then I'm thinking that *if* their deaths, by which I mean the deaths of these poor women, were in any way untoward, or suspicious, or

274

the result of foul play, then I've probably got the culprit already, as likely as not, walled up next door, wouldn't you say?"

He uncoiled this little speech like a string of Turkish Delight. There was work in the untangling of it, but he derived much satisfaction from the results.

I gripped my head in my hands. "No, no, no."

"*He confessed!*"

"There's been some mistake. I was there. You are wrong."

"*Wrong* now, am I? '*I did it*,' a man says, and I've somehow got the wrong end of the stick."

"This has to do with the ship's owners. Its backers. There were *slaves* on board, don't you see? The ship traded them in the Indies, and brought some back here . . ."

I fancied I saw the man stiffen at the word *slaves*, but the glitter in his eye was undiminished.

"And you believe that having gone to all that trouble to bring so valuable — not to mention risky — a cargo to our port, these owners are now summarily killing them."

"I —"

He rode straight over me. "You come from a trading family yourself, if I'm not mistaken, Mr Bright. So you above most should see that what you're saying is absurd! Your Bristol merchant would sooner . . . trade his better half, or first born, perhaps . . . than sell goods at a loss, much less destroy them entirely."

"There's a different sort of ruthlessness at work here. They've overreached themselves. The decision — to keep slaving — must have been cooked up two years ago. There were those who said they'd flout the new law then, and they've done it, only now they're scared of the consequences. The public mood has shifted. Punishment for these crimes is real. They're trying to cover the thing up now, and it seems they have the power to do so. First they get to the Dock Company, who suddenly lose interest in chasing their unpaid duties, and then, then they've got to . . ."

The Justice had stopped walking. He planted his feet, straightened his back, and stuck his fleshy chin out at me. "Go on man, say it, I dare you," he said softly.

But accusing him outright would serve no purpose, so I jinked sideways as convincingly as I could. "They have got to Joseph Blue. I'm not sure how, but it's the only satisfactory explanation. If he's saying he's guilty it's at someone else's bidding."

Wheeler lowered his chin; the udder swell beneath it bulged. "If anyone's *got to* anyone in this matter, you might want to pause to consider whether they've done so in your favour. Cry 'corruption' and the new broom might sweep you back into the fray. You don't want that. Not with you being so thick with the black during his murdering days. It's hard enough to hold you apart as it is, despite the incentive."

The rickety seat creaked beneath me as I leaned forward upon it. "The sailor was only present at the scene of these crimes because of me," I said. "The victims aside, it's him and Adam Carthy I'm concerned about. Not myself."

276

Wheeler allowed himself a smile. "Very worthy. But short-sighted, I'm sure."

"What do you mean?"

"It's the younger Alexander daughter you've got in your sights, isn't it?"

I felt my hands balling beside my thighs, and I leaned yet further forward on the chair, ready to roll up out of it and take the man by the throat.

"What of it?"

"Well." Wheeler pared some dirt out from under a thumbnail and flicked it to the floor. "Heston Alexander is a reasonable man, but I'd vouch he doesn't want himself tainted by these horrible events, even through a potential son-in-law."

As evenly as I could, I said, "Blue is innocent of these murders. If you won't reopen the case, I shall do so my —"

"Oh . . . damnation! Give it up. He's *confessed*. If you won't believe me, come next door and you shall hear it from the man himself!"

CHAPTER
SIXTY-ONE

Wheeler took his keys from their rack on the wall with the self-satisfaction of an orchard keeper picking the year's first apple. He jangled them cheerfully and beckoned me to follow him down the hall. We emerged through an unlocked door at the rear of the house into a cramped courtyard. Above us the sky was the blue-purple of a new bruise; night would soon fall. Three sides of the courtyard held gridiron doors, behind which stood cramped cells. Like the harbour, the courtyard managed to be both open to the weather and infused with a feral smell.

"Here we are," said Wheeler. Away from his desk the man was in his element. He selected a key from the bunch and unlocked the nearest door. I flinched upon seeing Blue. The Justice had taken his coat, leaving him in a hutch half open to the elements, its floor a shit-stained mess. He was holding himself awkwardly, as if to protect his midriff from a blow. We regarded one another. He took a breath and said emphatically, "Both men deserved their fate."

"I'll have you out of here."

"But he's admitted it. You just heard him," crowed Wheeler.

278

"He's admitted nothing."

Blue shrugged. "The Captain and Doctor Waring were evil men. It was my duty. I meted out what both —"

"Enough!" I cut in.

Wheeler laughed. "No use shutting the door now, Mr Bright. The savage is out. He has shot his civilised bolt!"

My eyes growing accustomed to the half-light, I saw that Blue's mouth was swollen and split, and that the hand he was cradling to his chest appeared broken, its fingers twisted.

"What have they done to you?" I asked, but I knew already. The sailor's thumb would have been screwed from its socket to evince this false confession. "Evidence got this way will not stand up," I said.

Wheeler snorted beside me. "Is that it? Your best retort?"

"Nobody will believe he means what he's saying."

Again the snort. "He's standing before you, confessing, and he'll do the same before the magistrate. He's seen the light, haven't you my friend?"

"I've heard no confession; he has merely —"

"Then you're deaf as well as blind."

Wheeler's smirk sat in the middle of his face like a knife-cut in a dough-ball. The man's complacency was infuriating. I took a half step backwards and surveyed the courtyard. Only one of the other three stalls stood occupied: an open mouth hung behind the grate to my left, and thick, working-man's fingers curled through its bars: Ivan Brook, no doubt. My own hands itched to make fists of themselves.

"You should tell him of the developments," the Justice went on, nodding from me to Blue. "The other murders, you know, of his black sisters in town. There might be some more confessing to be done yet!"

I chose my words carefully. "Leaving aside Addison and Waring, whose deaths Mr Blue here had nothing to do with, I must concede I was mistaken as regards the suspicious nature of those other cases, involving the women. You have sound explanations for those deaths, as you say. Mr Blue need not be weighed down further with unfounded accusations."

"That's more like it. No sense in complicating things." The Justice smiled. "The paupers are squared away."

A thought came to me. I said, "You have had the bodies buried already, I expect?"

"Eh? Certainly! The stench in this town works well enough without our leaving dirty corpses laying around to add to it."

"Who paid for the burials?"

"The Venturers, I believe, coughed up to have the unfortunates planted at arm's length. It's not as if the women's nearest and dearest were queuing up for the honour, and the powers that be never miss an opportunity to curry the town's favour on the cheap. A plot costs less than a pint of beer out at Horfield." Wheeler's smirk split further. "The name suits the purpose well enough, don't you think?"

280

Blue was wavering: I feared his legs would buckle entirely, and reached to steady him, but the Justice stepped between us and pushed Blue away, saying, "No hand-holding, unless you want to do it behind the bars!"

I willed Blue to stand up for himself. Together we could overpower this man. But as he slumped to the floor it appeared he had given up. Wheeler scraped the door back into its socket and locked it with a pathetic flourish, before ushering me away.

CHAPTER
SIXTY-TWO

I could not face returning to the Carthy household. The thought of little Anne and her mother there, waiting for him to come back, prompted a stab of guilt so sharp I fancied I could taste blood in my mouth. But I could not put my plan into effect until the small hours, so I resolved to walk both the time and my agitation away between now and then.

The streets were darkening, as emphasised by the dots of light in windowpanes, the occasional yellow slash out from under the doorjamb of a tavern, and haloes of brightness jerked here and there on the tips of lamp-bearers' poles. I threaded my way through St Nicholas Market and let my feet take me out to St Augustine's Reach. There the water looked like tar. I found myself drawn up the hill towards the cathedral. There was a rehearsal of some sort going on inside; the same snatch of organ music pumped weakly across the dark grass again and again. Since moving down to Carthy's I had not attended services here — or anywhere — regularly, but the three of us, John, Sebastian and myself, had flanked our father through sixteen years of Sunday mornings in this church before I left. The great embossed door stood ajar. I stepped inside, stood blinking for a second in the candlelight, then made my way over the smooth flags towards our pew. In here, the organist's practising was loud enough to be impressive, but as the phrase he was attempting to perfect repeated itself again and again I felt as if I were listening to a great orator who had lost his mind. There should have been reassurance in the pew's familiarity, hope in the vaulted ceiling, and solace in the great calm of the place, but when I shut my eyes to reach for a prayer, the enormous roof above me was immediately transformed into an upturned ship's hull, and the familiar feel of the wood beneath my hands was hatefully cloying, and the calm, the calm, was simply emptiness, vast and unforgiving as the sea.

I felt as if I were drowning.

The risk was that I'd pull people down with me.

I should do what I could to cut those closest to me free.

I reeled out of the cathedral; the organist may have been distracted by my footsteps, for he stuttered in his playing as I jinked back out into the night. Within ten minutes I was knocking upon the door of the Alexanders' house in Queen Square.

Spenser, the footman, drew it open, and pretended for a second that he did not recognise me. His face thawed unnaturally slowly and he responded to my request — that he announce me to Lilly — with a demonstrable lack of urgency. I was left standing upon the chequered tiles. Eight this way, eight that. My father taught me to play chess as a boy, and he never let me win, believing the victory would taste bad if he did. Yet if anything, the opposite was true. For many years after I became the better player, I held off winning for fear of how bad I knew defeating him would make me feel. The footman's delay worked to my advantage. I'd calmed down somewhat by the time Lilly, her hands clasped together with excitement, appeared.

"Oh, it's been days! They're just finishing up with dinner. Have you eaten? Would you join us? Or shall I have Spenser show us into the drawing room. There's cake!"

"Cake."

"Yes! It's a new recipe. Spiced ginger. And the icing is made with scrapings of orange peel!"

"Delicious. The drawing room, then."

This answer pleased Lilly. Apparently, it amused the footman, too. He opened the drawing room door with a voila and gave a complicit bow as he showed us across the threshold. This false solicitude gave him away. Knowing he would waste no time in telling Lilly's mother of my arrival, I cut to the chase.

"There's something I have to tell you."

Lilly rounded upon me and looked me over, nibbling her lower lip, and before I could continue she said, "And I you, I'm afraid." Her excitement had a nervous, unsettled quality to it, which made me feel suddenly protective. Or perhaps it was that any excuse to prevaricate was better than none. I nodded at her to go on.

"You mustn't be disappointed," she said.

"I'm sure, whatever it is, that I'll cope."

284

"But it has to do with the wedding. There's a problem, and it means a delay."

Lilly was beckoning me to sit down, and I did so, nodding gravely, but in truth it felt as if a weight had been lifted from my chest.

"I see. Well, I'm sure —"

Lilly perched on a footstool next to my chair and looked up at me, her eyes filmy. I gathered myself to suggest that she tell me all about the difficulty, but she leapt up and rushed to the door — in search of the maid with the cake, I suspected — before I could begin. Her silhouette, leaning out into the hall, her chin uplifted and expectant, was perfect, and I knew for sure that she was aware of it, and was deploying it now to hold my attention and steer us around whatever difficulty it was she perceived stood in our way. There was something futile and persistent about her which again stirred my affection, and her ringlets, in the lamplight, had a beguiling amber glow.

"What is it, Lilly?"

She turned back into the room slowly and her hands, which had been clasped together, dropped to her sides.

"The reception rooms, for the wedding breakfast . . . there has been some mix-up . . . a double booking . . . we shall have to put back the date."

She was looking at the nest of dull red coals, pulsing low in the grate, and not at me, and I knew that she was making this excuse up, and not for her own benefit; she was lying. What's more, she knew I knew this to be the case, and was prepared, if fleetingly, to reveal as much.

"I suspect this makes the revelation of your own news unnecessary," she said quietly, "for now at least."

"A double booking?"

"Yes. No doubt Papa could offer them more money to secure the rooms in our favour, but he knows the other interested party . . . something to do with a dinner for foreigners . . . and . . . it's perhaps for the best. Luckily the invitations have not been sent out yet. We can have them reprinted."

Those fine hands, still hanging disconsolately at her sides. I climbed out of my chair and took hold of them in my own. They were cool to touch.

"The reason I came by this evening is to explain how —"

"But there's no need now, is there?" she said, her fingers curling into mine.

"I think I owe it to you to be truthful."

"You can't help but be, Inigo. These past weeks, I've seen it."

"You've seen what?"

"At dinner the other night. The cutlery dancing on the table. And at the wretched poetry recital. Turning up late and distracted."

"And you think this signifies what exactly?"

"Please don't make me spell it out."

She sniffed and I looked down at her and she turned away. One of her hands slipped out from within mine. She used the heel of her thumb to rub at her cheek and sniffed again. "A delay just means a new date in the future, when we're, when you're —"

286

"But Lilly," I said, digging at my collar, which felt suddenly tight again. "I really must speak plainly, I must."

A bustling noise behind me caused me to tense in my boots ahead of Mrs Alexander's arrival.

"Lilly and I were talking . . ." I began.

"Yes. I can see that. And yet cake was demanded! I've brought it myself. See. Here it is. Cake! Lilly? Shall I cut it or will you? To what do we owe this unexpected pleasure, Mr Bright? I hope your arrival at this hour, and unannounced, doesn't presage bad news. Explain yourself!"

Something caused the coals in the grate to shift and collapse forwards upon themselves now, so that a small spillage of ash fell across to the hearthstone, and this gave Lilly the excuse to break away from me and tend to it. She looked small, bent forwards like that, her shoulders narrow. I stepped forwards to help her.

"Leave that, Lilly," said Mrs Alexander. "Heavens! One of us playing the domestic is surely enough. Now. Do carry on. What were you talking about?"

Without pausing Lilly said brightly, "The new dog, mother. Lo and behold, Inigo does care what we call it, after all!" She stood up and turned around and brushed herself down. Her lips were already fixed in a cheerful smile. She advanced to the sideboard and put a hand on her mother's shoulder, suddenly authoritative, so that for an instant I saw the true depth of her knowledge of me, and felt ashamed. "Here," she said, taking the knife. "Let me do that."

CHAPTER
SIXTY-THREE

Though a lamp would have helped me return to Stratton Street without splashing about in the mire, I was in no hurry, and a clandestine approach, even from this distance, seemed best. Skirting Back-Bridge Street I heard a commotion ahead and arrived adjacent to a house just as the argument within it spilled outside in the form of a barrel-chested woman in bare sleeves, her skirt awry. The door slammed behind her and she swore at it and turned around and fell silent immediately upon perceiving me. I held up my hands in a gesture of innocence, but she shrieked and began hammering at the door again. I put my head down and, blind-footed, hurried on my way.

I approached the Justice's quarters obliquely, pleased to note the four black windows in its face. To one side of the front door stood the pile of pallets upon which the Justice's cat had sought refuge from his daughter. As quietly as I could, I lifted the top pallet from the pile. Then I felt my way down the alleyway towards the rear of the building. Here was the back wall of the courtyard, a single storey of greasy brickwork. I leaned the pallet against this façade, put one foot on top of it, and thrust myself up to reach the top of the wall, where it met the sloping roofline. Without pausing to consider the consequences of failure, I hauled myself upwards, boots scrabbling beneath me. Chin, chest and midriff cleared the parapet; I swung a leg up to one side and banged my knee on to the ledge. Up and over I went, my coat-front dragging across the gull-shit, until I was kneeling on the back of the low roof. I spread my weight evenly on all fours and held myself still for what felt like a long, long time, listening and watching. None of the rear windows of the Justice's house proper blinked to life, and I heard nothing from that direction. The only noise was a muffled cough, which drifted up from somewhere beneath me, but just the one, before the quiet thrum of the town pressed down from above again. Slowly, moving one limb at a time, I crawled forwards to the front lip of the courtyard roof. The recess beneath me was a square of deeper darkness, a shadow within shadows. I took a deep breath, swung my legs out over the void, dropped from chest to chin to fingertips, and let go. Though I tried to cushion the impact by landing with bent knees, the heaviness with which my heels struck the dirt floor jarred my teeth in their sockets. I saw the cask slamming into the deck of the *Belsize* again. It seemed the commotion must surely have disturbed somebody, but though I lay still for further long minutes, I could still hear nothing but the wind sniping through rigging in the distant docks and the yip of stray dogs.

It would not be possible for me to climb back up on to the overhang of the roof from inside the courtyard: if this gambit didn't pay off, I'd be stuck here overnight for Wheeler to find in the morning. A trickle of sweat threaded its way through my eyebrow and into my right eye. Very slowly, I rolled on to my side, brushed it away, and stood up. Again the soft snort behind me, whether coming from Blue or Ivan Brook I could not be sure. The darkness was the colour of wet slate, but it was not complete. Rectangles swam toward me as I moved across the courtyard towards the rear entrance of Wheeler's lodgings. I reached the door, gripped the latch, held my breath, and eased it open. Utter quiet. I let the breath go, and stepped inside.

With one hand tracing the hallway dado rail and the light grey of my stockinged feet padding beneath me, I set off to the front of the house, found the front door, eased back its bolts, and stood it ajar. From there I headed to Wheeler's paperless office. To the right of his desk, on the wall, hung his pompous bunch of keys. I gripped the shafts so as to muffle any jangling, and lifted the bunch free. With the keys clutched to my chest, I soft-footed my way back down the hall, and was standing on one leg in the doorway, struggling to pull my boot back on one-handed, when the cat squirmed against my planted foot and very nearly undid me. Unsure of what it was for a second, I almost cried out. But no, I bent down and pushed the creature away and trod carefully across the courtyard to Blue's cell again. As stealthily as I could, I tried one and then another key in the lock.

"It's the one with the square shank, Inigo," Blue said matter-of-factly from within the cell's dark recess.

"Christ! Hush!" I hissed.

290

"He'll be drunk asleep by now," the sailor went on, his normal voice deafening to me.

"He has a family. Hold your tongue!"

"Still, Blue's right," a second, gravelly voice cut in. "If your slamming about all over the shop hasn't awoken him, a bit of talk out here is unlikely to make much difference."

"Please!"

Once Blue's door was open, I undid the labourer's. He was as innocent as the sailor, and besides, he'd be a help with what we had to do next. Both men's bravado quietened on the threshold of the house proper. We stole along the corridor and out of the front door, the cat a cut-out shape watching us from the stairs.

CHAPTER
SIXTY-FOUR

We were mud-encrusted to the knees, not to mention worn out, even before we began digging. The walk out to the hamlet of Horfield was along a road of rain-soaked clay: tough going in daylight, grindingly slow under cover of darkness. Still, I had plenty of time to explain my theory along the way. Ivan Brook took some convincing. His instinct told him that no amount of proving his innocence would add up to the benefit to be had from running away. But I suggested that in so fleeing Ivan would, in effect, be carrying out the court's transportation order in advance, and the labourer reluctantly agreed ("I was thinking more of Swindon than Sydney Cove") to wait until after we'd assessed the evidence before deciding what to do.

We searched the cemetery for fresh graves at daybreak, having passed the small hours in the groundsman's hutch, huddling back to back for warmth. As I scanned the field for newly turned earth, it struck me how far away I was from my own world of turned pages. The boredom of the Dock Company's files seemed a positive paradise by contrast to this: a slope of slantwise headstones and rotting crosses, the lot tumbling down to a scraggy hawthorn hedge, black against the eaten-out sky. Corpse-fed grass, knee-high and rank with dew, soaked my boots and obscured the view, but we discovered where the women had been buried eventually. Three oblongs of raised mud nosing the bottom of the slope as if intent on slipping their moorings and floating away.

The three of us gathered round the graves and looked down upon them in silence. Somewhere along the hedgerow a blackbird began singing. Ivan Brook was breathing heavily beside me. He passed the spade he had taken from the groundsman's shed from one hand to the other, then leaned upon it. I noticed that his knuckles were pale on the shaft.

I took the spade from him and he stumbled backwards a few paces, apologising to the ground.

The spade was heavy. I scraped at the topsoil of the nearest grave, once, twice, and again, fearing each time that the blade would bite something solid within the crust, which was ridiculous, as Blue made clear. He had taken a pick from the shed, but his torn thumb meant he was unable to swing it with any purpose. After three weak blows with it he paused, wincing, and said, "They sink even paupers below a man's waist."

I took off my coat and handed it to Brook and I dug to the sound of the blackbird's chattering. The deeper I dug, the more the broken ground seemed to smell of decay, though I suppose this was my imagining. My shirt, tight across the shoulders, was soon damp with sweat, and the hole I'd created was small.

"Here," said Brook gruffly, returning to my side. "Digging up the same corpse twice is abominable, but it's more painful still watching you try."

I stood panting next to Blue as the labourer's spade cut the hole square and then went deep, each bite precise and rhythmical and apparently effortless. There was a mesmerising quality to the man's movements. Only when I looked from the flowing spade-tip to his face did I see that he was weeping.

I rejoined my efforts. Blue dropped to his knees and helped scoop the loose earth from the grave with his good hand. The blackbird's song swelled and the sun tipped colour into the scene: oxblood earth, fir-green hedgerow, salmon sky. The hole stayed a filthy black.

Eventually, I uncovered sacking cloth. I flinched from it at first, then gritted my teeth and, working with Blue, prised the sack free. Together we manhandled it out of the hole and up on to the wet grass. Within minutes Ivan Brook had placed a second sack-covered bundle next to the first. He wiped his palms on his trouser legs after putting it down and — I could not help it — I looked back at his sack to see that one end of it appeared to be leaking.

The three of us worked swiftly to exhume the last body. It was in the freshest — and shallowest — grave. When we'd lain it next to the others, I motioned for the labourer to stand aside. He cleaned the tools on the grass, then used them as an excuse to walk back to the hut.

Blue watched him go. The whites of his eyes were yellow; his skin still looked grey. He turned his gaze upon me as I mustered the courage to open the first sack.

294

"I'll do it," he said. Then, as I protested, he continued, "Whatever's inside, I've seen worse."

The mouth of each sack had been roughly stitched with red thread. I shut my eyes and saw snakes. Blue ripped the sacks open and the snakes broke to maggots, dead in the long grass.

I tightened my jaw and stepped forwards.

Three dead women.

The first, here, charred and missing in the middle, so that she looked half-made, inhuman almost, but no, recognisably elbows, the skin heartbreakingly clean just there, and a black hand stretched out, and yes, I knew it, chained ankle to ankle, *manacles*.

The second, here, intact, her eyes shut, peaceful, asleep, but her stomach bloated, and there, the sole of this foot split to the yellow bone, and she was tall, elegant even in death, but there, on this side, her left thigh, just as the child said, *marked*.

And the third, here, her arm an unnatural shape, double-jointed or torn from its socket, and the eyes lidless, gone, something moving in the hole, making me look away, to the scarring round the neck, and the torn shin, and I crouched down by that leg see the same mark high on its thigh, yes, *branded*.

I looked to Blue and he shrugged his shoulders as if to say what did you expect? What did I expect? Exactly what I saw.

Three dead black slave women.

Manacles, markings, branded.

The same initials cut into flesh and metal.

W.T.C.

CHAPTER
SIXTY-FIVE

At that moment, as the two of us stood side by side staring down at the sorry corpses, I noticed that the blackbird had stopped singing. Turning towards where it had been, I saw Justice Wheeler advancing along the hedgerow. He had a pistol levelled at us and even from here I could see both that he was wheezing with the effort of moving doubled-up, and that there was a malevolent grin stitched into his face. Something about the narrow ridiculousness of the man hollowed me out.

When he saw that his approach had not gone unnoticed, he straightened up and strode the final paces bellowing, "Stay where you are! Attempt to run and I'll shoot!"

I put a hand on Blue's arm.

"Good morning," I said.

"Good morning? What in the name of Christ do you think you're doing, Mr Bright?"

"What does it look like?"

"Robbing graves! That's what. Robbing graves with a criminal! My God! I awake to find my prisoners freed, and I think of our conversation, and I think he'll never have done it, he'll never have gone straight there! But I come here and here you are! Incredible! You've done it

296

to yourself. Never mind not practising again, you'll swing for this. You're ruined!"

"I don't think so," I said quietly.

"What's that? Look at you!"

"It's not me you should be looking at, but them." I gestured at the corpses.

"You're standing next to a confessed murderer, Mr Bright. And another is at large because of you!"

"These women died at the same hand. They were shipped here together, tormented and killed. The link is *written* on them. You'd have to be blind — or *paid* — to miss it."

The Justice shook his head and snorted. "Step away, up the slope." He waved his flintlock at us.

"He's mad," said Blue. "Do as he says."

I glanced sideways, surprised by his conciliatory tone. Together we could rush the man; I doubted he'd ever fired his pistol in anger. But Blue's head was down and he was walking backwards, as instructed. Wheeler pressed on after us. The barrel of his gun shook as he wheezed closer. I found myself tracking the sailor up the slope. He picked us a way through the jutting headstones towards the hut we'd slept in and beyond it to the cemetery entrance. The blackbird's whistling started up again, fainter now, further away. I glanced back down at the hedge and saw smoke curling from a chimney pot in the distance. The town had woken up. We should have begun digging in the dark; it would not have been impossible to find the new graves then, if we had looked. I hadn't imagined Wheeler would be up

297

checking on his prisoners so early, much less that he'd figure out where we'd gone and set off in pursuit immediately, and in that way I'd underestimated the man. He was still coming on, panting harder.

He walked heavy-booted across the middle of a tended grave.

A shape materialised behind him.

Ivan Brook rushed out from within the plank-walled hut, the spade raised two-handed above his head.

Before I could react he had swung the flat of the blade down in a vicious arc. It glanced off the back of the Justice's head. Wheeler staggered drunkenly sideways but did not immediately go down. The pistol waved a bewildered circle as his legs fought to regain balance, but his thoughts were unconnected to his fingers, and no shot sounded. Seeing the man still upright Ivan Book quickstepped towards him and struck him again, harder still, a sickening blow beneath which he collapsed sideways into the headstone of the grave he'd just stomped across.

A high, hilltop silence followed.

Then Blue was bending down over the fallen man and Brook was inspecting the back of the spade and both of their faces bore much the same expression: they were marvelling at what they saw.

I could hear my pulse in my ears.

Finally the labourer cast the spade aside and said, simply, "That's me gone. No amount of proving my innocence can help now."

And Blue murmured, "I knew you'd do it, though."

Brook dusted down his coat-front, as if finishing a day's work, looked at me and said, "One good turn deserves another."

"It puts us both beyond the law," Blue said.

"All three of us," I said.

Blue flipped a thumb in the Justice's direction and said casually, "It's only him that can put you here. And he won't be able to if I finish him off."

"No," I said.

The labourer was already walking away.

"You're sure?" said Blue at length. He looked at me, his dark eyes unblinking and untroubled. "It won't upset me to do it."

He wasn't joking. The deep calm of the man was unequivocal. I found myself sputtering, "He may deserve it, but . . ."

"Addison deserved it. Waring deserved it," said the sailor gently. He looked down the slope. "Those women did not."

"But you're not saying . . ."

"The Doctor conducted experiments on board. The Captain let him. Between them they duped us. They made me complicit. Retribution wasn't possible in the confines of the ship. But on shore . . . There was no way I could let them get away with it." He returned his gaze to mine, his eyes liquid black. "I needed someone to know I'd done it. That's why I took you to Addison's lodgings. How was I to know that his corpse would have been meddled with?"

"Meddled with?"

"I left the man dead on the floor. Somebody else strung his body up."

"But why?"

"I don't much care. Neither does it upset me that I botched Waring. Murder doesn't sit well with me, and anyway, he died in the end. My conscience is clear now."

"But the women," I said. "You're not saying Waring killed them? Or Addison? The timing doesn't work."

"No. Yet in a way they were dead before they arrived. When you said you were investigating the *Belsize*, I assumed it had to do with the illegal trade, further up the chain, that you would get knowledge of who had taken possession of these women. The owners and traffickers. I wanted to help bring them to justice, too."

"I . . . no . . . it was just about import duties, port fees!"

"It was never about that. Your employer, perhaps, knew better."

The gentle certitude of the man, laying out his thoughts, contrasted completely with my fizzing uncertainty in those minutes. A thought was forming, but I couldn't make it connect; it was like a punch thrown in a dream. "But listen," I heard myself say. "The notes. On Addison's body, the faked suicide message. And . . . What was your involvement?"

Blue's eyes narrowed with incomprehension. He seemed to think I had lost my mind. "As I say, somebody else wanted it to look like suicide," he said eventually. "Not me. Whoever it is, this man here . . ." He nodded at the Justice, prone, his mouth a sagging O. "He's in their pay, and for that he deserves punishment. Yet you prefer me to leave him be . . ."

"He's not responsible," I said weakly.

"In which case," Blue looked from Wheeler to me and back again, "you're on your own. I must leave immediately."

"I know," I said, holding out my hand.

The sailor's calluses bit into my palm with the force of his grip.

CHAPTER
SIXTY-SIX

I dragged Wheeler into the shed by the heels, checked that he was still breathing, and laid him on his side, the better to bind his hands and feet with the groundsman's staking twine. Then I retrieved the axe. Blue and Ivan Brook had disappeared down the lane. I knew what I had to do, and I walked back down the hill to the hawthorn hedge determined to do it, but as I stood over the twisted, burned corpse, and gritted my teeth to do it, saliva flooded the back of my tongue and before I knew it I was reeling away to vomit in the hedge. The sight of my own weakness, in the shape of strings of drool hanging from my open mouth, enraged me. I spat, spun around, brandished the axe, and set to with it. One blow wasn't enough. Two, three. On and on, a howl held tight within me, I did it. I got the manacles free.

Then I covered the corpses and set off for town.

By the time I made it to the edge of the city, morning proper had broken. Achingly clear autumn sunlight illuminated the patchwork of roofs laid out before me, riven by gulls. As I descended St Michael's Hill the city's spires — the cathedral nearby, St Mary Redcliffe in the distance — appeared to rise up out of the mass, as if intent on bursting the taut blue sky. A woman, washing something in a wooden bucket on her stoop, looked up at me as I passed and, pleased with the day perhaps, she smiled at me. Was my predicament not written large enough to be evident? My boots and breeches were mud-caked, my hands were black, and I had a pair of manacles slung over my shoulder. Despite all this I smiled back.

But I stamped through the Dock Company's panelled hallway in search of Orton's office with my face set hard enough to dissuade the porter from all but weak protestations. His "You can't . . ." mewed in my ears as I banged open one door, then another, and checked the meeting room we'd occupied on my previous visits. All empty. I took the polished oak staircase three steps at a time, the manacles rattling the banisters, and the porter, having foundered to the half-landing, thought better of following further, and chose to duck back out of sight again. I found Orton behind the first door I threw open. He was already out of his seat in an odd and defensive half crouch behind his desk. He retreated a pace when he saw it was me, but drew himself tall: it struck me he'd been fearing a worse visitation. I advanced, the chains held out before me, and dropped them on to his tabletop.

He winced at the noise, then said weakly, "These are private offices."

I leaned over the manacles, turned one of the metal cuffs over, and held it out before Orton. "There," I said. "The Company mark. You can feign ignorance no longer."

"A Company mark. The relevance of which is . . .?"

"The relevance? They were used to chain a slave. A slave trafficked on the *Belsize*, brought to these shores not two weeks ago. Along with two others, she has since been murdered. Whatever you intended us to find in our examination of your records, this is where the search has led."

"But that matter is —"

"Closed, I know. Not at your bidding. You were told to shut us down. Justice Wheeler has similarly curtailed his investigations into the murders. Yet there's a connection. Whoever has taken Carthy feared he would discover it. If they know their secret is out anyway, perhaps they will give him up."

The man's face was down-turned, but I detected the flickering of a mirthless smile upon his lips. Eventually he looked up, and his eyes came to rest upon the metal device splayed on his desk. They skated away from it quickly. His papery hands, their cuticles frayed, had begun pecking at each other again miserably.

"The Dock Company does not exist in isolation," I said. "There's the High Steward and the common council men. I will report my findings beyond these walls."

Once again the pursed lips.

"The news-sheets, if necessary. I will inform the hacks."

Orton accompanied his desperate smile with a shaking of his head. "And who edits the editors, do you think?"

I dropped my voice. "There are good people in this town. You are one of them, I think. You wanted to root out the corruption which oppresses us all, or address it at least. That's why we're standing here. Whoever got to you, you know who they are. Send a message back. Ask for Carthy's release. Can you at least do that?"

"I know who they are, do I?" Orton tore into a thumbnail before going on, his voice cracking. "What I know is what I've been trying to tell you all along. It's in everyone's interests, yours most of all, to *walk away.*"

I glared at him. I picked up the manacles. How heavy they were, how brutal and despicable. To remove them from the slave woman's body I'd had to cut off both her charred feet. That was somehow this man's fault. I hefted the chain from my left hand to my right and swung them down on to the desk cacophonously hard, striking savage bite-marks into the leatherwork. Suddenly I could barely stand with tiredness. The black earth smell of those corpses seemed to rise from beneath my shirtfront. I shut my eyes and saw bloody splinters and broken fingernails and slumped sideways into a smoker's bow chair.

"Wait here," said Orton. His shoes creaked as he crossed the floor behind me. "I'll see what I can do."

CHAPTER
SIXTY-SEVEN

Little kindnesses count for something, no matter the circumstances. After waiting ten minutes in Orton's office, I turned to the door to see his maid hovering with a tray of bread, honey, and sweet tea. I had not realised my hunger, but despatched this offering in famished gulps. Then tiredness welled up again. I folded my arms on Orton's desk and dropped my head upon them.

And I dreamt that it was all over. There were broad leaves above me and the sun was dropping through them like the arms of God, illuminating white teeth exposed in a smile. Little Anne's. No, it was Lilly, turning towards me, her hair coiled golden at her neck. She was letting me go. Then the smile belonged to a woman with coffee-coloured skin who was looking down at me with eyes so kind and knowing that I felt like a child before her. I turned away and saw Carthy seated at his desk. Another shaft of liquid sunlight fell across the paperwork he was considering. He looked up and beckoned me over. Unmistakably, he was going to tell me about a new case. As if from above I saw myself walk towards him, a gull's eye view. I was wearing a clean shirt, so white it looked blue, and my hair was neat. "What is it, then?" I asked. "I'm all ears."

Before he could answer, Orton's door had creaked open and a hand was on my shoulder. I found myself blinking up at my brother, John. At first the familiarity of his face was as reassuring as the dream, but then the incongruity of him being there at all bit home. I rose and shook myself loose and two things struck me. First, that his affable grin had a rubbery, forced quality to it, and second that he smelled wrong. He'd been drinking.

"Come on then Inigo, let's get you home," he said, his voice steady enough.

"What are you doing here?"

"You look like you've slept in a bramble patch!"

"I . . . look . . . where's Mr Orton?"

He had obviously been waiting outside for he materialised as I said this. He stood by the door, ineffectual as a reed in the breeze, looking as if he were intent upon keeping out of reach. "I took the liberty of sending for —"

"I can see who you fetched! But why? Pleased as I am to see you, John, I'm here pursuing . . . a specific business."

John thumped my shoulder at this and let loose an inappropriately loud salvo of laughter. "Just come with me, Inigo. Father is waiting for us at home." His meaty hand fixed itself around my upper arm, and he made as if to steer me from the room.

"No, wait!" I said, shaking him off.

Orton had his head bowed to one side, almost apologetically. "Go with him, Inigo. I have done as you asked," he said.

I picked up the manacles and John took hold of me again and I found myself exiting Orton's office in front of my brother. There was something familiar and repellent about being so led: a reminder of the Bath Justice's strong-arming, perhaps? I almost wanted to appeal to Orton again. We had barely made it to the head of the stairs, however, before John, in a stage whisper, asked, "What use can that husk of a man possibly be to you anyway? You'd do better petitioning a scarecrow!" He burst out laughing at this, as if it had been a joke made by somebody other than him, and once again I sensed the drink in him. Orton had to have heard the remark. Even though it tallied with what I thought, deep down, I could not help feeling shame that he should have been privy to it.

Still led by John, I descended the staircase and made my way out into the street. The strange sensation persisted, that I had somehow walked this walk before. Oblivious to the chain and cuffs slung over my free shoulder, John continued prattling in my other ear about how Father would be looking forward to our return, but I wasn't really listening. I was thinking that if this was the way Father wanted it, so be it. I would present the manacles to him. He'd waxed on long enough about how the trade had run its course, but I wagered his face would tell the truth. Presented with such stark evidence, he would have to reveal his complicity and make some form of amends. He might even be able to get the investigation reopened.

"Yes, he'll be pleased to see you," John repeated. "But those things . . ." he glanced now at the manacles and pulled a mock grimace . . . "what on earth are you doing with them? A gavel would be more appropriate. Gavel. Funny word. You'd have to have a robe, too, for the judging. Isn't that what you want to do? Judge us all? What can the Dock Company matter to you, anyway? Gavel!"

Was I witnessing the effects of the previous night, or had he already begun drinking this morning? There was no way Father would tolerate such a display; yet how could he not know about it?

"Trade's the honest thing," John went on. "It makes money, which means jobs, sides of beef, etcetera. There's no honour in a luncheon got from nitpicking."

I was about to respond to this, but he dropped his voice three octaves in drunken emphasis and growled, "Anchovies to yams, and yams back to anchovies again. What a joke!"

"What did you say?"

"Import duties. You know, for you fellows it's all about form checking." Again he dropped his voice comically. "Anchovies, alabaster, yams and yellow-finches, and all the way back again."

Carthy had said something similar; I was sure of it.

A coincidence, it had to be, except for the voice. There was no mistaking that artificially gruff voice. Its twin, dark as opposed to jocular, but equally fake, had threatened me high above the city's rooftops. Coffee underscored with hard liquor. A strong hand forcing the sack over my head. Knife-tips and precipices.

I swung round and in one movement slammed John hard into the pavement railings. Though bigger than me, and heavier, I had taken him by surprise, pushing him backwards with enough force to drive the wind from his lungs. He blinked at me, struggling for breath. I leaned into him, a manacle in each hand, the chain stretched taut across his chest.

"You are a part of this?"

I worked the links up towards his throat. His eyes bulged. This close their whites looked a dirty pink. He coughed and struggled and coughed again, the brandy fumes sharp on his breath. Having given him away, the drink now made him guileless; though he was sputtering incoherent denials I knew I was right to accuse him, his panic-blinking said as much. He worked a hand up inside the chain and tried to lever me away; my forearms burned with the effort of keeping him pinned there.

"Own good," he gasped.

"What?"

"Father said."

I let the heat out of my grip and John managed a proper breath.

"Father said it was for the best, but . . ."

"Did you know about these?" I said, jerking the manacles up under his chin.

He twisted his head this way and that, whether in denial or disgust I could not tell.

"Did you?"

He began to cough again, wetting my knuckles with a mist of spit. I released him. He staggered forwards, hunched over, pitiful. His scalp shone dully through the hair scraped across the top of his head, and made me think suddenly of our father's bald head.

"Ingo," John gasped. "I'm sorry."

He had called me that when he was too small to say my name properly. He would follow me around repeating it. I was quarrelling with the wrong person here: John had never had an original thought in his head.

"Is he at home?" I growled.

John nodded.

I turned from him. The driver of a goods sled had paused behind us, I now saw, to enjoy our altercation. His horse blew in its traces. I glared at the man until he prompted the animal onwards. Metal runners ground insolently on the flagstones. With John trailing at my heels now, I struck out up the hill for my father's house.

CHAPTER
SIXTY-EIGHT

Approaching Bright House, I looked across the shoulder of Brandon Hill to the city's fourteen spires, still jabbing at the forget-me-not sky, but punctuated now by columns of smoke pulsing from the glass manufactories, tendrils of blackness trailing from stunted chimney tops. The clarity of the day just worsened the hellfire look of them. They were better suited to the city's familiar grey haze. I did not knock at the back door or pause to wipe my feet en route to my father's study.

He was reading a ledger, or pretending to, with his head bent disingenuously low over his desk, his shoulders and pate and one arm cut out by the brightness of the day, which poured in through the window casement in a solid block and fell across a wedge of the room like spilled whitewash. I sensed he'd reached for the book on hearing our arrival; it felt as if he wanted me to interrupt him with words in order that he might then pointedly delay his answer, so I said nothing, just let go of one end of the manacles and allowed them to swing from my hand. Eventually, he spoke.

312

"I gather from Mr Orton that you have become . . . embroiled despite my counsel."

"Counsel? You've offered more than that."

"Very well. Despite my warning, then."

"You set my own brothers against me."

"Our interests lie together," he shrugged. Then he looked back down at the ledger and turned the page, oblivious to its contents: pornographic pictures would not have held his attention in those moments. Indeed, he glanced straight back up again as John slumped on to the ottoman beside the dusty bookcase. John hung his head. Father's affection for him came at a price: what hold did the old man have over my brother that he did not have over me?

"John," Father said now. "You don't look well. Why not retire to your room?"

Amazingly, my brother swam back on to his feet, muttered his thanks, and took his leave. Father regarded me complacently.

"You're concerned with nobody's interests but your own," I said.

"That's not true."

"The very essence of this trade —" I lifted the manacles "— depends upon it. You were privy to the *Belsize*'s illegal slaving. Instrumental in it. Weren't you."

Ignoring the restraints, Father looked straight at me, the brightness falling across one side of his face, chipping splinters of light in his right eye. "How do you think that the fortune which has enabled your legalising, never mind moralising, was made?"

"You yourself declared the trade defunct."

"Pre-abolition, it was. But like anything else, a shortage of goods increases demand, and therefore profit. It was an opportunity —"

"It was what it always was. Inhuman. The only difference now is that it is also illegal."

Father turned his face toward the window, so that sparks now flew in both his eyes. "Oh please," he said. "It's as old as man itself. There's nothing illegal about owning slaves. It's only the getting of them which is in question just now. And as soon as the sugar stops flowing, mark my words, they'll find a way of making that part lawful again. In the meantime, there is money to be made. Lots of it, you understand, because of the financial exposure. That is all business is about, Inigo, in the end. Profit and risk."

Here he was, trotting out the same old hackneyed justifications, glib as a pamphlet. Up until now he had concealed such opinions from me. Why? Because he knew I disagreed? What of it? This wouldn't be the first issue over which we'd stood at loggerheads.

From upstairs came the sound of Sebastian's piano. The noise had been there a while, I think, but I only became conscious of it now that he'd switched to playing something quick-fingered, light and jaunty. It set my teeth on edge.

"You're worried," I said softly. "You know that I will make this wrongdoing public. You've feared it all along."

Father shook his head and inspected the back of his hand, flexing his fingers as if they were stiff. "No, you won't," he said.

"The women the ship brought back here. You knew about that, too, didn't you?"

"That . . . venture . . . does seem to have been a mistake."

"A mistake? They've been killed. Whether to cover up their existence, or . . . I don't know . . . but their blood is on your hands."

At this Father let out a gentle laugh, and recommenced shaking his head. "Inigo, your sympathies —" he began, and his tone, and the laugh, and twittering piano upstairs, enraged me.

"I'll make it known," I cut in. "I'll see you punished."

"No, you'll desist," Father said.

I stared at him. The shards of light made his brown eyes almost orange. They were unblinking and filled suddenly with a hostility beyond irritation.

"As I was saying, your sympathies are understandable, given the mulatto whore your mother was."

Sebastian's music seemed to slow down. I felt very still, calm. Here it was. An odd sense of reassurance descended.

Father was searching my face for a reaction, and his voice rose when he appeared unable to detect it there. "The sacrifices I've made, and continue to make, for you. But I'll tear it all up, I will! You stand before me, threatening me, but it will amount to nothing. Your . . . enquiries were fruitless. Understand that. Because if a word of your little discovery becomes public knowledge, I will see to it that your true heritage is exposed. Polluted. The fruit of a half-blood plantation whore, tupped in drunken folly. I have stood by you, raised you as if you were a true son. Yet Lilly Alexander will walk away, trust me. And your professional life will be finished, before it has properly begun."

"This morning," I started, and my voice sounded as quiet in my head as his had sounded loud. "This morning I freed two prisoners awaiting trial for murder from Justice Wheeler's lockup. Then I robbed three graves. Finally, I took part in an assault upon the Justice himself, leaving him bound hand and foot in a gravedigger's shed. I think my prospects, both professional and marital, are already beyond repair."

In fighting to recompose himself, the corners of my father's mouth twitched, as if at some private joke. "Do you think judges any less swayable than clerks, Inigo?" he said at length.

"No. Nor do I think newspapers immune to corruption. But I doubt very much they can all be bought at the same time."

He did not deny this, but inspected the back of his hand absently again, and finally shut the ledger on his desk with an air of having reached a decision.

"You're worse than he is," he said.

"Who?"

"At least he's predictably obstinate. I thought, no I hoped, you had better sense."

"Who do you mean?"

Father slid the book forward on the desk and planted his elbows wide. His fists bounced together, the left one in shadow, the right crawling with bright liver spots. "Why your master, Mr Carthy, of course."

"Carthy? You know of his whereabouts?"

"He is safe."

"What do you mean, safe? Don't tell me . . . that you're responsible for Adam's absence?"

"On the contrary. He came to see me. He was a step ahead of you. I imagine he thought you'd catch up eventually. And so you did. He clearly holds you in high regard."

"I hold him higher still," I said through gritted teeth.

"I know, I know. And that is why, even if you have a cavalier disregard for your own good fortune, you will not want to see him harmed."

"Where is he?"

"As I say, he came to see us. He has been encouraged to view things afresh."

"Where is he?"

Father turned his palms upward. They glowed pink, and his face above them appeared to reflect the colour. Whether in triumph or repressed agitation, his blood was up.

"You turned my own brother against me," I said.

"It was safer than using somebody else. Men in that line of business have a habit of getting carried away."

He said this softly, as if expecting me to recognise a kindness in what he'd done. I think it was then that I realised he had lost his senses. The air in the room had a muffled, stale quality. Sebastian's piano playing petered out upstairs, breaking first into chords, then individual notes spaced further and further apart, as if the instrument was slowly giving in.

"Can't you see," Father was saying now, "I'm just trying to do what's best for the family? That's always been my aim."

I stared at him, and saw a man capable of saying or doing anything in pursuit of his own ends. Which were what? Turning a profit, the success of the firm. It did not make sense. He'd been no more than ordinarily ruthless in furthering his mercantile aims for as long as I could remember. Certainly he'd not — to my knowledge at least — pursued an illegal scheme such as this before.

"And I shall not be swayed from doing what is best for us all, regardless of your mewling objections, Inigo. If the only way to halt you in your folly lies with your good friend, Carthy, then, unfortunate as that is, so be it. He is safe, for now. But if you publicise your findings, I shall be unable to vouch for his continued safety in the future."

The manacles were still hanging from my right fist. I let them drop to the floor entirely now, for fear of acting upon the burning impulse to wreak damage — and hurt — with them there and then. I think the only thing that held me back from lashing out was the knowledge that Carthy would not have done so. The answer lay with him. Like a man trapped in an upturned hull, I had to force myself to sip at what air there was in the study, fighting not to lose control.

"You underestimate Mr Carthy," I muttered.

Again Father appeared to struggle against an inclination to grin.

318

"You do," I said, my voice rising. "You cannot vouch for him at all. Even if I keep my counsel, and he is released unharmed, you cannot be sure of his silence in the matter. In fact, if I were forced to take a bet upon it, I would say he will be all the more likely, for having been interfered with, to report our findings himself! Though you try to dress the thing up in terms of a bargain, he won't be bought off. He's cut from more principled cloth."

Now Father did smile broadly enough to reveal his stained incisors. "Oh Inigo," he said. "You really have no idea. *Everyone* weakens eventually. We're all susceptible to a change of heart. Should you be fortunate enough to see him again, I think you may find Mr Carthy . . . so altered."

CHAPTER
SIXTY-NINE

Oni cradles the man's head in her lap. He is still now, his breathing more regular, his features sharpening in the swollen mass of his face.

He still hasn't eaten. But the real danger comes from his having drunk so little in the four days he's been with her, only what she's been able to run into his mouth, most of which has leaked straight out again. He has not surfaced for long enough to concentrate.

Oni is not surprised to see this violence directed against one of their own. She witnessed it often enough on the ship. Though they use race as a means of distinguishing slaves, at its heart the men's cruelty is colour-blind. The oddness of their having directed it at this man, she considers, has more to do with his clothing than his skin. Ordinarily, fine stitching offers protection. On board, those with the brightest buttons fared best. But this man's transgression, whatever it was, tore through the shield of his frock coat easily enough, it seems.

Since he cast this poor soul into her cell, the man has come for her on three more occasions. Each time is worse than before. His cruelty feeds on itself. When she failed to satisfy him he turned to her pain. Beyond that lay sight of her spilled blood. Then, as his horrible, mottled hands closed around her neck, and the room's edges blurred, what light there was shrank to a merciful dot. His panting was, for a moment, overrun by the birdsong. Even the burning of his fingers around her throat spread out into the warm glow of sun on her bare shoulders.

It tasted and sounded and felt like an invitation: give in, stop breathing, the sensation said.

And were it not for the invalid, she would gladly have accepted this fate. But he needs her. She knew that the man had put him with her to die. On board the ship all captives were forced to eat, and even exercise. Yet the devil cast his fellow white man face down in the straw here, unconcerned whether he starved — or thirsted — to death.

Oni fought to breathe and the dot of light grew brighter. The devil-man finished. He let go and her mouth filled with bile. She forced the room back into unforgiving focus, rolled up on to one arm and looked back along the brick wall to where the invalid lay where she had left him, unmoving and slumped on his side. She hated him for making her come back.

The devil hitched himself back into his trousers and rubbed his hands across his face. He was breathing as heavily as she was. Before he left he looked down at her, a quick devastating glance empty of malice, lust or shame.

Oni sat up, fetters tinkling disingenuously. She crawled over to the invalid as the door banged shut behind her. She gathered him up on to her lap.

Now she dips her fingers into the water bucket again.

CHAPTER
SEVENTY

"W-w-what do you mean *if* Inigo sees Mr Carthy?"

I spun around to see that Sebastian had stolen into the room while Father was speaking. His lips were ashen, his face silt grey. Neither of us had noticed him; I saw Father's head jerk-to angrily.

"And w-w-what do you mean a-a-altered state?"

In a voice dripping with soothing intent, Father said, "Sebastian. I expected you to keep to your quarters, at least until you were feeling better."

John, still moving with an underwater languor, re-entered the room behind our youngest brother. Father's confidence was draining even as the colour mounted in his cheeks. A tick appeared under his right eye. John retook his seat on the faded ottoman. Father blustered on, saying, "And you too? What is the meaning of this? I told you to retire to your room."

John said quietly, "This involves us all. We must hear what is being said."

The lack of colour in Sebastian's face was alarming. He looked as if his blood had been let. I went to him and took hold of his birdlike shoulders. "It's all right. I know what's going on. No matter what he has involved you in, I know you are not to blame."

322

He blinked amazedly. Father had risen from his creaky chair, and now moved to the trophy wall, beneath which stood his inlaid filing cabinets. "Well. Perhaps you're right," he said carefully, addressing my brothers in turn, and then me. "If we're all together again, then let's reach a joint understanding, finally. Let's talk the matter through. As I promised you both that I would, I've been apprising Inigo of the firm's recent investments. He has concerns, but together I'm sure we can see a way to ameliorate them."

There was something catlike about his feigned unconcern in those moments. He was ignoring a danger, yet something inside him had coiled tight — to spring away, or fight.

I steered Sebastian towards a chair, but he shook me off and said, "W-w-what do you know?"

"Everything," I said. "I know about the Bright & Co. stake in the Western Trading Company and the *Belsize*. I know the ship sailed the golden triangle. I know of its illegal trading in slaves. I know three females were brought in error — or a mistake of judgement, at least — to these shores. I know whoever wanted them changed his mind. I know they ended up murdered."

"Murdered?" said Sebastian.

"The three bodies, recently found, were all black women, and all connected with the ship. I have evidence."

"But the labourer took one, and then the s-s-suicide, and the woman dead of exposure. They were freed, but lacked the capacity to . . . f-f-fend for themselves."

323

"Quite so, Sebastian," said Father. "They lack the capacity. But Inigo here is still intent upon putting the savages' needs ahead of our own." I glanced up at him. He was leaning on the filing cabinet awkwardly; despite the bluster he could not even stand up straight. "As I feared, he intends to pursue Mr Orton's agenda of making the firm's involvement in the trade public. I was just in the process of persuading him otherwise."

"Three slave women?" muttered John. "What about the fourth?"

Father, his back to the three of us still, stiff in his black frock coat, laughed softly and said, "There was no fourth."

"Yes, there was. There is."

"Nonsense. Sebastian, help John back to his room —"

"She's down below now."

"He's delirious."

"With Carthy. The two of them all but dead. I have seen them with my own eyes."

"Silence!" Father thundered.

He was still leaning across the filing cabinet. No, not leaning, reaching. I guessed his intent a fraction too late and stood powerless as he spun around swinging his twelve-gauge up into the crook of his arm. Its twin barrels wavered from Sebastian to me accusingly. My hands rose automatically from my sides, spread to placate.

"It is enough," Father growled, "that this corrupted mulatto bastard should seek to destroy us . . ." the gun's twin barrels dropped to my feet and rose back to my chest again ". . . but no true son will do the same. Now . . ." he swung the shotgun at Sebastian and John . . . "the two of you will retire. Neither of you are in your right minds, it seems. You will permit me to sort this out."

John stood up from the ottoman, his head bowed. He crossed the rug, his footsteps heavy, motioning at Sebastian to get up. Father stepped forwards after him, the gun now trained on me again. He would pull the trigger; I could see it in the firm line of his mouth. The depths of my brothers' complicity drained me of words with which to remonstrate. But as John reached my side he dropped to one knee swiftly and, before I could register what was happening, he had grabbed up the iron restraints from where I had let them fall. He swung round and the chain unfurled and caught the barrel of Father's shotgun, smashing it to one side, the gun discharging in the process. The shot was deafening in such confines. Father staggered backwards and John was upon him, the manacles taut across his chest, blue smoke enveloping them both. I sprang forward to help, and managed to wrest the shotgun from my father's clutches as John forced him down to the floor.

The air hung heavy with the burnt metallic smell of gunpowder. Compared to the blast, the sound of Father's hobnails raking the floorboards was scratchy and thin.

"The sea chest," John grunted. "There. Look for a brass ring. The keys are on it."

Father was still struggling, but ineffectually. Though by no means frail, he simply hadn't John's heft. I

325

turned to look for the keys and found that Sebastian had already yanked open the chest. He was rummaging within it furiously, casting padlocks, lengths of chain, and restraints aside. A choking sensation took hold in me. It felt as if I had swallowed a hunk of gristle which my throat was powerless to work down. Finally Sebastian surfaced holding a brass ring hung with black keys. "This one?" he asked.

John turned and nodded. Seeing the chest's up-flung contents he glanced at me. The knuckling sensation intensified in my chest as I selected a length of chain, two pairs of restraints, and a padlock and key. Father's railing took on a bewildered, pathetic strain. I could not look him in the eye. My hands were shaking. John and I worked in silence; we chained Father's wrists to his ankles and padlocked the end of the chain to itself, having first run it through the fireplace's wrought iron grate.

Despite all that he had done, the sight of my father chained on his side, his lips twisting with empty threats, sickened my heart.

The three of us left him there.

Led by John, and moving as if through a dream, we descended through the scullery, beyond the big house's empty basement rooms, and into the catacomb of its cellar. The final door we came to, beyond which lay the coal hole, had been reinforced with a crude iron strips. It was bolted top and bottom. The familiar dock-stench had a rank and decaying quality down here. John drew the bolts back with an apologetic force which told me he'd done it before. Then he turned the key in the lock.

My eyes had adjusted to the cellar-gloom, but could not at first break apart whatever was slumped against the vaulted brickwork at the end of the coal hole. Clumps of matted straw were strewn on the damp floor. Inching through the muck, my hand to my mouth and nose against the smell of excrement and sickness, I accidentally stubbed over a wooden bucket, prompting the shape to shift within its blankets up against the far wall. I advanced again, steadying myself with a hand on greasy bricks. One figure became two, a black woman seated with her back to the wall, and a prone man, his head clutched to the woman's belly. I knelt down beside the pair. At length Sebastian returned with a candle. Together we disentangled Adam Carthy from the slave woman's embrace.

Epilogue

There's a seagull standing on the wall not three feet from my table, just the other side of this windowpane. If I move my head a fraction one way or the other its defiant outline bends and blurs a little. Imperfections in the glass. I raise my coffee cup, still watching the bird. Its beer-bottle neck twists this way, registering the movement with unblinking eyes, monumentally unconcerned.

Across the street, the curtains on the top floor are still drawn. Adam Carthy has yet to rise from his bed. He sleeps late most mornings, and retires early, but he's gradually regaining his strength. Anne is his greatest comfort, of course, and precisely because she does not try to comfort him. Young children don't accept weakness in their parents. Even when he was at his most broken, she could do nothing but ply him with normality, and demand that he wake up and read to her. His first words, on pulling through his month of darkness, were to Anne. "You need to learn for yourself," he told her. "A is for anchovy."

We have not returned to work. The clients have been understanding. No doubt Adam will take up the reins again, when he is well enough, but I shall be unable to assist in any official capacity. Although Justice Wheeler has apparently been persuaded to drop his charges against me, the part I played in helping Joseph Blue and Ivan Brook escape could not go entirely unpunished. For paying the law so little respect, I have been struck from the list of Bristol's attorneys.

It was acknowledged that I had tried to right an injustice, and Ivan Brook has been exonerated in absentia, but Blue, wherever he may be, still stands charged with the murders of Captain Addison and Doctor Waring. He confessed to those crimes, after all. Though he made his righteous motive clear to me, I had still not fully believed him guilty, not until my brother John explained the notes — Carthy's and Addison's — to me. John wrote them himself. On hearing of the Captain's unbalanced demeanour, Father sent John to scare Addison off, or ensure his silence by other means. When John discovered Addison already dead — apparently strangled — he was fearful an investigation might focus unwanted further attention on the *Belsize*, and determined to rearrange the scene so as to suggest suicide. He never imagined Carthy's ransom note would fall into the same hands. Though loyal and willing, strategy has never been John's strongest suit.

But it's not just my wrongdoing in releasing the prisoners that has turned some of the town's masters against me. I am a murderer's son, and I am tainted. From his first interviews with the authorities, Father was at pains to discredit me by all means possible. He began with the secret of my mixed heritage. Nobody has referred directly to this accusation, save Sebastian, whose vehement denial had the odd effect of making me certain that Father had spoken the truth. It makes sense. The face I see leaning down to me in dreams has, for as long as I can remember, been of a dusky hue.

In any event, the disgrace brought upon our family has been enough to fulfil Father's prophecy: the Alexanders lost no time at all in disentangling themselves. I have seen Lilly once, in the company of her mother, whose official line was that circumstances made it best that we put off our plans. Needless to say, her puckered little mouth twisted happily around the word "indefinitely". The strange thing was the look I shared with Lilly as her mother laid down her decree: clear-browed relief. She giggled nervously when we said goodbye, and pushed a strand of sunlit hair behind her pink ear, and in that moment she had never appeared more serenely beautiful — or profoundly unsuited — to me.

If Mary has heard the rumours, and with her sense of what's what I've no doubt that she has, then she's not been outwardly concerned by them. She still regards me — like a joke she enjoys retelling — with a mixture of warmth and amusement, and bumps into me on purpose when delivering coffee to my table. Some folk swamp superficial concerns. She was the only person to tell me she was sorry to hear that my father had died.

He took his own life three weeks after his arrest. At least that's what the news-sheets reported. He'd been before the beak for a preliminary hearing the day before, and it is possible that he hanged himself after seeing the strength of the case against him. Perhaps it dawned upon him then that he would never again walk free — even following transportation. But I am not so sure. His true motive, like the real workings of this city, remains largely opaque to me. All I know is that he was not the sort to give up even in the face of a lost cause.

It's more likely, I think, that those he colluded with in the Western Trading Company were determined to limit their exposure to further damage. They are attempting to depict the *Belsize* as a rogue ship, exploited by Addison to his own ends, and with the Captain dead, and the ship's log a fabrication, they may yet succeed in escaping much of the real blame. Addison's suicide note would indeed have played into their hands. If anything the slave-murder case has offered the city a distraction from the more endemic evil in its midst: so far the magistrates have appeared less than vociferous in pursuing the slave-trading charge. They say there is not enough evidence. When Mr Carthy is well enough to take up the cudgels again, he will at least have my chronological record of the Company's dealings, secure beneath Anne's rocking horse, to make a start with.

And Oni, the last slave woman, will bear testimony one day. The fear in her eye when my father appeared before her, even in chains. I blink now and see the bodies of her disinterred friends, splayed on the wet grass. My own father . . .

At present Oni is convalescing in Mrs Carthy's care. Upon hearing how Adam and the woman were found together, Carthy's wife lost no time in taking her in. Beatrice made the mistake of expressing distaste at this development, and found herself on the front step within the half hour. Oni now occupies the guest bedroom Aunt Beatrice vacated. In time, I imagine, she will want to return home. There will be money enough in Father's estate to see to that, come what may.

I say that Mary was the only person to offer me her condolences on the death of my father, but that's not quite true. I also received a letter from Edie Dyer, in which she commiserated with both my loss and involvement in such an abominable course of events, and praised, as she put it, the strength of mind it must have taken for me to see the thing through. Anything but! I was propelled by many things. If a sense of duty towards Carthy, and via him to the truth, came into it, those motives were cut with low curiosity, antipathy toward my desk job, and a self-destructive streak. In her letter Edie also repeated her offer to comment on my drawings. That's three times she has asked now, and when I penned my reply I found myself, for the wrong reasons no doubt, agreeing to show her those few sketches I'd managed which might merit her attention.

And yet, on looking them over again last night in search of a workable selection, I discovered what I always do, that they are no good. The only thing that can be said for them is that they make me want to try again.

I glance back through the window, see again the seagull standing sentry on that wall. It lifts a wing and rams its beak deep into the soft feathers of its breast, so that for a moment, from behind, the gull appears to be headless. Then it stretches out its neck and flaps both wings, white and grey and black-tipped, with its beak stretched screamingly wide. These images will do for a start.

But before I return to my room in Carthy's house to scratch them down in ink, I have first to keep my appointment at the barber's shop. I have resolved to stick with a fuller head of curls, but they need trimming all the same.

Also available in ISIS Large Print:

Fate & Fortune

Shirley McKay

1581, Edinburgh. Running from his new responsibilities as head of the family in St Andrews, young lawyer Hew Cullan arrives in the vibrant capital of medieval Scotland. There he plans to publish his late father's book and quietly endure the completion of his legal training under an old family friend. Life in the whirl of Edinburgh is full of dangers and distractions for Hew. Beautiful women, fashionable living and the treacherous world of the law threaten to turn his head. But a brutal murder and hints of a long-hidden mystery draw him into a deadly game against an unrepentant foe. When the game is murder, can Hew Cullan play to win?

ISBN 978-0-7531-8892-7 (hb)
ISBN 978-0-7531-8893-4 (pb)

The Equivoque Principle

Darren Craske

When a series of gruesome murders coincides with the arrival in London of Dr Marvello's Travelling Circus the performers find themselves caught up in some rather sinister goings-on. Prometheus the strongman winds up behind bars and it falls to ringmaster and master conjuror Cornelius Quaint, ably assisted by his Eskimo valet Butter, to investigate the killings and to clear his name. But Quaint, an irresistible mix of Sherlock Holmes and Harry Houdini, soon finds that these seemingly random killings are actually linked to dark secrets from his own past. Secrets that he might not be prepared to face.

ISBN 978-0-7531-8722-7 (hb)
ISBN 978-0-7531-8723-4 (pb)

Snow Hill

Mark Sanderson

"Friday, 18 December, 1936. I went to my funeral this morning . . . "

So begins the diary of Johnny Steadman, an ambitious reporter on London's Fleet Street. When he gets a tip-off about a Snow Hill policeman's death he thinks he's found the scoop that will make his career. Trouble is, no-one at the station seems to know anything about it . . . or they're not telling.

Johnny's one lead takes him to the meat market at Smithfield where he encounters violent death up close and personal. Undaunted by this chilling message, his investigation drags him deep into a web of corruption reaching further than he imagined.

Johnny must risk everything to save his closest friend and expose a ruthless killer. But to bring them to justice he must first go undercover. Six feet undercover. After all, a dead man cannot be tried for murder . . .

ISBN 978-0-7531-8702-9 (hb)
ISBN 978-0-7531-8703-6 (pb)

Washington Shadow

Aly Monroe

September 1945. Bankrupt and desperate, Britain sends John Maynard Keynes to Boom-Town Washington to beg for a loan. Under cover of the back-up team, agent Peter Cotton is sent to investigate the break up of America's wartime intelligence agency.

Cotton finds himself caught up in a world of shadows involving an extraordinarily attractive girl from the US state department, a Soviet ex-tank commander claiming to be his opposite number, a contrarian African academic, an ambitious, quick-tempered boss from the world of misinformation . . . and an Anglo-American conspiracy that will change the world of post-war intelligence for ever.

ISBN 978-0-7531-8662-6 (hb)
ISBN 978-0-7531-8663-3 (pb)